Things We Do For Love

Things we do for love
First edition: June 2023
Vered Neta

Layout & formatting: Arjen Broeze, Kingfisher Design

ISBN Paperback: 978-1-61947-081-1
ISBN Ebook: 978-1-61947-084-2

VERED NETA

Things
We Do For
Love

Happy Families Are Not All Alike

Dedication

This book is dedicated to Yael and Keren. Without you this story could not have been written. You have shown me what true family is all about, and for that, I am eternally grateful.

Acknowledgments

Writing may be considered a solitary profession, but the truth is that no book can come to fruition without the help and support of numerous individuals. I am immensely grateful to all those who aided me in bringing this book to life, as without them, it would not have been possible.

First and foremost, I would like to express my deepest gratitude to Lucy V. Hay, my mentor, coach, and dear friend. Her unwavering encouragement, feedback, and invaluable input were instrumental in helping me shape this story. Lucy, thank you for always believing in me and for being a guiding force throughout this process.

I would also like to thank Elinor D. Perry-Smith, my first editor, who ensured that, as a non-native English speaker, I was able to express myself in a way that was fitting for the story. Additionally, I would like to express my appreciation to Arjen Broeze from Kingfisher Design for his expert assistance in navigating the technical aspects of publishing a book in today's world.

To the wonderful community on the Bang2Write platform, including Fiona Leitch, Carmen Radke, Lucy Linger, and so many others, thank you for providing me with writing advice, feedback on earlier drafts, and most importantly, weekly encouragement to keep going. You turned my writing journey into a shared adventure and created a safe space for me to share my work. Thank you to each and every one of you.

Lastly, I want to express my love and appreciation to my beloved husband and best friend, Jonathan (Nisandeh) Neta. You have always been my biggest supporter, encouraging me to believe in myself and reminding me that I can achieve anything I set my mind to. Thank you for being a constant source of love and inspiration in my life.

Chapter One

⊂℞ DAISY ℘⊃

The taxi jolts to a halt.

'Why are we stopping?' I lean forward so the taxi driver can hear me through the glass window.

'Traffic.' He says in a bored voice.

It's a typical day for him, but not for me. I can't be late, not today. I have to get to this appointment on time.

'For once in your life, Daisy, be on time' I can hear my Mum's voice in my ears: *'First impressions are important!'* I can feel my heartbeat rising and my breath becoming shallow just thinking of her.

'Are you sure you want to do this?'

A calmer voice surfaces in my mind. A voice I learned to trust, with the years, more than my Mum's tone.

I don't have time for this now. I pay the driver, get out of the taxi, and start my power walk. I'm late because my last client of the day had a major breakthrough. I didn't have the heart to tell her that her time was up and she should leave. That's not the way therapists - or rather *good* therapists - work, according to my book of conduct.

Just as I'm around the corner I see Mike waiting for me. He doesn't seem bothered by the fact that I'm late. He leans against the wall of the grand house with showy letters saying, "Dodson

Fertility Clinic". His foot braced against the building, scrolling through his phone, Mike looks like an overgrown teenager.

He's oblivious to others' curious looks as they pass him. No one in their right mind would guess this chubby-looking guy with his old jeans and T-shirt is one of the sharpest minds in the City. Mike's natural home is more Canary Wharf than Harley Street.

In that sixth sense way of his, Mike raises his head from his phone and waves to let me know it's ok. It does not make me feel better. I quicken my step, but before I reach him for a hug, my bag flies open. Files, papers, and other rubbish fall to the ground. Mike swoops down and picks it all up for me.

'You're on time.' He kisses me.

I laugh. 'We both know you mean *Daisy Time* and not Greenwich Mean Time.'

'It's all the same to me.' Mike shrugs.

I look up at the grand entrance of the clinic, adorned with pillars and stone lions. The whole place screams elegance and money. In contrast, I'm out of breath, red-faced, and looking like a mess. I blot my clammy hands on my wrinkled skirt. I take a deep breath, straightening my belt and scarf in an attempt to look as composed and professional as possible.

Mike flashes me a reassuring smile. 'Are you ready?'

'As ready as I'll ever be,' I reply.

ᛒ IRIS ᛒ

Iris Bach-Dillen elbows her way through the crowded train to find a place. Even approaching her 60s, Iris is a woman on a mission, even when that mission is inconsequential.

At last, she finds a compartment with space. She takes a seat and opens her laptop and mobile phone without even looking at her fellow travellers. Her usual mantra plays in her head: *'No time to lose! So many tasks, so little time.'*

Her constant inner judge calls out when she glances over her list of 'To-Do', highlighting the most urgent tasks. Iris picks up her phone and dials 'DAISY'.

Daisy does not answer. It's not the first time she's tried calling Daisy today; her irritation turns into resentment. Feeling despondent, Iris lets her gaze roam around her compartment and the people in it. Her face reflects in the window of the train. She looks outside, drinking in the beauty of the landscape the train passes through. Lavender fields stretch into the horizon between rolling green hills.

'Why can't I stop myself from running all the time? The whole idea of moving to the countryside is that I would leave the rat race and slow down. But somehow, no matter what, I never enjoy the moment of being with nature and the beauty of it all.'

Iris sighs, allowing herself to close her eyes and lean back. For a while, all she feels is the movement of the train. It puts her into a trance. Though her body shifts into a relaxed state, the voices in her head keep going.

'I wonder if a day will come when I can let go of my need to run

everything and stop being a control freak like everyone says I am. What was it Mum always used to say?'

'Iris, you can't make everyone like you all the time!'

She opens her eyes. A teenager that reminds her of Joy sits in front of her. The girl is reading 'Anna Karenina'. Iris smiles; that's just like Joy as well. There aren't many youngsters who still read physical books. Without thinking, Iris leans forward.

'You do know he got it all wrong?' Iris says.

The girl looks at her, surprised. 'Who?'

'Tolstoy. Not all happy families are the same. Everyone is happy in their own way.'

The girl has no idea what Iris is on about. She smiles civilly and continues reading.

Feeling embarrassed, Iris tries calling Daisy again, but the call goes to voicemail. She dives back into her long 'To-Do list' to avoid catching the girl's eye again for the rest of her train ride.

ॐ DAISY ৪০

'What did you think?'

I hear Mike saying something, but I have no clue what he is talking about.

'What?' I ask to gain some time to think.

'What's your verdict on Dr Hamburg?' Mike repeats.

I go into my automatic mode of apologising and giving excuses. 'Oh... sorry... I was miles away.'

'I noticed!' Mike says with a laugh. 'So...?'

'I don't know,' I murmur. 'It felt as if I'm talking to a technical manual. I couldn't connect to him at all.'

'I guess it's what professionals are'. Mike responds.

'I want a professional and a human being. He was a total jerk. Judging me for waiting until this age to have kids!'

'So it's a "no" from you. I agree.'

I can breathe easier knowing Mike is on the same page concerning the clinic.

'The only problem is, we're back to square one on this issue,' I mention.

I can see Mike has something on his mind. Knowing him, he is looking for a way to assert it as politely as possible. I can literally hear the wheels whirling in his brain. I can't take it any longer.

'Spit it out!'

'Don't be upset... but why don't you ask Iris? She has experience with giving birth late in life and did well.'

I shake my head so hard; my ears practically start ringing. 'No one knows yet.'

The look on Mike's face tells everything. He never had to deal with my family's lack of understanding of personal boundaries. It has taken me years to establish those borders. If I tell them too early, I know they will ride roughshod over me.

'I'll have to tell them this weekend,' I mutter more to myself than to him.

'Do you think they'll object?' he asks.

'No, but I want this weekend to be about Dad, not about me. The truth is, I don't have the energy to put on a happy face and do the whole Bach Bunch routine of one big happy family.'

'Then we can find an excuse and not go.'

Mike doesn't really know my family, even after all these years together.

'It's Dad's eightieth birthday, and we worked so hard on this. Besides, Iris will kill me if I don't show up.'

Mike squeezes my hand reassuringly. 'I'm sure your Dad will understand. And if you do tell them, I'm certain he'd think it's the best gift you could give him.'

'It's not Dad I'm worried about. It's Mum, and she'll have a new excuse to start controlling our lives.'

This reminds me I switched off my phone hours ago. I turn it on and nearly choke.

'What's wrong?'

'Loads of missed calls from Iris. You'd think someone died. Most likely, all she wants are more stupid details about the damn party.'

Mike roars with laughter. 'You'd better call her back, or she'll have a heart attack!'

I think it over. 'No. I want to go home, take a shower and wash this appointment off me before I call Iris.'

CR HEATHER BO

Heather Bach could have been a beauty queen if she'd wanted. But she and fashion were never friends, which could explain why it took longer to perceive the beauty behind her plainness. Even well into her forties, she managed to maintain a slim, youthful figure and striking looks. Zoe, her girlfriend, had said she couldn't take her eyes off Heather from the moment she'd met her.

Heather and Zoe cuddle up together in their compartment as the train passes through the countryside.

Heather is not looking forward to the coming weekend. 'I just want it to be over as soon as possible so we can return to Berlin.'

Zoe looks like a young Amazon. She has an open face and ready laughter, two reasons why Heather was attracted to her. She knows Zoe balances her seriousness.

'It won't be that bad!'

'You say that, now. Wait till you meet my Mum.'

'I'm excited to meet your Mum,' Zoe replies.

Heather grits her teeth. 'Why on earth do you want to meet her – or my family? You're out of your mind! You could have a marvellous weekend in Berlin. Instead, you're stuck here with me.'

'I'd have to meet your family, sooner or later, if we want this relationship to go anywhere. If so, what better way than your Dad's party.'

'Some might call it a party. I call it a show, especially when Iris is running it. I'm telling you now: you don't want to get to know my family.'

Zoe stares at Heather. 'I suppose it's a case of the old saying, 'you can choose your friends but not your family'.

'They also say blood is thicker than water,' Heather snaps.

Zoe looks away, hurt. Heather gazes out the window. The train's PA system dings with an announcement.

'Next stop, Oxford station. Please don't forget to take all your belongings.'

When the train enters the station, Heather stands up to take their suitcase, and her eye catches a familiar face on the platform.

'What the hell is she doing here?' She cries out loud in a cold voice that could freeze the fires of hell.

Chapter Two

○ろ DAISY 乙○

As usual, there isn't a parking place on our street when we arrive home. Mike drops me outside and continues his mission impossible task of finding one. I enter our house only to face a pile of glossy brochures from various fertility clinics. I bend down to pick them up to find myself looking straight at Oggi, my beloved dog. He greets me with his usual enthusiasm, licking my face and barking with joy at my return. Everything forgotten, I roll around with him, enjoying every second.

'You missed me, didn't you? You deserve a walk; you've been locked up in this house for too long. But first, I have to shower, and then I can take you for walkies. Can you hold on that long? Well, you'll just have to! I'm off to have a shower. Oh, who's a good boy....'

I climb the stairs to my bedroom with Oggi behind me when my phone rings. I know who it is and am too tired to answer it. I don't have the patience for Iris now.

'What the hell do you want now?' I mumble to the empty air, knowing very well Iris will have a long list of questions at the ready. I know the call will feel like an interrogation, and I don't have the energy or time for it. *Oh well, here goes...*

'Hey Iris, what's up?'

'Where were you? I've been trying to reach you for ages! How come you're unavailable on such an important day?'

I can hear Iris barking on the other side of the phone. Iris clearly has forgotten I'm past forty and not her little sister anymore.

Just like old times. But I'm not going to rise to her bait. I don't have time for her control-freakery. Let's just finish this as quickly as I can.

'Ask your questions, Iris,' I say, attempting to hide my irritation with my cold tone.

'I want to negotiate the costs of catering,' Iris says, 'So I need to know how many people have RSVP'd. Also, is Heather taking care of the music? Do you want to say anything? I wrote a few things, and I think Heather has prepared something, so I want to know if you're going to say anything.'

I don't really listen to Iris. All I want is to have that shower and spend some precious time jogging with Oggi. But I know trying to stop Iris on a roll is like trying to stop an avalanche — no way of doing it without burying myself in lengthy explanations.

'Hello, hello? Are you there? Can you give me those numbers?'

Her majesty has finished her monologue.

'Iris, really, I just got in. I need a shower. Give me half an hour, and I'll call you back!'

I can hear Iris swallow. 'Sorry, Daisy! Talk to you later!'

She hangs up. I stare at my phone, surprised at how abruptly Iris ended the call. *That's a first.*

Distracted, I start leafing again through the clinic brochures when I notice the time and drop them down to rush into the shower I promised myself.

❦ IRIS ❧

Iris still holds her phone when she gets off the train. She feels awkward and irritated to the point she can endure the pain from her exchange with Daisy. She tries hard not to micro-manage but is obviously doing it without even noticing. She wants to forget that call as fast as she can.

She glances up for airport directions and drags her suitcase and oversized bag along the platform. The walk allows her to steam out some of that irritation. She passes through the check-in counter. She doesn't speak to the ground staff hostess, only waving her boarding card and joining the long line for security checks.

She checks the screens for her gate. But nothing has shown up yet. She looks for a place to sit, so she can see when her flight is listed. Once she finds the perfect spot, she sees a message from Nate on her phone.

'You're still the LOVE of my life.'

Iris blushes like a teenager who'd just gotten a message from her first boyfriend. *He still does it to me. Even after twenty-five years together, my heart still misses a beat. When will I get over the feeling that I'm not worthy of him?*

As these thoughts run through her head, she quickly types back, 'Can't think of anyone better to spend the rest of my life with, even when you're a pain in the arse sometimes.'

Once she presses SEND, she realises she hasn't heard from Joy about when she'd be arriving at Gatwick. She is hoping to get some time together with her on the train to Oxford for a mother-daughter occasion. She speed-dials JOY, smiling broadly when she hears her beloved daughter on the other end.

❧ JOY ☙

Joy Dillen rushes through Gare Du Nord train station, looking for her platform. She is a 20-year-old quicksilver woman with a sharp tongue, like her maternal grandmother, Verity. She has also inherited her mother's 'take-no-prisoners' attitude, especially when she's on the go. Even burdened with an extensive art portfolio, fabric samples and an overnight backpack, she can keep up with her mother's phone calls without losing sight of her objectives.

She knows her mother expects her to be in Gatwick today, but she has other plans. Though she adores her Mum and treats her Dad with wary respect, she is happier living away from them. She can run her life on her own terms.

While most of her friends are still in university and enjoying their parents' financial support, Joy refuses money from the bank of Mum and Dad unless absolutely necessary. Such dependence is immature. That said, lately she has been suffering from guilt concerning her relationship with her parents.

Joy had not been honest with Iris and Nate but hadn't been able to tell them the whole story just yet. Though she is officially registered as a fashion design student in Paris, for the last six months, she has been working crazy long hours in a big fashion house in Paris as an assistant to one of the rising stars of haute couture.

I can't miss this opportunity! She'd learned more in a week in this job than in two years at university. But she also knows that though she will get a much better experience and education this way, her family expects her to get a proper degree. Hence the guilt: she can't bear disappointing her family. She'd been avoiding talking to Iris for weeks, but she'd have to take that call this time.

'Hi Mum!' And before Iris can say anything, she adds, 'I've got good and bad news. What would you like to hear first?'

'Always the good news first. Who has time for bad news?'

'The good news is that I'll be on time for Grandpa's party.'

'That is good news! And the bad?'

'I'll arrive in Oxford tomorrow!' Joy says, her tone cheerful. 'Don't worry - I fixed the flight. I'm your daughter, after all. After watching you run the world all these years, I've picked up a few of your tricks!'

Iris is baffled. 'Is something wrong? Why can't you come today, like we planned?'

Joy finds her platform. The train is about to leave, and Joy runs to catch it on time. 'I have to make a detour, which is really important for me... Just wish me luck, ok, Mum?'

'Of course, darling, but....'

Joy cuts her off. 'I'm going to miss my train! Is Dad with you?'

'Are you mad? He and your Grandma under the same roof would drive me crazy.'

Joy burst out laughing. 'True. Grandma says he's missing the family gene, and I tend to agree with her. Ok Mum, gotta run, please don't stress too much! Remember, it's supposed to be fun. Love you!'

Joy hangs up.

⌘ IRIS ⌘

Iris looks at her screen. *Fun! What does that mean, and when was the last time I actually did something just for fun?* She thinks, silently fuming.

Iris gazes at the screens, hoping to see her flight, but nothing is showing yet. She looks at her watch and realises the thirty-minute wait Daisy promised her passed. She calls Daisy again.

⌘ DAISY ⌘

I step out of the shower feeling refreshed and energised. Just as I expected, the shower let me wash off the humiliating meeting I had earlier in the fertility clinic.

Now all I want is to have my time with Oggi. Some people relax while reading a book; some have a bath; some drink wine; others do meditations I find ridiculous and pretentious. For me, the best way to unwind is by taking Oggi for his walk. He is the one creature (apart from Mike) I love unconditionally. I adore watching him play, getting excited over everything he spots or sniffs.

This part of the day is my 'me-time'. It gives me an excuse to jog. I can process my thoughts when I am active. It is as if my body does the thinking for me, not my mind. If it were up to me, I would have chosen a career involving physical activity, but growing up with my mother, I knew that was not an option for me. We were all expected to graduate from a prestigious university with a first-class honour's degree and a profession my mother could boast about. Being a mere gym instructor was never on the books for me.

'Don't get me wrong, I do love my work, and I know I'm good at it, but at the end of the day, what makes me happy is when I run with you. You make me feel alive,' I whisper to Oggi as I put on his leash.

My mobile starts ringing. I know it's Iris with her never-ending demands. I hesitate. I want to let Iris wait until I get back from my walk; on the other hand, Iris may ruin my time with Oggi by constantly calling me. I take a deep breath and answer. Before Iris has an opportunity to say anything, I interrupt. 'I don't have those numbers for you.'

'Typical!' Iris asserts. 'Typical of you, you're just like Mum… leaving everything to the last minute. You are truly her daughter.'

I can't take any more of her righteous superiority over me; I completely lose it. 'Thank you for that helpful observation! But, you know what? Let's see how you manage Mum, even for a few days. I haven't seen you do that. Interesting how I've been stuck here taking care of them all these years without any help from you, smart-arse!'

'Fine. I'll see you tomorrow … I hope.'

I hear Iris utter through gritted teeth. I know I've hurt her, but I don't care anymore. I just want my time with Oggi.

❧ IRIS ☙

Sitting at the airport, Iris realises, not for the first time, something has to change. But she doesn't know how to achieve it.

She never expected to hear such forcefulness from Daisy. In her mind, Daisy is the soft, receptive one who keeps the family boat from rocking. But this time, Daisy's response had been like a splash of icy water on Iris's face.

Iris felt frustration wash through her. It is as if no one is taking this event seriously. She, as usual, is the only one who wants it to be perfect.

It's as if I'm the only one that cares.

She knows it is ridiculous, but she feels as if someone 'up there' is doing Her best to make Iris' day as miserable as possible. Nothing is going well for her. Her flight still does not show up, so who knows when she will arrive in Oxford? She isn't going to have time with Joy, and now she will have even more work to do, all because her sister didn't follow up on people.

Iris looks up at the screens only to see her flight is delayed.

'Fuck, it's not my day!' Iris whispers, glancing around in case anyone has heard her swear.

Just what I need to make this day even more stressful

A black taxi stops at the entrance of an impressive Victorian house on the outskirts of Oxford. Iris steps out of the cab and takes the view in. She hasn't been back home for a long time.

When she thinks of the word "home", this is it: the red terra-cotta brick, the cast-iron gate and the railing leading from the street into the small front garden.

The porch with its beautiful stained-glass door is still stunning. Magical light plays on the decorative tiled floor of the lobby, courtesy of the sun's rays. That pales into insignificance next to the unforgettable lush Wisteria covering the house's front. Each year it needs trimming to prevent it from taking over the whole entrance and blocking it. Iris smiles when she remembers fighting with her Mum about it; she'd said it would be wonderful not to trim it and have an adventure when you hacked through it to get to the door.

'Good God!' Verity said. 'Whatever would the neighbours say?'

Adventure was one thing, but looking respectable was much more important for Verity. The Bachs had their standing in the community to consider. Iris walks towards the house, noticing touches of neglect. That was out of character for her parents.

This would never have happened if I had lived here. Well, I guess I can't complain. I haven't been here to take care of anything.

Iris knows what is coming. She takes a deep breath and whispers, 'Let the games begin...' as she rings the bell.

Chapter Three

☙ HEATHER ❧

Heather is busy putting the finishing touches to the video and photo album she made for her Dad Sol's eightieth birthday. She enjoys doing it. It is her way of showing how much she admires him - and there is a lot to admire.

What she respects most, and also never can understand, is that he is still married to Verity after all these years. He even seems still to love her.

Anyone who loves Mum so much must be someone special.

The last few days at home had not been easy for her. It looked like all her memories were stored in the house itself. It was as if she had opened Pandora's box just by coming back here.

It all started when she and Zoe disembarked from the train to find Verity waiting on the platform. Heather hadn't been ready for it. Zoe took control of the situation before it turned into World War Three. If Heather is honest with herself, Verity still pushes all her buttons.

Heather knows she must have had some good times in this house, but she keeps hearing her mother's voice, screaming at her, or criticising everything she does wherever she goes in the house. Above all is her never-ending demands to do the 'right' thing, to which Heather never agreed. Any attempt to challenge Verity ends in miserable defeat. It only cemented Heather's attitude to life of being cautious about anything she says or does.

To her astonishment, Zoe hit it off with her mother from the first moment. Her mother is charmed by Zoe's easy-going nature and readiness to laugh. Zoe takes Verity off Heather's hands so she can prepare everything Iris demands for the party.

It's great for me, too. I wouldn't have been able to stay here that long otherwise.

Iris is about to arrive any moment. Heather cannot remember when Iris wasn't giving orders left, right and centre. She is always in charge of things, even when absent. Heather has no desire to change her, but it is irritating that even at her age, Iris still thinks she has the right to tell her what to do and how to do it.

The doorbell rings. Walking to open the door, she mutters to herself. 'Get a grip, Heather. It's been years, and people change. Maybe this time, Iris won't be so bad? Perhaps she's mellowed with the years, and we won't get the Sergeant-Major routine now she's back. She's your sister. She means well. If she runs the whole show, it will get Mum off my back when Zoe isn't here. Let's give it a try.'

Heather opens the door and spots Iris pulling out some ivy growing between the cracks. *So much for change!*

'Thank God you're here! It's been such a long time... wow!' Heather hugs Iris, hoping effusive compliments will carry the moment 'You look really well.'

'Well. I hope I look better than this place!' Iris retorts.

'Still can't handle compliments, I see!'

'Compliments are a novelty at our age, don't you think?'

Walking down the hall towards the living room, Iris cannot help herself. She detects every speck of dirt. It looks as if no one has cleaned the place for a long time. *That's weird, so much not the place I know.*

Arriving at the living room, Heather watches Iris's face finally break into a smile. The house is still breath-taking, the highlight being the huge French doors leading into the most spectacular garden. The room looks like a nineteenth-century Parisian cultural salon taken from a movie. They both can remember people being entertained here and various intellectual talks taking place. Ghosts from the past still occupy the room.

'Such a pity I arrived so late. I would have loved to go out and see the garden. When I think of home, the garden is the place I miss the most.'

'Plenty of time to see it tomorrow.'

If you miss this place so much, why haven't you come more often?

Heather manages to bite her lip. Iris is rapt with admiration, taking in the room that had always fascinated her. Heather watches her start detecting the broken doorknobs, the old newspapers piled up, and dirt around the fireplace. She frowns. She turns to Heather. 'Where is everyone?'

'Well, you know Dad, he's in his study and Mum… who knows? Somewhere in the house. Thank God for Zoe! She keeps her busy and out of my way. I don't know how I would have survived these last two days if she hadn't kept Mum entertained. I don't get it, but she likes Mum! She even enjoys her company. For the life of me, I don't understand how anyone could!'

'Well, Mum can be charming when she wants to,' Iris says, 'I guess I'm in my old room?'

'Did you expect something else? I thought Joy was coming with you. Where is she?'

'I thought so too. She'll be here tomorrow. No idea why. She was so mysterious on the phone. I hope everything is ok.'

Heather grins. 'She'll be fine!'

'I know, but still...I swear that kid could charm her way out of a murder. Don't know where she gets it from.' Iris says in her usual sarcasm while walking to her room.

Iris enters her old room and scans it with her gimlet eye. Heather knew that, like her, Iris could hear conversations she's had in this room.

So many dreams are still trapped in these walls.

'Daisy tells me you did a remarkable job on that album for Dad. I'd love to see it. Where is it?'

Heather smiles. *We're on familiar territory now. We're back on a project. Safety beckons...* When it came to more personal issues, there was too much-undisclosed business. It was like a bomb waiting to explode in the family. *Better not go into it. Stick to the predictable.*

'It's in the living room. I'll show you.'

She and Iris return to the living room where a huge album rests on a table, full of old photos and letters of congratulations people sent their father for his eightieth birthday, sharing a piece of history from their lives with him.

'It's beautiful. You've created something amazing. I'm sure he'll love it.'

'I thought I heard the doorbell! Who is it?'

Verity Bach sweeps into the living room. At seventy-eight, their mother keeps her slim figure and youthful looks. It's not that someone would take her for a thirty-year-old, but Verity's energy, the way she dresses and how she moves through life, makes everyone ignore the lines on her face and only experience the force of nature she is.

Zoe follows Verity. Heather notices her partner's beauty and youth takes Iris aback. Zoe rushes to Iris, giving her an intense and loving hug. That throws Iris out of balance. She never expected Heather to be with someone who expresses feelings openly and physically. Heather realises Iris always thought she was only attracted to intellectual, cold people.

Well, maybe people do change.

'Iris, when did you arrive? No one told me you were coming!' Verity complains, giving Iris a cold, appraising once-over. She turns to Heather. 'Why didn't you tell me Iris is coming?'

'We did, Mum.'

Verity cuts her off. 'When will you learn to express yourself accurately? You should take elocution lessons!'

Heather bites her lip. Verity turns to Iris with her arms outstretched. Iris cringes very slightly.

'I'm so happy to see you, darling! Let's have a look at you.'

Verity examines Iris from head to toe. Iris stands awkwardly as if for an audition. Heather notes that Iris, the powerful woman, disappears. All that is left is a little girl trying to please the adults.

Verity sniffs. 'You've gained weight. It's not healthy. I've always been slim. You get that from your father's side of the family, being fat. You should know better, darling: a woman can never be too rich or thin. Fortunately, I've always been both!'

'I think Iris lost weight since we last saw her.'

Verity turns sharply on Heather. 'No one asked you, Heather! What would you know about it? You could have been a beauty queen with your figure and looks, but you make the utmost effort to be a frump. How you ended up with someone as attractive as Zoe is beyond me.'

Heather's face remains impassive, but she clenches her fists.

Verity puts her manicured hands on Iris' shoulders.

'All women should look their best. Look at me! You should make the extra effort at your age. It's not your fault you weren't given much to work with.'

Iris shuts her eyes. Heather finds her mother's casual cruelty hard to swallow. The words, *some things never change,* echo in her brain.

Iris smiles brightly. 'I'm probably wearing the wrong outfit... Where's Dad? Let's reel him out of his study and back into the real world!'

It is an effective distraction strategy. Iris takes Verity by the hand, and they walk out of the living room together. As they go down the long corridor that leads to Sol's study, Iris glances back at Heather and mouths 'thank you' to her.

Zoe is stunned by the exchange she just witnessed. She had gone through life avoiding confrontations as much as possible. As a foster child, that was the best strategy. She had turned it into an art form, deflecting any kind of confrontation by being funny and sweet.

Seeing Verity lash out at Heather and Iris in front of her was shocking.

The last few days with Verity had been an absolute pleasure. It was not at all how she had imagined it.

All the time she'd been with Heather, she only heard negative remarks about Verity, so she was expecting to meet a dragon lady. But when they arrived at this breath-taking house, all she saw was an elderly, well-preserved woman who was longing for company. She had fascinating stories about her early life, which she loved to tell: her parents' farm, her grandparents' lovely house in suburban London, the swinging sixties, meeting Sol, and how she dedicated her life to his career. Although she repeated the same story several times, she was such a good storyteller that it was like watching your favourite movie each time. She was able to describe people and events vividly. She didn't expect this kind of cruelty from her.

All she could do was give Heather a reassuring hug. She appreciates Iris's deflection, taking Verity away.

She's a much stronger woman than I could ever be. I probably would just freeze like a deer in headlights.

Zoe saw how this impressive woman could turn cold and cruel, lashing out at her own flesh and blood. It was like watching Mr Jekyll turning into Mr Hyde. Now she understood why Heather didn't want to return to this place.

Chapter Four

❧ SOL ❧

Solomon Bach - Sol, to his family and friends - is working in his study. Some might call it a study, but to him, it is his private haven. It was where he could spend eternity quite happily if it were up to him.

Sol loves his profession with a rare passion. Even after sixty years of research and study, he can still find a new aspect in his field of history that excites him. More than that, he enjoys developing new theories to solve questions. Finding the appropriate texts and historical evidence to prove them thrills him beyond measure. Above all, he relishes finding evidence to discredit theories that were proven incorrectly due to sloppy research.

He still remembers the first time he was introduced to the magical world of ancient scripts and how fascinated he was. It was like finding a treasure map and finding the key to unlock what was written on it. It was his first love.

His second is Verity.

His study is his fairyland. He can get lost there, only to find his way back after adventures amidst the fragile manuscripts and dusty books.

It is a typical scholarly room. The room is full of bookshelves from bottom to top on all walls. The heart of the room is his antique Victorian writing table.

He can precisely remember the day he found that table, more than sixty years ago. He'd taken Verity on their weekly trip to the Cotswolds. They'd had this tradition of scouting for treasure in antique markets, mainly because they were young and broke.

They were strolling through the streets of one of the old villages when Sol noticed the table standing outside an antique shop. He was drawn to it as if the table was calling him. However, by the time he got close to examine it, another person had stepped in and was enquiring about the price from the shop owner.

Never before had Sol felt so compelled to purchase something as he did at that moment. Nevertheless, the asking price was way higher than he could afford. The other man didn't seem to mind. He would never have bought that table if it hadn't been for Verity. Her ability to captivate people and negotiate most charmingly was something he was incapable of.

Verity had stepped in and started talking with the owner, ignoring the other man, and taking the owner's attention away from him. She entertained him with anecdotes and stories, and within minutes it seemed as if she was a long-lost friend of the shop owner. As her sparkling conversation continued, the other customer lost patience and left the shop. That was when she started negotiating the price of the desk.

Sol had watched in amazement. It'd looked more like a tennis match than a negotiation. In the end, Verity managed to get him to lower the price to something they could afford, but not before she'd invited him for dinner at their place as a sign of appreciation. It had been the beginning of a beautiful relationship with that particular antique shop owner, which had lasted for years. His name was Graham. During the years, they filled their home with other pieces purchased from him. Verity had a knack for creating and keeping friendships alive for years.

Buying the desk had been a symbol for Sol of the strength of his partnership with Verity. Neither came from wealthy families, so her ability to negotiate on everything had meant a lot during their years together.

Verity's family were farmers who struggled to keep a roof over their heads. Sol's family were refugees who escaped Germany at the last minute before World War Two broke out.

His father had been a famous doctor, but he was stripped of all positions once Hitler came to power. He was not allowed to work in any prestigious institution, despite the fact he had been highly sought after as a private physician to the upper echelons of the Nazi party. He'd seen the writing on the wall for the Jews and took a request from Mussolini's office to treat a friend. He had escaped Germany with Sol's mother, Sol and his brother and sister.

They were scheduled to return via London, where his father maintained a good relationship with the Council for Assisting Refugee Academics, who had arranged for them to stay in the UK. Their only possessions were the clothes in their suitcases when they left Germany for what they thought would be a short visit.

Although he was only six years old when they arrived in the UK, Sol remembers the warm reception they got when they first came to Oxford, their first home.

The last two years before they left were marked in his brain.

Overnight, his friends refused to play with him. His best friend was not allowed to come to his home. Each time Sol had seen him at school, the boy turned his back on him, later joining others in bullying him. He didn't understand what he'd done to deserve it.

Only years later, he realised that it had nothing to do with him personally but with the fact that he was Jewish. Even the teachers joined in. One day, his parents told him he couldn't attend school. Jews were no longer allowed to go to school. He was relieved.

But the harassment didn't stop there. Wearing the yellow star on his clothes made him an instant target wherever he went. His mother wouldn't allow him to go down the street anymore on his own, in fear for his life. The most traumatising incident was not one he experienced personally but witnessed.

He was standing at the window at his parents' home, looking outside, when he saw his parents' neighbours being forced to clean the pavement in front of their pharmacy, which was opposite Sol's house. The chemist ran the shop with his wife. They were kind people, always watching out for the elderly and the ill.

Sol felt his face flush with shame as he watched the once-proud couple kneeling on the pavement, scrubbing it clean of dog excrement, while SS guards and a mob jeered and laughed at them. Sol hadn't realised they were Jewish too. The wife raised her head, tears in her eyes and looked directly at Sol. A guard hit her in the face with his rifle butt, and she collapsed amid the dirty suds and filth. Sol could see the blood on her face.

Now in Oxford, it was strange. Instead of being rejected and feeling like an outsider, they were suddenly the centre of attention: the distinguished physician and his charming family. Given the physician's proximity to the ruling party, they held a certain cachet. Everyone had wanted to help them settle down.

From an early age, he'd known he could never follow in his father's footsteps in medicine. The very thought of blood made him faint. Even so, Sol loved it when his father sat with him, and they read books about natural science and biology.

Hoping to encourage Sol to a medical career, his father brought a frog home to dissect. At first, it seemed exciting for Sol, but blood oozed out when he cut into the frog. He blacked out. He woke up to find himself on the floor. Sol was instantly transported to seeing the chemist's wife to his degradation.

From that moment, it had become the family joke. His sister, Miriam, tormented him by splashing her clothes with red poster paint, telling him she was bleeding, only to see him weaken and faint.

No, medicine was not on the books for him, which disappointed his father. He resigned himself to Sol's interest in more bookish pursuits. As Sol grew up, he found his bloodless sanctuary in the Classics.

He could still recall the thrill he felt when he'd first entered the Bodleian Library. It was like stepping into a magical world where you could wander where you wished. Nowhere in the world was there a better place for him to explore his passion for new material in ancient scrolls than in the Bodleian Library and Ashmolean Museum.

Oxford had been a magical place for Sol from the moment

they arrived. The combination of ancient buildings and open fields around them was enchanting for him. He enjoyed both worlds. He explored the beautiful old buildings that looked like they had come out of fairy tales, then went out and roamed through the forest, where he imagined himself as a knight on a quest.

Very quickly, his parents found a small place on Woodstock Road near his Dad's workplace at the Radcliffe Infirmary. The small apartment was in an impressive old Victorian mansion now divided into separate flats.

The Bach family could only afford the basement flat, traditionally allocated for the servants. Most days, it was dark in every single room. But its saving grace was the big kitchen, where the family assembled as much as possible. It was used as a living room and dining room, where the children would play and obviously, where meals were cooked. While growing up, the kitchen was where Sol associated most with family life.

The other advantage of the flat was the direct exit to what used to be the kitchen garden of the old mansion. Though neglected, the small garden still provided fresh herbs and a place for Sol, his brother, and his sister to play.

Their mother encouraged them to play outside as much as possible, and the garden was an excellent place for their burgeoning imaginations, freed from the constraints of discrimination.

His father was absent most of the time, but they knew that this was not because he was a bad father or didn't care for them but because he was a good doctor and cared very much for his patients.

The Bach place at Woodstock suited them as a family so much that his parents stayed there until they passed away in the eighties. Sol himself stayed there until he married Verity.

Verity had not been willing to live in a place that was associated with servants. She always aimed higher. The fact that she came from a poor farming background strongly motivated her to get a place that would look respectable and impress other people. Appearances were important for Verity.

The house Sol and Verity found was outside central Oxford but close enough to a bus stop, which made it easy for Sol to get into Oxford on days when it was raining. Otherwise, he preferred cycling to his college and library. The house itself had the same feeling as his parents' home, only this time because it was in a suburban area, the price was so low even they could afford it.

Little did Sol know that within a few years, property prices would rise so high they'd be living in something worth a fortune. *On the other hand,* Sol thought, *maybe Verity knew, with her sharp business sense?*

She should have been a businesswoman, but no respectable woman could have done that in those days. No, Verity did what was expected of her and became a teacher, first in a primary school, later becoming headmistress of one of the private schools in Oxford. No wonder she was permanently exhausted.

However, as she always stated, her primary role in life was to pave the road for Sol's success. She ensured he rose through the College ranks, becoming a prominent figure in the social circles of the college and the City. She did this by throwing splendid parties. Their place, though outside the City, became the hub of all the important social gatherings. People were happy to meet at their home, whether they were the Dean of the college (for intellectual discussions) or fun-loving partygoers (for the excellent food and vintage wines). They held summer parties in their amazing garden.

Verity was the queen of hostesses. She knew how to create a fantastic evening for any event. People enjoyed her charming company, sparkling wit, and innate good taste. She knew how to make every conversation lively and stimulating. She would focus on whomever she was talking to, making them feel they were the most important person in the world, and then she would lead them by the hand and introduce them to someone else, with whom the most charming conversation could then take place.

'If I have one skill, it's connecting people,' she would tell her daughters. But most of all, she brought fun and light into Sol's otherwise serious life. Sol could not imagine how his life would have been without Verity. *It would have been very dull,* he thought to himself when he reminisced about his life.

History and the Classics were fascinating, but at the end of the day, you want someone to share your life with. He lived with dead people and memories of a grand past. Thanks to his clever wife, his life was full of laughter and excitement. Sol was unaware that he had made no physical effort in this endeavour. Verity did everything; she earned her own money, raised their daughters, ran the house, and organised every aspect of Sol's career.

Lately, he had been thinking a lot about his life. He'd been strong-armed into this party for his eightieth... *or maybe it's just because I'm getting older*, he thought. *Where has the time gone? Eighty used to be so old, but I certainly don't feel that way*. He certainly didn't look that way, either. He still cycled the four miles to Oxford as much as he could. Whenever there was a party, he was the last one dancing. These days, unfortunately, it wasn't with Verity, who was the one who taught him how to dance so many years ago. Today, she preferers sitting and talking with her friends and not dancing with him, so he ends up dancing with his daughters at family celebrations. Sometimes he dances with younger women who Verity keeps inviting to their many social events.

'Are they undergrads?' he would ask.

'No, darling!' Verity would say, laughing. 'They're professors!'

Sol would shake his head in wonderment. As he got older, his colleagues got younger. He was much given to this sort of reflection.

Even so, he feels that his biggest successes are not the awards or prestigious positions he's held in life or even the fame in classical circles. No, his greatest successes are his beloved daughters, of which he is most proud. Each one of them, in her own way, has become someone he admires. It isn't that they followed his career with their life choices, but they were all independent, powerful women with full lives, contributing to society. They are his biggest achievement, he feels. Again, Sol is unconscious of how little he has had to do with their day-to-day physical lives.

He does regard himself as a lucky man. He has a wonderful marriage, great children, and work that feels more like a passion. He's seen much of the world and travelled far beyond his dreams, primarily due to Verity's lust for life. Verity always felt she was missing something and that there was something even more interesting somewhere else - wherever there was, it was never here.

She kept pushing him, her kids and herself to move forward and see what was around the corner. She is the fire that keeps him burning. *Without her,* he thinks, *I would have been satisfied staying in one place for the rest of my life, focusing only on my research and manuscripts.* But Verity demanded more from him, which wasn't easy and often irritating, but today he knows it made his life a thousand times richer.

Sitting in his study, his table covered with books, manuscripts, papers, and an old-fashioned box-like computer, he appreciates that his life wouldn't have been half so rich without Verity.

All those thoughts made him emotional, which takes him by surprise. Growing up, he was not used to showing and expressing emotions. It was not until he met Verity and her family that he first encountered a different way of dealing with emotions - loud, raw, and passionate.

At first, he was shocked, then intrigued, fearful even, but after sixty years with the woman and her family, he got used to it. He could always escape to his study if it all got too much. He used the same strategies if Verity and the girls were arguing. His study was off-limits.

'Daddy's working, girls!' Verity used to shout. And they would be ushered from outside his door.

He raises his head from his papers and looks through the

big French doors that lead from his study into the lush garden. Even at night, it is an enchanting sight with the small fairy lights Verity had insisted on installing long ago.

Not bad for a little refugee boy, he thinks.

He hears some noises from the corridor leading to his room, but lately so many people have been going in and out of the house, he tries to block them out and focus on his work.

When he hears the soft knock on his door, he is surprised. Everyone important to him knows never to disturb him when he is in his study. He cannot imagine anyone in his family disobeying this mandate.

But when the door opens and Iris walks in, saying, 'Happy Birthday, Dad!' he cannot be happier. Iris is the only one of his daughters who used to be intrigued by his research. He never understood why she abandoned her academic studies and moved into business. Life as an entrepreneur is so unpredictable.

∽ IRIS ∾

For Iris, her father's study has always exerted a special kind of magic on her. It was like entering another dimension, where space and time have their own rules. She always thought that no matter how many books her father purchased, there would always be space for them in that room. It is as if the room stretched to accommodate the never-ending procession of books.

Iris gazes at Sol and experiences a massive surge of love for this man. She can never understand how he always stays calm and kind despite what he had to go through in his early life. She admires him.

She recalls the days when she wanted so much to follow in his footsteps, only to discover that Oxford is not an easy place for a woman to reach the top, especially if her father is a respected academic. Though she loved her studies, she realised that if she ever wanted to make a name for herself, academia was definitely not the way to go. Not that building your own business and running it is easier, but there at least the fight is in the open.

At university, she discovered the fight was always behind your back, and she'd never been good at diplomacy and politics. She was much more of an in-your-face person, certainly when she was younger. Iris knows it was a disappointment for Verity that she dropped out, but it was the first time in her life she had chosen to do something that would make herself happy.

Well, thank God Heather brought them pride by getting her PhD. At least one of us maintains the family tradition of being a scholar. Thank God it wasn't me.

Iris hugs Sol and observes how fragile he feels.

He's getting old. There was a time, not so long ago, when I had to stretch to hug him. Suddenly the man has shrunk.

Sol would probably say he needed to watch his weight, but there was more to it. It was as if the air, and life, had been knocked out of him. She wonders if his escape into the past might have taken its toll, drawing his energy for the present out of him.

'Let's take you out into the world of the living, Dad. Let's have dinner, and you can tell me about your latest research.'

Sol could not have been more pleased to hear these words. 'At last! I can talk intelligently with someone about my work!'

Iris is surprised to hear him speak in such a blunt way.

'Come on, Dad! Heather is the one with the PhD - and MA letters after her name, not me. I'm sure you can talk to her about your research.'

'It's not the same,' Sol insists. 'She comes from the scientific research world, but you understand how classic research works. It's different. She could never get excited about finding a new archaeological site in a place no one expected it to be, or uncovering ancient cities that could shed some light on a life lived two thousand years ago. You could! You always got excited by turning rocks over to discover what was underneath or finding a scroll or document in an archive that no one paid attention to. I never understood why you never completed your PhD. You had such a great topic and good research!'

Verity hovers at the door. 'But we're very proud of you. I never imagined you would achieve so much in your life!' she declares.

Iris gapes at her mother. Hearing such praise from Verity overwhelms her. Sol beams, oblivious. *That's weird. I had to reach my sixties to hear my mother compliment me. That's not the woman I know.*

She could still hear the sting of disappointment in her Dad's words, but that was something she'd learned to live with. Sol knew when to let things lie.

On the other hand,... Mum, as always, prefers one child over another.

'I think all your children have done great things, Mum,' Iris comments briskly. 'After all, we had fantastic role models in you two. Now let's have dinner. I'm starving! There was so much junk food while I was travelling. I haven't eaten a thing all day.'

Chapter Five

᚛ IRIS ᚜

In most houses, if you ask the occupants which room turns the house into a home, they'll have their own idea of which room it should be. For some, it's their living room, where they can relax at the end of the day to watch their favourite TV show or movie. For others, it's their bedroom, where they feel safe and protected, cuddled up under the blankets as if fulfilling a long-hidden desire to return to the womb. For some, it's their bathroom, a place of privacy and rejuvenation.

For Iris, the heart of the house is the kitchen.

'Nothing is more homely,' she'd say, 'than a kitchen. This is where real life takes place!'

Food and cooking are, for her, the epitomes of what a home is. The kitchen is the heart of the Bach family life. The living room is for showing off and entertaining guests. The kitchen is raw, real, where the Bachs are fully realised as human beings. Growing up in this house, she couldn't recall a time when the most crucial moments of their lives didn't take place in the kitchen. There's a reason people say, 'If you can't take the heat, don't go into the kitchen.' The Bach kitchen was always hot – food being prepared, the steam from the kettle, family arguments.

Verity loved the kitchen too, though for her, it was a practical means to an end. There were always children to be fed or guests to be entertained. Whenever Iris came home, the fridge was stocked with the best food, plus delicious leftovers from Verity's parties. It was food any restaurant would have been proud to serve, and it had all been made by Verity.

Iris believed that for Verity, food equalled love. She would show her love through her cooking. No matter how much you ate, there would still be another dish Verity had prepared that, if you didn't try it, would mortally offend her. Iris joked that she'd grown up on Verity's weekend party leftovers, as she made so much that even the most gluttonous guests never finished it all, so the whole family could be fed on it for the following week without her having to cook again. All she needed to do was warm it up.

Thus it was how the Bach girls ate lobster thermidor, canapés, crostini, gravadlax and steak tartare every week during party season. *Very effective,* Iris used to think later on in life when she had to cook for her own family, who refused leftovers and wanted only freshly made meals from scratch.

When Iris, Verity and Sol enter the kitchen, Zoe and Heather are already setting the table for dinner. Iris opens the fridge, expecting to find the usual numerous Tupperware boxes full of food for them to enjoy, but all she sees are half-empty shelves.

She closes the door and gives Heather a questioning look. *What's going on here? That's really weird.* Heather shrugs. Verity is oblivious. Iris's heart misses a beat. This is scary. Iris takes out whatever she can find in the fridge. Fortunately, there were eggs and salad ingredients. That was hardly up to the extravagances of the past, but it would have to do.

'Would omelettes and a big salad be enough for everyone?' she says, smiling. 'Meanwhile, Dad, why don't you tell me what you're working on these days?'

Sol is happy to answer. He usually left the dinner table conversation to Verity. Small talk has never been his forte - another reason Verity was such a great partner for him. But if you ask him what he is working on, all reticence will vanish. It is as if he downloads all his thoughts and ideas into the other person's ear. He can talk about the latest obscure artefact that has been discovered for hours, citing all the articles and books written on the subject.

This evening, he is even more delighted that Iris asks him about his work than usual. Now he can talk about the latest book he is writing.

'I was asked to write an article for a book that will be published in memory of Professor Brown. You remember him, don't you?'

'Sure,' Iris replies, trying to recall when she'd last seen Professor Brown. It had to be over thirty years ago. *God, where does the time go?* 'I didn't know he died! When did that happen?'

'Oh, six years ago. Just like that. I saw him in the library on Monday, and we discussed some new developments in C14 dating technology. The next day he was gone. He died in his sleep. Best way to go at our age....'

'Dad!' Heather cries. 'You're not ready to go. You're healthy and strong. He wasn't. He had high blood pressure and diabetes. I always remember his wife trying to control his diet. Poor woman.'

Sol ignores Heather's outburst. 'Anyway, I was asked to write

43

an article for a book the college is publishing in his name, but you know me! It started as an article, but now it's become a full-length book. So now I'm trying to figure out how to give an extract for Professor Brown's book, and at the same time have a full manuscript for a standalone book on the topic. It's truly exciting!'

'Pffft!' Verity mutters. 'No one ever reads these books or even buys them. Who cares if something is an original manuscript from the fifth century or a fake one from the eighteenth? At the end of the day, if no one buys those books, you can't pay your bills.'

'Ah, my practical wife!' Sol says, smiling at Verity.

Zoe looks shocked. Iris and Heather shoot looks at each other. They are both outraged at how Verity is so unappreciative of his work and the child-like excitement it evokes in him. She is always convinced that poverty lies just around the corner—a symptom perhaps of her rural upbringing where bad weather could destroy crops.

Heather helps Iris prepare the dinner, muttering, 'bitch!' under her breath. Iris frowns at her. Sol is oblivious. Verity, on the other hand, now has the attention she needs.

'Professor Brown still owes me a mink coat. He told me the royalties of the first book he and your father wrote over fifty years ago would be enough for your father to buy me a mink coat. I'm still waiting.'

Heather is unable to contain her anger at Verity any longer. 'Yes, we know, Mum. You tell us this story every time someone mentions his name.'

Verity's eyes narrow at the challenge. Zoe glances around for a clue as to how she should react.

'It's called the art of conversation, Heather,' Verity bites back. 'Something you have no clue about, even with all the education we've provided for you. The least you can do is shut your mouth and listen, hoping you might learn something....'

Iris steps forward and puts a hand on her mother's shoulder, distracting her. 'Mum, help me bring the food to the table. I couldn't make as much as you do, but I think it will suffice for tonight,' Iris utters, a big bowl of salad in one hand. 'I was expecting the usual fridge full of meals, but it appears you haven't been entertaining as much lately!'

'Oh, all right, dear,' Verity reacts as though nothing had happened. The silence during dinner was unbearable. Zoe keeps her eyes on her omelette. Heather picks at hers, fuming. Sol is miles away, thinking about his book.

'Let's talk about tomorrow's party!' Iris announces to break the awkward silence, making everyone jump slightly.

'What party? I'm not aware of any party! It's not written in any of my diaries. What are you talking about?'

'Mum... We've been working on this for the past three months. It's Dad's eightieth birthday this weekend, and we're having a lunch party in the garden the day after tomorrow. We thought it would be nice to celebrate just as a family tomorrow.'

'How come no one's asked me about this? It's my house, my rules! Or have you forgotten that? Now, who's the forgetful one? Besides, he's my husband. How come I haven't been consulted?'

For once in her life, Iris is left without any quick response to her mother's accusations. They'd been planning this weekend with her and Sol for months. How is it she has no recollection of it?

Something's not right with Mum. This is more serious than short-term memory loss. She needs to be re-examined.

'Mum!' Iris contends, attempting to control the spiralling thoughts in her head. 'You and Dad made the list. It was difficult with your huge circle, but in the end we managed to limit it to eighty people.'

'This is ridiculous!' Verity shouts, throwing her napkin on her plate. 'I want to see who you've invited. You probably forgot the most important people. You have no idea how to plan such an event. Besides, I hate it when you lie to me! You all lie to me. You think you can decide everything for me and use the excuse of my short-term memory loss to run my life. I will not have it! Stop lying to me!'

Zoe looks like she's close to tears. Sol puts his hand over Verity. She shrugs him off. Verity has never been one to keep calm when she isn't happy with how things are going. The only person who gives back as good as she gets is Iris. The quiet, cosy family reunion is seconds away from being blown to pieces.

'Don't you dare call me a liar!' Iris asserts. 'I have the list in my room. Is that what you want me to do now? Bring it down so you can see what's written in your OWN handwriting?'

As usual, the only person able to relax Verity is Sol. He puts his hand gently on Verity's shoulder. 'Let's all relax,' he mentions softly with a smile. 'Nice to see that some things never change! It only takes twenty minutes for the two of you to blow up the neighbourhood.'

'Darling, I never wanted to make a big deal out of this birthday, but you insisted, and in the end, you came up with this brilliant idea of inviting eighty people to symbolise each year of my life. I think it is a fantastic idea. And, as usual, our girls came together to help you make this happen.'

And then a transformation happens. Verity gazes at Sol with eyes full of adoration. 'If you say so... you always were my memory. What would I do without you?'

Zoe lets her breath out.

'We get to live another day...' she whispers to Heather, who has also been holding her breath. Heather laughs out loud, which allows everyone to join in and move on.

Later that night, once Verity and Sol have gone to bed, Heather, Iris, and Zoe sit in the kitchen chatting, avoiding anything controversial. However, once Zoe declares she is going to bed, Heather refills Iris's wine glass.

'Did you know it is as bad as this?'

Iris shakes her head. Heather frowns.

'What did you expect once they diagnosed her?' Heather says bitterly.

Iris looks surprised. 'But they said it is just a short-term memory issue. They didn't say she has dementia or Alzheimer's. We all lose short-term memory as we get older, don't we?' She is really hoping Heather will confirm this belief. Her mother is all fire, focus and determination. Nothing can win against Verity, especially something so quotidian as dementia.

Heather is silent for a moment. She'd never seen Iris so clueless. Iris is the pillar that has held the family edifice up all these years, so it surprises Heather to see her so helpless and concerned about something so obvious to Heather. *I can't believe Iris could be under any illusions.*

For the first time in her life, Heather senses she is the adult and Iris is the child. This is a new experience for Heather, who has always perceived Iris as a controlling extension of their mother.

She comprehends Iris is still holding on to the image of Verity they'd all had growing up. But that is not the woman of today.

'What did you understand when they gave us the diagnosis of short-term memory loss?'

Iris shrugs her shoulders, trying to formulate an answer. 'The truth is I didn't give it much thought. It didn't mean much to me. I thought it was the usual - forgetting names, where you put your keys, or can't recall whether you met someone on Tuesday or Thursday. You know, the things that happen when you have an active, busy life after turning seventy-five. But this isn't what we're talking about here. I mean, how is it possible she's forgotten all the conversations we've had in the last two months? How is it possible she forgot she wrote that list? How is it possible she forgot I sat with her, and we went through her address book one person at a time to choose who to invite? Trust me. It was a huge list! Do you know she even keeps lists of people she invited to all the parties through the years so she can compare who she invited and who invited them back? We went through everything!'

Heather is amazed to see Iris in such a state. 'You really didn't understand that the term' short-term memory loss' is just another way of defining dementia?' she suggests softly.

'No, I didn't. But doesn't that mean it's going to get worse?'

'Yes, it does.'

'Then we need to find a way to help Dad handle this. He can't take care of her. She's the one that takes care of him! How can he reverse the roles? We need to get him some help.'

Heather remains silent. *Here she is, all bossy and deciding what's best. And to think I felt some sympathy for her for a moment!* 'Did you consider asking Dad if he wants that kind of help?'

Iris stares at Heather. If looks could have killed...

'Have you seen their fridge? Since when is our family fridge as empty as that? Who's doing the cooking when we're not here? Dad probably eats in the college refectory, but what about Mum? And what does she do when he's in the library? She could set the house on fire just because she warmed something up and forgot it was on the stove. She could go out on her usual bike ride and get lost! Don't you see how dangerous this situation is? And you expect Dad to put his life on hold to care for her?'

Heather sighs. 'I'm not saying the situation is good. I am surprised about the fridge, too. Right now, she's only in the first stages of the disease. We'll need to send her for another test to define what type of dementia she has. If it's Alzheimer's, then we can predict its trajectory. If it's another type, we'll know what to expect. But right now, the only people here are Dad and Daisy. Do you see Daisy taking care of Mum? I don't think so, given their history. We should be grateful for the fact that she's still willing to come up once a week. And by the way, let's give Dad some credit. He's not that helpless! Why not trust him to look after Mum for a change?'

Iris listens to Heather attentively, appreciating there is truth in what Heather asserts. She is in her old habit of taking care of everyone without checking if that is what they want.

She smiles at Heather. 'You're right. I'm on automatic pilot. Maybe it's not such a bad thing that Dad takes care of Mum after all the years she's been taking care of him.'

Heather chuckles. 'Time for bed. It's going to be a long day tomorrow. Let's get some rest.'

She leaves Iris sitting in the kitchen with her own thoughts. The house is silent. The thoughts in Iris's head rise in volume as her worry about Verity increases. As usual, she distracts herself by washing up the dishes.

Chapter Six

CR VERITY BO

Verity wakes up in her bed.

Well, at least I think it's my bed.

Lately, she isn't sure about many things. Mornings were never her favourite part of the day - she is an owl, not a lark. Iris used to wake the girls and get them ready for school, giving her a few more delightful moments in bed. There is always a party to plan.

Today, she could hear voices in the house. *Is it the girls?* She wonders. *They haven't been around for a long time... No one comes to see me!*

She weeps a little, overwhelmed with self-pity. And then it struck her that the voices were those of mature women. Verity thinks, these notions tumbling like rocks in a landslide.

They aren't girls now. Are they successful in what they're doing? I do hope so... What's the time? What day is it? What year? How is it that time passed so quickly?

At that moment, a ray of light enters the black hole of her memory. The events of the previous evening came rushing back. She argued with Iris in the kitchen—big mistake. Verity cringes at the memory.

Of all her daughters, Iris is the one she trusts the most. *I even called her a liar!* Why did I say it to her? She feels her face grow hot with embarrassment. It is Sol's eightieth birthday celebration this weekend. She can't understand how she could forget all the discussions she had with Sol and the girls in preparation for it. *Was that why Iris was angry with me?*

She is happy Iris and Heather are back home to help her. *Parties are in my blood!* Lately, she felt like she is at school again, repeating tasks and learning. *I used to be the teacher,* she remembers with sadness.

She sits up and looks around for… *where is it? It's small, with lines. I write in it… my notebook!* It was nowhere in sight. Anxiety clutches at Verity's heart. Someone has stolen it, obviously.

'Hello?' she calls, her voice quivery and uncertain. *Notebooks are good. They help you keep track of everything and everyone.* She didn't want to worry Sol, so she never told him about her notebook, scribbling lists of things and people she needed to remember when he wasn't looking. And now the damn thing is gone.

Sometimes, when she can't find her notebook, she grabs any spare piece of paper, writes on it, and stuffs it in her purse to copy it into her notebook later. But no matter how many notebooks she has, they keep disappearing.

Verity shakes with sudden fury. *It's that cleaning woman!*

But when she pictures herself telling Sol about it and him smiling with sad regret, asking her for proof. Humiliation washes over her. She would rather die than tell him she is becoming forgetful.

Long ago, they agreed that the household was her exclusive domain. She vowed she would never bother him with any domestic issue. He must be free to pursue his career. She smiles to herself, thinking about Sol. She used to joke that Sol was her memory; he had such a keen mind, especially for dates. It was their party trick.

'Darling, where were we on August 9th, 1987?' she would ask him while their delighted guests turned to hear Sol's answer.

'Hmm, let me think,' he would say, stroking his chin. 'Ah yes, we were on safari in Kenya! Elephants ate ripe pears off the ground that fermented in their stomachs and made them drunk.'

One of the girls would check in their father's extensive diaries or Verity's journals, and of course, Sol would be correct. But these days, it was no laughing matter. *Where are my journals?* She wonders.

She gets up and opens the wardrobe. No journals there. Instead, beautiful chiffon gowns are hanging there, many in their dry-cleaning plastic bags. Verity fingers them, awestruck. Then she sniffs.

All right for tea with the Queen, I suppose.

Another shaft of sunlight pierces the darkness: the day she and Sol met. Verity stood next to her dresses, lost in the memory.

When she first saw him in the bookshop where she was working, she'd been struck by his dark hair and tall frame, but most of all, she'd been impressed by his request for a rare book about Albrecht Dürer. She knew immediately that this was the man for her. He was cultured, educated, and intelligent. His hands were soft and pale, the hands of a professor, not a farmer.

If there was one thing Verity was afraid of, it was ending up like her mother, working herself to death on a farm.

Her mother had grown up in the genteel middle-class suburb of Streatham in London. She'd been expected to marry well but somehow married a farmer she'd met at a dance, much to her parents' disappointment. Verity was always amazed to see how her mother, who'd been glamorous and sophisticated, enjoyed getting her hands dirty, planting seeds, and taking care of cows and chickens.

Trips to her Streatham grandparents filled the young Verity with dissatisfaction. She became embarrassed by her country bumpkin parents. That was no life for her. She couldn't wait to get out of the small village in Sidcup, where everyone knew each other, warts and all. In many ways, it was as hidebound as the stultifying suburban life her mother had escaped from.

It was the fifties. Verity wanted to see the world. Leaving her small village behind to study and work in Oxford was her first step. London was too big for her. She'd end up a small fish in a big sea. But Oxford was just big enough (and at the same time small enough) that she could carve out her own niche. She smiles at the irony of it. She'd upset her mother in much the same way her mother had upset her own parents. When she told her dad she wanted to move to Oxford to study and become a teacher, he'd been proud of her.

'Going up in the world!' he'd declared. He sold some livestock to give her some money.

Her mother, on the other hand, had nothing encouraging to say. 'What do you want to study for? Get married and have children. Give them a country life!' she'd announce. The subtext being that Verity was returning to a life of snobbery and bourgeois values. The very things Verity's mother had rejected.

She was right; Verity longed for a middle-class life where she could employ a cleaner and throw parties, dazzling people with her repartee and charm. And now here was this educated, good-looking man gazing at her, who embodied the life she yearned for.

He was a serious student, far more intellectual than Verity, surrounded by smart and wealthy friends. It seemed as if he was living in his own private world. That was a challenge Verity loved: to enter his world and drag him out of it. She charmed her way into his orbit by not only tracking down the Dürer book but also cycling to his rooms at Magdalen to drop it off.

For his part, Sol was awestruck by Verity. She was fresh-faced and pretty, embracing the latest fashions but also serious about books. She taught him how to dance, enjoy the theatre, and especially the movies. Sometimes they took her father, who loved Charlie Chaplin and Laurel and Hardy. He would frown at the French New Wave films they would get him to watch. For her father, movies were his escape from farming life. Her mother never came, preferring the company of her cows and chickens.

Verity always held that movies were her education. She learned how to talk and behave in England's brave new world of the sixties. She studied how the women dressed and how they spoke. Even her accent changed from farmer's daughter to city sophisticate. They watched 'My Fair Lady'. Verity saw herself as Eliza Doolittle, with Sol as Professor Higgins. She practised her charming smile in the mirror until her face hurt.

Meanwhile, Sol laboured under his own parents' expectations, not only academically, but also of him marrying 'the right sort of girl'. They met her and saw through her mannered, cut-glass vowels at once. She wasn't even Jewish.

'Sidcup?' Sol's mother had said. 'I don't believe we know anyone from Sidcup.'

Verity wished she'd lied. She could have said Streatham. At least that was in London. But it was too late. They didn't like her. Her heart sank. But she needn't have worried. Sol was madly in love with her. She loved Sol even more for standing up to his parents, even if it had resulted in a standoff. They asked Sol not to come home for a while.

So, Verity asked his father, Professor Bach senior, to tea. Sol's father was no more immune to Verity's blandishments than Sol, and besides, Verity made him think of the pretty young female medical students he gave tutorials to. Verity had come straight to the point over the Earl Grey and Chelsea buns.

'I may be from a poor farming family, but I can assure you Sol and I are going places. He will go far, and I will be at his side every step of the way, cultivating the right people to further his career,' she expressed, passionate with determination.

She and Sol's father knew that to succeed in Oxford, it wasn't enough to have a sharp mind, prodigious intellect, or be prepared to work hard. It was about connections. You had to understand the politics, something Sol was detached from. He believed that if he discovered a sensational new manuscript that turned modern thought on Anglo-Saxon history on its head, it would get him promotions with their attendant glory.

He did, but only because Verity manoeuvred the right people close to him at her famous parties. She connected him to all the influential people of the age: dons, journalists from all the broadsheets, eminent writers and thinkers.

That was the one thing I promised his father, and I kept that promise.

Verity ran her hand over the dresses, liking how the plastic covers crinkled. She once gave Sol a sign for his desk that said, 'Behind every great man stands a great woman'.

Making sure Sol was successful was not just pure altruism on her part. Verity genuinely enjoyed the benefits that came with each promotion or successful publication: sabbatical years at universities in New York, Boston, Sydney, and Berlin, as well as field trips to enchanting places like Greece, Italy, France, Algeria, Morocco, Egypt and even Russia.

They were away with their family so often and with such complicated itineraries that Daisy used to joke, 'Well, if it's Wednesday, it must be Paris.'

She'd never regretted leaving her little village with its narrow horizons. Yet that village had had a hold on her for years. She never lost sight of the humbleness of her origins. Remembering her mother's words about country air, Verity took the girls every summer to spend quality time with their country grandparents. They loved running wild in the fields, helping Grandma to milk the cows and feeding the lambs with bottles. Verity's mother was only too delighted for Verity to take off with Sol for a well-deserved holiday, which meant spending some glorious weeks either in London going to shows and museums or travelling in Europe.

In later years, after her parents' deaths, the village was taken over by second-home owners. Never one to miss a trick, Verity did her childhood home up with Iris's help. She got it featured in a Sunday magazine via one of her Oxford connections and sold it at a considerable profit. Verity could hear her mother spinning in her grave. Her father would have approved of her initiative, she felt. *Finally, the farm brought in some money.*

She flinches, hearing shouting from downstairs. 'Where's Mum?'

Who on earth is shouting? Verity opens the other side of the ample wardrobe, only to be faced with small post-it notes. It catches her by surprise.

She tuts. *That cleaner has to go,* is her first thought. But when she starts reading them, she realises it is her own handwriting. On one note it says, 'My name is Verity Bach. I've been married to Sol Bach for over 55 years.' On another, it mentions, 'I have 3 daughters - Iris is the oldest, then Daisy, then Heather. Yet another reads, 'I have one granddaughter, her name is Joy, and she is Iris's daughter'. She is surprised to read the next one, 'Iris's partner is Nate. They've been together for 25 years but are not married.' Another: 'Daisy's partner is Mike, and they are not married.' 'Heather is single. She lives with Zoe.'

That's strange, she reflects. *How come none of my girls is married?*

She scans the rest of the post-it notes. Some of them are scrawled and illegible. One flutters to the carpet. She bends to pick it up. It is in Sol's neat handwriting. It reads, 'Your notebook is under your pillow. I love you. Sol. X'.

Chapter Seven

❧ IRIS ☙

Iris wakes in her old room. It takes her time to realise where she is. At first, she finds herself waiting to hear voices all over the house calling for the start of the day: Verity screaming at the top of her lungs, ordering everyone to get moving, Heather and Daisy laughing in their room, and Sol, quietly pointing out to everyone the obvious, which is that they are running late.

But none of this takes place. They are only ghost voices in her mind, she grasps. The only one who is trying to catch up with time is her.

That brings her back to the harsh realisation there is still so much to be done before the big celebration. Though she ran the plans through Daisy and Heather several times, things are not yet finalised, and she needs clarity. She only has a few hours before the first guests arrive.

As a perfectionist, nothing gets her more stressed than knowing not all details are in place.

'You have to get up!' she tells herself, but though her spirit is willing, her flesh is weak. *Funny how age does that to you. I can still get up, but only accompanied by a whole symphony of bones cracking.*

It takes her longer than usual to go through her morning ritual; exercise, shower, meditation, and affirmations, but finally she is ready to enter the kitchen. Heather and Zoe are there, and from the look of it, they finished their breakfast and are talking to each other.

'Morning, have you any idea when Daisy is coming?' Heather shakes her head, indicating she has no idea and continues talking with Zoe.

Iris frowns. She hates being left out of a conversation. 'We need to agree on several things for the party tomorrow. I want you to have a look at the seating arrangements and see what you think.'

'Whatever you say. I don't think it's such a big deal. Why do you make a big deal out of every small detail? All I want is that Dad will have a fun birthday,' Heather replies.

'Whose birthday is it?' Verity inquires, breezing into the kitchen.

Iris tries to find the right words to answer that question without creating a scene like they had the previous night.

Iris realises that having Verity at home while she is organising the last details would be a challenge. She will constantly repeat herself. *I have to get her out of the house until the rest of the gang comes, and we're ready for the family celebration.*

Zoe looks at Iris and winks, letting her know she understands her challenge.

'It's Sol's birthday,' Zoe says to Verity. 'But I didn't bring anything appropriate to wear to such an event. Would you mind going out shopping with me? You're much better at this than Heather. Besides, I'm sure you know all the best shops.'

'I'd love to do that, Zoe!' Verity replies, beaming. 'I'll ask Sol to give us a lift to town. He can spend some time in the library, and we can meet him after our adventure. You made my day Zoe!'

Verity hurries out of the kitchen to tell Sol about their plans.

'Thanks Zoe, that was brilliant! You're a lifesaver.' Says Iris with a heave of relief.

'She's my lifesaver,' Heather remarks. 'It is a genius move, but are you sure you want to spend so many hours with her?'

'I think she's fun,' Zoe retorts.

'Fun is the last adjective I'd use to describe Mum,' retorts Heather.

'You're too hard on her; it would be good for you to be less strict.'

Iris watches this exchange between Zoe and Heather. She is full of admiration for Zoe. She is able to deal with Heather's rigidity and Verity's whims, despite the difficulties of the previous evening. *I hope Heather doesn't scare her away. It appears that even Heather's icy heart is melting.*

Once Zoe, Verity and Sol leave the house, Iris opens her iPad and shows Heather the colour-coded seating arrangements in all their glory. Heather doesn't even bother to ask any questions. Iris explains with enthusiasm all about the different colours, what they mean, and the criteria she uses to seat people next to each other.

The doorbell rings, pulling Heather out of her thoughts and stopping Iris's monologue about the seating arrangements. Before either of them can get up, the door opens, and they hear Daisy's voice: 'Hey there, Bach Bunch! Where the hell is everyone?'

❧ DAISY ☙

I stride into the kitchen just in time to hear Heather sighing with relief.

'Thank God you're here!' she cries out, wringing her hands in supplication. 'Iris is obsessed with the seating arrangements. Please help me!'

For a second, I'm anxious. 'Where's Mum?' I check, with some irritation.

'Zoe volunteered to take Mum and Dad out of the house for a couple of hours, so we can finalise the details for this weekend,' Iris answers, in her usual 'teacher' voice, as if we're still kids in school and need to be disciplined.

I didn't feel like fighting her. 'That was smart. How did you manage to get her to do it? On second thought, you are the only one that could put Mum in her place.'

'This time it wasn't me, it was Zoe, but we need to make use of this time and iron out the last points.'

I really didn't have the energy for more planning. I know Iris has dotted the i's and crossed the t's, which will be a waste of our time.

'Your plans are always perfect. Let's just have some fun before duty calls.' I suggest.

I hoped this would be enough flattery for Iris to let go of the boring details. Iris glances at her iPad 'Fine, who's going to start?'

Both Heather and I breathe easier after hearing this. To my surprise, Heather, who is typically the slowest of us all to respond to any action, jumps up and makes a beeline to the fridge.

'That's a good enough reason to celebrate! Let's bring out the bubbly. I'll go first.' It seems Iris is just as surprised as I am to see Heather in such a cheerful mood.

Heather brings a bottle of champagne and three flutes to the table, opens the bottle like a pro and pours it out, handing the flutes to us. We settle down to talk, the alcohol cutting across our usual tendency to bicker.

'So, is Berlin suiting you better these days?' I ask Heather.

'Berlin is fantastic! After three years, I'm finally starting to enjoy all the great vibes everyone's talking about. My work pays the bills, which leaves me time to explore the city. But the best thing in my life is Zoe,' Heather says as her face softens. 'She moved in a few months ago, and I could never have imagined I would enjoy living with another person so much. Me! Can you imagine it?'

'No!' I utter simultaneously with Iris. We all laugh.

'I mean, I'm such an introvert, yet here I am, having fun and enjoying every second with this wonderful human being. Sometimes I look at myself in the mirror and say, 'who are you, and what have you done with Heather?' I can't recall a time in my life when I was as happy as I am now. I honestly didn't feel like coming here this week, but I suppose family comes first.'

I gasp. Not because I disagree with that statement. I know I preferred staying in London to being here this weekend, but I also know Heather's statement will trigger Iris. I brace myself to the counterattack from Iris.

I'm right. Iris nearly chokes on her drink. For Iris, family is sacred. Nothing comes before family. I anticipate the speech that is coming even before Iris opens her mouth.

'How can you compare a weekend in Berlin with Dad's eightieth birthday? It's only going to happen once in a lifetime. Obviously, family comes first! Really Heather…'

I sense I must step in before this cosy scene we are having will be destroyed by Heather's aggressive response. *I always have to play the UN between those two. It's about time those two accepted each other.* 'Let's calm down, Iris. No one doubts Dad's birthday is important, but not all of us share your sentiments about family. If you asked me, I'd also prefer to go to Berlin.'

I can see Iris gritting her teeth, which means she is going to hold herself back from proving her point about the importance of family. To my relief, her next sentence allows us all to relax, but I am not happy it is directed towards me.

'So, what about you, Daisy? Any news we should know about?'

Though I prepared myself to share my news with the family, I'm not ready to do it now. But I realise I have to. I use the old-fashion way of ripping the Band-Aid in one stroke.

As usual, when I become the centre of attention, I turn into this shy person and wish the ground would swallow me up. *How old do I have to be to accept attention without embarrassment?* I look around and notice Heather and Iris are still staring at me, waiting for me to speak. *Well, it's now or never.* Taking a long gulp from my drink, which almost makes me gag,

I take another deep breath. 'Yes, there is some big news, but I need you to keep it between us for the time being. I can't handle it if Mum hears about it before I'm ready to tell her.'

Heather and Iris look at each other. They both nod.

'Mum's the word! Pun intended...' Heather remarks. We burst out laughing.

'Come on - out with it!' Iris orders me.

'Mike and I have decided to get pregnant,' I mumble into my champagne.

'What?' Iris bursts out. Heather looks dumbstruck.

'I'm trying to get pregnant,' I repeat myself.

The silence in the kitchen is ear-piercing. I don't have the courage to look them in the eye, especially Heather. I notice how I stop breathing and can hear the old grandfather clock ticking away in the hall.

When I finally get the courage to look at them, I can see Iris raising her glass to me and squealing like a child.

'I'm going to be an aunty!' she squeaks enthusiastically. She puts her hands on my stomach as though I am already pregnant. I think I'm going to throw up from her childish outburst.

Heather rolls her eyes at Iris's response. She glares at me. 'Do you know what the risks are at your age?'

Heather's pragmatic response is what I need to hear. *I knew I could depend on her.*

'Yes, I do, and I'm shit-scared. But I really want to give it a try.'

Heather glares at me, thunderstruck. 'What happened to the 'I never want to be a Mum' speech you've been giving us all these years?' she splutters, looking most put out.

That's what I was afraid of. I know my decision to get pregnant will break the unspoken pact Heather and I had of not becoming mothers. I am certain Heather feels betrayed by me, and it's the one thing I dreaded the most. I don't want to let her down. I don't want to lose her as my closest friend and ally.

I focus on Heather and take her hand.

'Things change, Heather,' I utter as gently as possible. 'Mike and I really want a baby. We're aware of the risks. We know the odds are against us, but we have to give it a try. We don't want any regrets later. It's now or never. Please be happy for me; it will mean a lot.'

I hold my breath and look at Heather, pleading for her approval. It takes a few seconds when I can see Heather allowing herself to smile.

'Obviously, I'm happy for you. I just don't want you to get hurt or disappointed. Unlike Iris, I know the odds and see the risks.'

I can hear Iris seething. But I don't care. Heather is the one I need for this journey. I don't care what Iris has to say. She will never understand me. She always wanted to be a mother, while for me, this is not yet something I embrace entirely. I only don't want to miss my last chance to become one.

'Don't listen to her,' Iris announces. 'I gave birth at thirty-eight, over twenty years ago. Women of forty-five are doing it these days. Don't think negatively!'

I knew she would come up with that argument. Mike keeps reminding me of it as well, but my focus is on Heather.

'I know what my chances are, and honestly, I'm not sure if it's going to work. Please help me, Heather. I need you.'

'Just say what you need. I'll always be there for you,' Heather answers.

I sigh with relief.

'For a start, I'll need someone to explain all the medical procedures in layperson's terms to me.'

Heather laughs. 'That's not a problem. In fact, that's easy.'

It is precisely what I need to hear. I cannot express how grateful and relieved I am to hear it from her. All I can do is fall into her arms and give her a long hug. The whole room disappears.

❧ IRIS ❧

From the moment Daisy steps into the kitchen Iris's old feelings of being an outsider and not being understood come rushing back to her. *'How is it that those feelings always come back to me when I'm back here with my own family'* She notes with pain searing below in her belly.

First, it is the dismissing way Daisy treats her need to finalise all the details to make sure Dad's celebration is perfect. Then it is the manner Heather talks about this celebration that makes it sound like a duty being forced on them rather than an opportunity to enjoy their family.

What hurts her most is that, once Daisy drops her news like a bomb explosion, instead of looking at Iris as someone with some experience in getting pregnant and having a child, she turns to Heather as her source of knowledge.

Looking at Daisy and Heather hugging each other, Iris feels redundant. She stands up, clears the table and washes up, hoping it will help her get over the pain in her stomach, the knot in her throat and the sting of tears in her eyes. *I have to stay composed. There's still a lot to do today.*

She chuckles to herself as she hears in her mind's ear her favourite heroine, Scarlett O'Hara, says, 'After all, tomorrow is another day.' When she gets a grip of her emotions, she turns around, only to see Daisy and Heather still hugging and whispering to each other.

The ache is so intense she has to walk away from the kitchen into the one place that is always her refuge: the back garden.

Once she steps outside, it is as if she's been transported to a different dimension. The Bach garden is her secret place, where she can escape all duties and the agony of daily life. It allows her to enter the imaginary world of her books. She used to say her best friends are books. People always disappoint or offend you. Books never do, not even the bad ones.

The garden is as beautiful as she remembered it, though, again, she can see it hasn't been taken care of for a while, but it has an overgrown charm to it. *It makes it more like a proper secret garden,* she muses.

She walks to her favourite place, a bench underneath an old oak tree. She sits down, able to breathe freely. *Some things never change,* not for the first time. It is as if returning to her parents' house turns her into a teenager.

Sitting on the bench, she can see the kitchen. She watches Heather and Daisy talking to each other, oblivious to the fact she isn't there anymore. *Nothing new about that.* Iris closes her eyes and relaxes into the soothing effect the garden has always had on her.

The quiet sounds of the wind in the leaves and the scent of the flowers somehow take her back in time. She is fourteen again, hiding in the garden reading her book, wishing she can live an exciting life like the heroines she is reading about, when Verity's sharp voice snaps her from her dreams.

'Iris? Iris! Where are you? I thought I told you to take care of Heather and Daisy. Have you seen the mess they've made in their room?'

The young Iris jumps up from the bench.

'They promised they would be quiet,' she mumbles as Verity stares at her.

'When I tell you to take care of them, it doesn't mean leaving them alone!'

Iris struggles for a suitable response but doesn't need to bother.

'No excuse. Go and clean that mess. I don't have time for it. I have to get to school, and I'm already late. You'll have to give them dinner and put them to bed.'

Iris finally finds her voice. 'Why is it always me?'

Verity gives Iris a serious look and sighs heavily.

'Do you see anyone else that can do it? It's time you grow up and pull your weight around here. I'm counting on your help with your sisters.'

Iris is crushed by her mother's expectations. 'But what about me? Why can't I have a normal life?' she demands, sadness making her bold.

Verity has the urge to slap her recalcitrant eldest child. She'd just about had enough of this nonsense. She glances at her watch and realises that, as usual, she will be late. She hurries away from Iris.

'You do have a normal life,' she says over her shoulder. 'And as long as you live under my roof, you'll do what I tell you...

take care of your sisters! Are we clear on that? I have to run now!'

Iris watches Verity disappear in her mind's eye. She flinches when she sees Daisy standing in front of her. She observes she still has tears in her eyes, so she quickly turns around to look at the flowers behind the bench she sits on.

❧ DAISY ☙

Heather and I are still talking when we hear Dad, Mum and Zoe returning from their shopping. Zoe is cheerful and describes what great fun she had with Mum, something I can never imagine.

Heather and I always agree that spending more than the compulsory polite thirty minutes with Mum is like spending time with a dragon. Here is a bright, young woman that insists Mum is fun to be with. *'She has to be special to think that way. I'm so happy Heather found someone as special and unique as her.'*

A few minutes later, the doorbell rings, bringing in Mike and Joy. My unstoppable niece is a chip off the block of her mother. She can take care of a whole host of armies without a blink. She manages to get Mike to pick her up from the airport, which is out of his way, and drive her to Oxford to be here on time.

The truth is, I'm sure Mike enjoyed the ride with her as she is a source of endless stories that would put Scheherazade to shame, and Mike always loves a good story. No one better than Joy for this task.

We are ready to leave for the clubhouse for our afternoon punting when I spot Iris missing. When people started arriving, I didn't see her, and I thought she was back in her room finishing all the details we didn't feel like going through when we were talking in the kitchen.

I go to look for her but can't find her. After a while, I see her in the garden. I walk towards her, but she is lost in thought. When I approach, I detect she is crying. It isn't something I've seen often when it comes to Iris. It surprises me.

I watch Iris's futile attempt to hide her tears with amazement.

'Here you are. Where were you?'

'I was walking down Memory Lane,' Iris responds.

'Well, time to come back to the present. Joy is here, and so is Mike. We're ready to leave for the afternoon punt we organised for Dad.'

Iris looks alarmed to hear it. I'm certain Iris has no clue what time it is. *Another small revelation about my sister. Never thought I would see the day that Iris would lose track of time.*

Iris, being Iris, manages to assume her efficient persona without a problem or hesitation.

'So, Joy did make it in time! Great. Let's get this party started!' she declares. Within seconds she is marching across the garden at a speed I can hardly catch up with.

Chapter Eight

෨ IRIS ๘

When Iris and Daisy approach the living room, Iris hears Joy taking control of the discussions. *That's my girl,* she reflects with genuine pleasure. *No one dominates a conversation like my daughter.*

Sure enough, when she enters the living room, Joy is centre stage, telling one of her amusing stories at eighty miles an hour, holding the whole room's attention and making them all laugh. *It's as if she needs to entertain everyone all the time.* A familiar voice whispers in her head, *I wonder where she learned that.* Her intrusive thoughts annoy her. *Thank you for sharing, but I don't have time for you now, so go and take a back seat.*

Iris stands at the entrance door of the living room, gazing at Joy, feeling proud of herself. *In the end, I did a good job with her.* If there is one person on Earth Iris does not try to control, educate, or coerce, it is Joy. A long time ago, she discovered that if she wanted to have a close and loving relationship with her daughter, she had to let her do her own thing, even if she didn't approve or believed it wasn't in Joy's best interests.

Somehow with Joy, Iris had managed to live by the words of her favourite poet, Khalil Gibran: *'Your children are not your children. They are the sons and daughters of life's longing for itself. They come through you but not from you. And though they are with you, yet they belong not to you. You may give them your love but not your thoughts, for they have their own thoughts. You may house their bodies but not their souls, for their souls dwell in the house of tomorrow, which you cannot visit, not even in your dreams. You may strive to be like them, but seek not to make them like you. For life goes not backward nor tarries with yesterday. You are the bows from which your children as living arrows are sent forth.'*

Looking at Joy now, in her mother's living room, Iris experiences a surge of satisfaction and accomplishment. Joy seems to be enjoying herself. It isn't an act. She is as natural as a fish swimming in deep water.

Joy suddenly turns around and catches Iris looking at her. She rushes to hug her. 'Told you I'd be on time!' she whispers into Iris's ear as she hugs her.

'Never doubted it, but you'll have to tell me the reason why sometime,' Iris replies.

Now that she had her few seconds with Joy, Iris could look around the living room and see who else was there. Sol and Verity come in and sit down on the sofa. Zoe sits beside Verity as if she has always been at her side. Heather is standing behind her, giving her an occasional neck massage. Daisy and Mike are huddled together on another sofa in the living room. Iris is always surprised to see Mike at her sister's side.

It isn't that she didn't like Mike - no one in the world can resist his charm - but he is definitely not the one she expected her sister to end up with. He is a good head shorter than Daisy, chubby, with a beard that looks like it contains remnants of his last meal. He is very fond of his food. The fact that he is charming and brilliant at what he does always comes after you get over the shock of his unkempt appearance.

His looks never seemed to bother Daisy. It is Iris who is irritated at how Mike looks. *I'm just as superficial as Mum when it comes to judging people. No doubt I get it from her. Well, it's good Daisy doesn't, because he's really good to her.*

Suddenly, that irritating voice in her head is screaming at her: *Enough talking! You're on a schedule today, so stop daydreaming!*

Iris springs to attention. 'Hey guys, let's get to the college for those boats. Otherwise, we're going to miss our slot!'

'What are you talking about?' Verity asks.

'We thought we'd start the weekend celebration with us doing what Dad loves most and what he's great at… punting!'

The look on Sol's face is the biggest reward Iris can receive at that moment. He is delighted.

'Let's get going, I've reserved two boats, and if we're not on time, they'll give them to someone else. Joy, Mum and me will be in one boat with Dad and everyone else in the second one. I hope you have a good rival for Dad!'

Heather laughs at the sound of that. 'I'm not sure I'm in the same league as Dad, but I'm going to give it a go.'

Iris sees Mike lean towards Daisy. 'Was I supposed to volunteer?' she can hear him ask in an anxious tone.

'No! Heather loves punting, and the truth is… she's not bad at it. Not as good as Dad, but good enough.'

⪭ DAISY ⪬

An hour later, I find myself sitting in the punt with Mike and Zoe, watching Heather punting. I could see Mike was grateful he didn't have to take on that role. Dad is a genuine master at punting; he makes it look so effortless, but anyone can see there is an art to it which takes years to master.

I'm looking at Dad as if through Mike's eyes, and it's obvious that Dad is remarkable for a man of his age, punting with such elegance and strength. Suddenly Mike whispers into my ear:

'You'd never think he's eighty. I hope I'll be as sharp and strong when I'm his age.'

'Punting means giving up sweets and exercising more, and I'm not talking about exercising your fingers on the keyboard,' I answer him back.

Mike chuckles as he's well aware of his sweet tooth and the last one to deny it. He was the one that came up with his own nickname, 'Mike the Hobbit.'

When I look at Heather, it appears she's doing well in her attempts at punting, but I can see the effort it takes. There are moments where we nearly bang into the bank before she can get control of the punt back and steer it back to the centre of the river. When she does, Zoe, with her never-ending humour, cheers her and makes us all hooray for the save of the day done by Heather.

ℭℛ VERITY ℰℭ

Verity is sitting with Iris and Joy in the other boat. Verity always loved the times she and Sol went punting. It gave her the feeling she was some kind of character from Jane Austin's books and made her feel like royalty. Not to mention that Sol was so good at what he was doing, it filled her with pride and a sense of achievement, though she was not the one doing the punting. She knew she was the one that encouraged him to master it. It was one of those things that made him stand out in the usual group of scholars. He was not just a scholar; he was a master at punting as well.

Now she sits in the boat observing the conversation between Iris and Joy. She doesn't mean to be eavesdropping, but it is hard not to on such a small boat. It never ceases to surprise her how close Iris and Joy are. She still remembers when Joy went through her rebellious puberty stage, she still called Iris 'The Best Mum in the World'. Verity told Iris that no matter how many mistakes she might have made as a mother, it shows she clearly did some things right.

Looking at her daughter and granddaughter, it seems as if Joy considers Iris a trusted friend, confiding in her on issues she never dreamt her daughters would ever talk with her when growing up - or even as adults from the pieces of conversation she heard.

Joy is discussing issues like boys, sex, dreams, and her future. Every time Joy shares her thoughts with her mother, Verity feels a pang of jealousy for such an open and honest conversation between mother and daughter. She grasps she would have given anything to have such a close relationship with her daughters, but it seems that it wasn't in the stars for her to have one like that. Not that she had any kind of a role model for such a relationship. Her relationship with her own mum was cold and distant one.

Joy is sharing some fun experiences she had in her studies.

She mentions friends whom it looks like Iris knows or at least pretends to know. Verity cannot recall any of her daughters' friends - she isn't even sure whether they even came to visit Iris, Daisy or Heather when growing up. *How come none of my daughters inherited my skills at socialising?* She wonders, not for the first time.

Verity allows herself to drift into her own thoughts when she catches an interesting sentence Iris says to Joy that brings her attention back to them.

'Education comes in all kinds of ways,' Iris tells Joy. 'A degree isn't the only proof of an adequate education these days...'

This startles Verity. *That's not how we see things in this family*, getting angry.

'It might not be proof, but having a degree is always better. People take you seriously when you have one, and your chances are better when searching for work after graduation, so don't listen to your mother!' she announces.

'Mum, do you even know what Joy is studying?' replies Iris.

Verity sniffs in response. 'It doesn't matter. The fact is that you need a diploma to get on in life?'

'Mum, although I agree with you that having a degree is a good thing, these days it's not as important as it was in the past, especially in what Joy is studying. In her line of studies experience and connections are much more important and valuable than graduating. They are now offering her a paid internship in one of the best fashion houses in Paris. That's much more valuable than any piece of paper.'

Verity doesn't know how to respond to Iris's argument and knows very well that she needs an alley who Iris values, so she diverts the conversation to Sol.

'Sol, what's your view on this issue?'

Standing on the box of the punt and being the diplomat he always is, Sol knows very well not to get involved. 'Well, you know, your mum and I are from a different generation, we lived in a different time, and therefore the criteria to make such decisions is different for us. I will not pretend to understand how the world works today. I will only say Joy needs to make her own decision. She understands the modern world better than we do.'

Sol's comeback leaves Verity speechless. This is definitely not what she expected to hear from Sol, who has devoted his whole life to academia. Degrees were crucial for him.

By the look on her face, Joy is also surprised to hear such an answer from her Sol. Verity knew that if there was one thing she drilled into all her children and granddaughter, it was that being a Bach meant one was expected to have at least one degree and some letters after your name before you hit the job market. She cannot recall anyone in their family who has not completed undergraduate and postgraduate studies with first-class honours.

'I'm surprised to hear you say this grandad, but I'm relieved. Having to hide my desire to quit University hasn't been easy, but I knew I had to do it. I also knew I had to tell Mum and you guys about it. Mum always told me that no matter the situation, she and Dad rather hear the truth from me than a lie. Hearing you say this makes me feel so much better about myself. Thank you.'

Verity doesn't know what to say. *There is change in the air, and I can't stop it... am I changing, or is it the world that is changing, and what would I be in such a world?*

☙ DAISY ❧

We were approaching The Vicky Arms, a well-known establishment in Oxford. It has been serving people food and drink for two hundred years. The building itself looks as if it is taken from a movie. On a summer's day like today, it looks at its best, I reflect. With Wisteria decorating the walls and the verdant flowerbeds around it, nothing screams traditional English country house like the Vicky Arms. *No wonder Iris chose this place for our family dinner. As always, she thinks of every single detail – she loves making a point and a show of how a family has to look like*

Before I met Mike, I thought all families were loud, bickering and dominating. When I met Mike, I discovered that some families are different. His father died when he was twelve. His mother hasn't been the same since. Mike had to take care of his mother and younger brother. Though capable of living independently, his mother relies heavily on him to take care of her.

As the years passed, his mother became increasingly needy, to the point that if a day passed and they didn't talk, she got scared and left a dozen panic-stricken messages.

This is why we had to find a house not far from hers, so she will be able to visit us whenever she has the urge to do it. Mike keeps repeating that one of the reasons he's forever grateful to me is that I don't resent his mother's dependency on him. Not only do I not resent it: I like being around his mum. I know he would never admit to it, but he finds his mother's behaviour embarrassing, while I keep telling him that his mother is nothing compared to mine.

When we enter the Vicky Arms, the waitresses immediately recognise us and lead us to our table. Dad and Mum are regulars here, and I reminisce on all the years we used to come here regularly.

Once seated, James, the head waiter, approaches the table with a big smile, welcoming Dad as if he's his long-lost friend.

'Professor Bach, I insisted on serving your table tonight. We have a new selection of wines and would love to hear your opinion on them.'

If there is anything else that can make Dad talk for hours, beyond historical facts and old manuscripts, it is wine. He loves wine and loves educating others about the best way of cultivating vineyards, the different types of grapes and what makes each variety unique, and all the other thousand little details that go into the art of making wine. 'Viniculture is as ancient as the world,' he often reminds us when we complain that we've had enough of listening to all those boring details instead of drinking the wine.

'Bring it on, James,' Dad declares with a hearty laugh. 'We're having a big celebration tonight. And wine delights the human heart.'

When James next approaches the table, he has a bottle and the wine list in his hand. 'I thought I'd bring you my favourite, but if it's not to your liking, I've brought the wine list, so you can choose something else.'

James opens the bottle with a ceremonial flourish, allowing Dad to smell the cork, which he appreciates very much.

Heather and Zoe giggle.

'Pour the wine!' Zoe mutters. 'Why waste time smelling the cork?'

Iris frowns. 'It's part of the fun. Let him enjoy it.'

Heather scowls, feeling Zoe's harmless remark has been attacked. 'It's just so pretentious - so not like Dad,' she remarks coldly. 'It's the one area where he's fallen into arrogance, and it's difficult to watch.'

'Oh please! He's always been soft when it comes to wine. It is his way of fitting in with all those snobbish professors in the early days. He has an excellent cellar. Let him have his fun!' Iris replies.

After tasting and approving James' choice of wine, Dad has James serve us while Zoe and Heather make all the right sounds of enjoying the wine.

Mum suddenly stands up, raising her glass. 'It's time to toast this lovely evening that, without our daughter, Iris, we would not have been able to have. I am so fortunate to have such a fantastic daughter….'

Silence falls on the table as we all comprehend Mum does not recognise the rest of us. Within a fraction of a second, she notices it and her words fail her. Mum shakes and sits down.

As always, Dad comes to rescue her from her embarrassing moments. He immediately stands up to cover the awkward moment. 'What we're trying to say is that even though this occasion is to celebrate my eightieth birthday, we feel it is only an excuse to have all our family together in the same room. Nothing brings more happiness to your mum and me than seeing all of you together. Let's raise a glass to family!'

It takes a few seconds for us to recover. We all raise our glasses.

'Happy birthday, Dad, and here's to the whole Bach Bunch!' Iris declares.

Chapter Nine

ಂ HEATHER ೞ

I drank too much wine last night! But who could blame me? The embarrassing scene Mum created, Heather thinks when she wakes up the following day. Turning over, she gazes fondly at Zoe, sleeping soundly beside her. *The beauty! I need to count my blessings from now on and stop looking for negativity everywhere I go.* She gently drapes her arm over her lover and shuts her eyes in contentment.

A knock on their door yanks her back to reality.

'Wake up, sleepyheads!' she hears Daisy yell. 'We have a full day ahead of us, and Iris is calling the shots already. I need your help.'

Daisy's voice wakes up Zoe. She rolls over to embrace Heather. 'Hi there, gorgeous. Duty calls.'

They get out of bed and start getting ready. Each time they pass, they touch each other tenderly as if to say, 'I'm here for you.'

ಂ IRIS ೞ

Meanwhile, Iris has been up for hours, phoning the caterer, the florist and the band to ensure they all arrive on time. Iris at work is like a general sending troops marching into battle. By the time Heather and Zoe have finished their breakfast, preparations are in full swing for the celebration lunch.

Various deliverymen, including the marquee installers, are in full swing in the garden. Iris instructs them on what, where and how, when she stops to direct two bakers who arrived carrying a huge cake with the word 'Solomon' written on it.

In no time at all, the marquee is up, tables are set, and food is laid out. Iris is checking and altering each table as if she is the head butler in some fictional period TV show.

At the same time, Iris notices Daisy running around, and from the look of it, she's taking care of people who might be insulted by her double-checking. Iris remembers that Daisy once told her that kindness goes much further than her sergeant-major act? *Maybe it's good that she does it, so service would be good later that day.* Iris thinks to herself.

She then recalls she has asked Heather to take care of the technical part of the day and walks towards her. Heather is talking with the technical team about how best to show the video she made of Sol's life. Heather and Zoe have worked for days making the film from hundreds of old photos of Sol, Verity, and the Bach clan.

Iris hurries towards Heather. 'Did you test the mics and sound?'

'I know how to do these things without you micro-managing me!' Heather answers in a sharp tone.

Iris is a bit taken aback by Heather's response. She is about to return to the house when she remembers something else she wants to check with Heather. 'By the way, did you want to say a few words for Dad, or have you left that for me?'

Heather stares at her. If looks could kill, Iris would drop down dead.

'We agreed ages ago I'd be saying a few words for Dad on behalf of us all, so what's new? Why can't you trust me?'

Iris is hurt. 'All I want is for everything to go like clockwork!'

'You're right. My bad. In any case, I wrote a nice speech. If you want, I can show it to you.' Iris apprehends it is better not to pursue this topic if she wants to enjoy the day.

'No, I'm sure you wrote a beautiful speech. So long as Dad's happy.'

She walks back to the house, still fixing small details, like a napkin out of position or a flower vase not in the middle of the table. *I just want things to look great. Why can't they understand that?* She wonders petulantly for the hundredth time that day.

She stands at the big French doors that lead from the living room to the garden and surveys the scene. All is ready and on time. She takes a deep breath and whispers, 'Let the games begin.'

⟶ DAISY ⟵

Like a well-rehearsed orchestra, we, the Bach girls, take our position and slip into our roles as the first guests arrive. Years of having to help Mum host her famous social events in this house made us a well-trained team.

Once the doorbell rings, I lead the guests through the house into the garden, where Heather welcomes them with some small talk and humorous anecdotes. When the guests are faculty members, I take them to Iris, who, as always, remembers what questions to ask them about their latest research, adding just the right compliments to flatter their professional egos. *She really learned well from Mum on this issue,* I had to admit to myself.

I also know that these days, she had to do research on Dad's colleagues in advance, as she's been away from the scene for such a long time. *Thank God we created that guest list, and she was able to prepare herself.* I smile to myself. *But then again, that was another of Iris's well-thought-of details on her list to make things perfect.*

The first to arrive is Graham and his wife, Betty. They have been our neighbours for years. Heather and I were friends with their daughter Amy, but that was years ago.

'How is Amy these days?' I hear Heather ask when she leads them to their table. 'Last I heard, she moved to New York!'

'Oh, my dear,' replies Betty. 'That was nearly ten years ago! She returned and lives in the Lake District now, in charge of nature conservation there. You know Amy; she never was one for the city. I could never understand why she moved to New York! I think it was her worst year ever. She came back as soon as she could. It took her a few years to find herself, but she finally found a job that allowed her to do what she loves best, being in nature all the time.'

I can see Heather's face tighten. I know very well what she's thinking. Being a Bach girl does not allow you to do what you love. You are expected to get your degrees, even if you don't like what you study. Experimenting with different careers was not an option. *Oh well, at least in Heather's case, she got the degree they all expected her to have. That's a small compensation for being unhappy,* a self-pitying voice adds in my head.

'Where is the birthday boy?' I hear Graham say.

'Probably lost in thought in his study, as usual!' Heather laughs. 'I'll go and let him know you arrived. It is great seeing you again. Enjoy yourselves.'

I now have to focus on another couple that arrives and lead them to the buffet table. While standing in line for the food, I hear Iris talking with Professor Frank Cornell and his wife, Julie.

Professor Cornell is one of Dad's oldest colleagues. They had a special relationship, as Julie is one of Mum's closest friends. Julie describes how each time Dad leaves the house, he needs to write a note for Mum, but Mum still phones her to check if he's with Frank. Julie is concerned about Mum's condition, which everyone in their social circle has started to notice. It seems as if the only topic people can speak about is how Dad has to take care of Mum. *What's wrong with that? She's been taking care of him for over forty years. Why is it so bad that he would take care of her in their old age?* An angry voice in my head asks.

'He's two weeks late on the deadline for the new book. It's starting to harm his reputation,' Frank adds.

Big deal, I'm thinking, but the look on Iris's face shows me that this is a big deal. But when I hear her following sentence, I'm irritated by it. I know she is only trying to keep up appearances, but I don't like the implication of it.

'I spoke with Daisy about getting someone in to help with Mum, but Dad will not hear about it.'

Iris notices another faculty member stepping into the garden. 'Excuse me for a minute,' she says to Frank and Julie.

Going around the garden and welcoming everyone, I notice Heather having lunch with our cousin Ruth.

Again, when I walk around, I hear Ruth expressing concern about Mum and Dad's situation. 'I'm concerned about Sol. He doesn't have a life anymore. He has to write a note to Verity each time he leaves the house. If she doesn't find it, she phones me and asks if I know where he is. She makes it sound casual, but I hear the fear in her voice.'

It feels as if everyone in Oxford has rehearsed the same story to tell us. I don't know how Heather feels, but I feel attacked by it. As if they are blaming us for the situation.

'But Mum is still active. She plays Bridge twice a week and is involved in Oxford Now...' Heather is trying to give this as an excuse, but Ruth cuts her off mid-sentence.

'It's obvious you haven't been around lately. Oxford Now was axed last year. You, of all people, should know things change very quickly for people with this condition. I don't understand how you allow her even to drive!'

I can see Heather is offended by Ruth's comments. She obviously feels criticised just as I do, and retorts by confronting the other person in her usual way.

'You know how it is in this family. How long did it take you to get your dad to stop driving?' she remarks coolly. Our uncle, Ruth's father, had been pulled over for driving erratically and had lost his licence.

Ruth is crestfallen. *Oops, Heather forgot how deeply Ruth took her father's death a few months ago,* and obviously, her tactless reply brought back the sadness of losing him.

'You're right… I guess once we managed to get him to give up the car, he lost his will to live and was only waiting to die. It was the hardest part.'

I can see Heather regrets responding so harshly in her next sentence. 'From your experience, what can we do to help Dad?'

'Bring someone to live in who will take care of Verity and support Sol. You have no idea how demanding care is with this kind of disease. If you want, my dad's carer is looking for work. She's amazing, and Verity already knows her, which would make it easier for her to accept,' Ruth mentions without hesitation.

At this point, I notice how late it is. I look around, and I cannot see Dad anywhere. I know Iris is probably getting stressed about the timeline of the event.

'Have you seen Dad?' I ask Heather.

'Last time I saw him, he was with Iris and Professor Gray.' She replies.

'Well, he's not now. I can't see him anywhere. We need to start the speeches!'

I cross the lawn towards Iris, who is standing in the middle of a small crowd, entertaining them with her witty stories. I stand close to Iris.

'Have you seen Dad?' I whisper to her.

'I saw him walking to his study a few minutes ago'.

I hurry towards the house when I hear Mum screaming from the study. 'Help, help! Someone help me… Something's wrong with him!'

I sprint towards the study; I get there at the same time as Iris. We both burst into the room. Mum kneels beside Dad, who is face down on the floor, his hands twitching. Iris gently turns him over to see his eyes rolling back in his head as a seizure storms through his brain.

'Call 999!' she shouts at me. Mum is in total shock and can hardly move. I dial 999 with trembling fingers.

Chapter Ten

❧ IRIS ☙

Once the ambulance has left with Heather, Verity and Sol, Iris is left facing the stunned guests. Daisy followed the ambulance by car. The guests rally around. Iris is inundated by many offers of support. *As always, I'm the one who has to clear up the mess in this family!* She thinks. *But maybe it's better this way...* It suddenly dawns on her that each of the Bach daughters is taking the role they are best at.

Heather went to the hospital as she was the only one who could get accurate information on Dad's condition and be able to explain it to the others. Verity insisted on going; there was no way of stopping her. *I must say, she was in good form, quite like her old self, even if she only thinks he fell down and got a bump on his head.*

It is why Daisy followed them, to keep Verity occupied so Heather could get as much information as possible. *Those damn doctors! Why do they always act so superior to anyone else? Unless it's someone who can actually speak their language. Well, if anyone can put them in their place, it'll be Heather.*

Iris nearly pities anyone who'd try doing that to her sister. 'God help them,' she whispers. *Now, back to business.*

'First, I must take care of the caterer, his team and the AV people. Make sure they clear the place out and bring it back to normal. Then I need to tell Nate I'm not coming back for at least two weeks… oh God, do I have any important meetings coming up? I'll check. ok… who can I ask to help me with all this? Yes! Joy…'

As Iris goes through all the logistics out loud, Joy, Mike, and Zoe dash towards her.

'What needs to be done?' Joy asks her.

That stops Iris's chaotic whirlpool of thoughts. She is back in her element. 'Great, thanks! Joy, contact dad and tell him I'll return in two weeks and check with the airline if I can change my flight at no extra cost. Mike, check Daisy's appointments in the coming days and cancel them. Zoe, ask the caterer to pack the food in containers so we can take some for Mum, Heather and Daisy in the hospital and keep the rest for us for this week, so no one has to bother with cooking….'

The list goes longer and longer. Mike and Zoe are amazed at Iris's ability to deal with it all. For Joy, this is no surprise, she'd seen her mother do this for years, but for Mike and Zoe it's quite overwhelming. They both agree it is impressive and intimidating at the same time – though, exactly what is needed now. It is good having someone like Iris around when crisis strikes.

Zoe jokes that even when everyone is running around like headless chickens, Iris is the only one able to catch the chicken and make a great dinner from it.

When Iris goes through the garden to see whether the workmen are dismantling everything correctly, the caterer approaches her.

Iris understands that even if the final accounts could be

delayed, she will still have to give tips to the crew for the day. To her surprise, the caterer says he will take care of it and not worry about the bill.

His words are like music to her ears. 'Your Mum's been our best client all these years. I owe everything to her. She kept referring me to other people. I owe my success to her. Please, keep me posted on how the professor is. If there's anything I can do, let me know.'

Iris is touched. She never imagined such a generous gesture from him. 'Business is business' has been her motto all the years she ran her companies. But obviously, Verity has managed to cast her spell on him. She managed to make him a friend.

Next, she calls Daisy for an update on what is happening in the hospital, but Daisy is not responding. *No point calling every five minutes; it'll only irritate her.* Iris sends her a WhatsApp message and keeps on working at the house.

She walks into the house and bumps into Joy. 'Dad asks if you can call him when you have a minute. I arranged a flight for you in two weeks' time without any extra cost.' Joy pauses for a minute as if hesitating and then spills it, 'But Mum, I need to return to Paris today. There's no point in me staying here. I'll just be in your way,' she says.

Iris looks at Joy, knowing she is right, but in her heart, she wants her daughter to stay. It will be a comfort. More than anything, she wants to cuddle up with her in bed like they did when Joy was small. But Joy is an adult now and doesn't care much for hugs. Joy hugs her mother, but only because she knows Iris yearns for it.

'Alright darling,' she says sadly.

The rest of the day, Iris is busy clearing up the remains of the party and answering phone calls from concerned friends and colleagues. When she finally manages to get through to Daisy in the hospital, all she gets from her is that Sol is still unconscious.

Never was Iris so aware of how fragile her family was than during these hours of clearing up. She regrets she is unable to stay longer. The demands of her business, and Nate, will not allow her. She can return when Sol is back home - not that she knows when that will be. That means someone has to take care of Verity. *Who is going to do that?*

Daisy hates being in the same room as their mother. Heather has her life in Berlin and clearly will not be able to do it. *Not that I'd trust Heather to take care of another human being. It's good Zoe is with her. Stop being so hard on Heather and give her a chance!* Another voice chimes: *Fine, but the problem remains, there is no one to care for Mum! I must find someone to do it, at least temporarily, until is back. I can't solve it now; this is the time for Scarlett O'Hara's famous words…*

'I'll think about it tomorrow. After all, tomorrow is another day!' she murmurs. And with that, she is able to relax.

❦ HEATHER ❧

Heather cannot believe she is back in the same hospital she left years ago. Sitting in a consultation room waiting for the head of the Neurology department to come and update her on Sol's condition, she grasps the irony of the situation. If it had been fifteen years ago, the patient would have been waiting for her.

John Radcliffe Hospital has been her home for more than twenty years. Spending nights in that place is not a new experience for Heather. The novelty of it is that this time she spends it as a family member and not as medical staff. She suddenly starts to see things in a different light.

When she left, she knew she had to do it to keep her sanity. *It was time! I paid my dues. I needed a new challenge, not what Mum and planned for me... The worst thing that could happen to someone is that they become great at something they don't like.* It was what happened to her. She's been a great neurologist but hated every single moment. Now here she is again, on the other side of the consultant's desk.

It is a frightening experience. She never appreciated how intimidating it was for the family members waiting for her to give them the verdict on their loved ones. She'd been too pre-occupied with the accuracy of her diagnosis; she never thought for a moment how emotional it was for them. It sure feels like payback now.

She keeps perfectly still, waiting for her old colleague to update her on her father's condition, contemplating the mysterious ways life works.

⪧ IRIS ⪦

A pair of lift doors open at the far end of a long hallway. Iris hurries out, pulling a small suitcase behind her. She has a bunch of flowers tucked under her arm as she scans the room numbers.

It has been the longest night of her life, staying at home while everyone else is in the hospital. No one bothered to update her. She experienced, as always, being excluded. *No matter how old I am, that feeling of being an outsider never leaves. That's what I have to work with.* Therefore, she left the house as early as possible to bring whatever she thought Sol would need for a long stay in the hospital.

'Be prepared,' she tells herself. The old Boy Scout motto is also hers. But what she doesn't expect is how she feels when entering Sol's room.

Sol is asleep. The only thing that shows something is wrong with him is an IV drip tube stuck into a vein on the back of his hand. Daisy and Verity are slumped, trying to doze, on bedside chairs. They both look worn out. They evidently had a sleepless night.

Verity looks lost and confused. Daisy is at the end of her tether. Being with Verity the whole night has definitely not been the best thing for her.

'Where's Heather?' Iris asks.

'She's with the doctors. No one is willing to give us an update on his condition, so Heather decided to use her old connections. Better than us waiting for their daily rounds.'

'Good to hear Heather's being active,' Verity remarks. 'She's finally putting all those years she gave to this hospital to good use! Not that I understand why they're keeping him here. He just fell down and bumped his head, that's all! No one dies from one small bump! The only thing I don't understand is why he isn't waking up. Do you think they've drugged him?'

Daisy makes faces at Iris behind Verity's back. Iris understands Daisy's frustration. 'It's a more complicated, Mum,' she answers Verity. 'I think Dad's had a stroke!'

Verity stands up from her chair. 'No, no, no... I saw what happened. He fell from his chair and bumped his head on the floor, nothing too serious. Don't tell me I don't know what happened! The only thing I don't get is why they aren't releasing him yet. That's what Heather needs to find out. She should insist they release him so we can go home and get on with the party.'

Knowing her mother, Iris understands there is no point in saying there is no party to return to, let alone normal life. *We're not in Kansas anymore, Dorothy, but how can I explain that to Mum?*

'You're absolutely right,' she responds. 'We all want to go back to normal, but until they release him, how about you and Daisy go back home? I'll stay here with him. You both had a long night. You can use some proper sleep.'

Daisy gives Iris a relieved smile.

'Iris is right,' Daisy adds. 'I have to go back as I have some appointments I need to cancel.'

'No need, I've taken care of it. I asked Mike to check your diary and cancel them.'

'Who gave you the right to ask that of Mike? Do you have any idea about the concept of the word privacy? You're just like Mum, no consideration!' Daisy snaps at Iris.

Iris is stunned by Daisy's attack but bites her tongue. 'I'm only trying to help!'

'No one asked you! You and your control-freakery!'

'I'm sorry. I'm only trying to think of everything.'

'Well, don't. I'm taking Mum home. Hopefully, we'll get some sleep.' Daisy gathers her and Verity's things together.

'Make sure you…' Iris starts to say but stops herself mid-sentence as Daisy glares at her.

Once Daisy leaves with Verity, Iris sits beside Sol's bed, looking at him. She cannot fathom how life will be without him around. It isn't as if she lived close by all these years, but somehow the knowledge he is living his life reassured her that all is well in the world.

Sol is her anchor. She used to say that parents give their kids wings to fly and roots to know where they came from. Sol has definitely given her roots. She always knew he had her back, despite the path she chose.

⊂⊃ IRIS ⊂⊃

Suddenly the door to the room opens, and Heather steps in. She is as pale as the walls of the room. Iris urges her to sit.

'Did you manage to get any information from the doctors?'

Heather sinks into the chair and looks at Sol. Watching Heather closely, Iris has the feeling she can almost see the blood draining out of Heather's face, which gives her the chills.

'Where's Mum and Daisy?' Heather asks.

'I sent them home to sleep. I think you need to go home too and get some sleep after the night you had! I'll take the day shift. You can come back in the afternoon if they don't release him by then.'

'They won't release him by then, for sure! We'll be lucky if they release him in three months.'

98

'Three months?' Iris repeats, not sure she hears it correctly. 'It can't be that bad?'

Heather takes a deep breath. *That's not good. Heather is never shaken by medical information and has years of experience delivering tough situations to family members. I guess it's different when it's your own family.*

Iris watches Heather warily, knowing trying to rush Heather to explain is a big mistake. She knows Heather moves at a much slower pace. Every word and action is calculated three or four times before being expressed or acted upon. Where Iris shoots, Heather aims. So, she waits to hear what Heather has found out, though inwardly she is screaming, *Come on, speak!*

Finally, Heather manages to compose herself. 'Dad had a stroke which left him paralysed on his left side. He doubtless will be unable to walk again or use his left hand. We don't know what damage he has in the brain or if it affects his mental faculties. This can only be assessed later. The implication of hemiparesis is that he will have a hard time reading, writing, or understanding…Can you imagine without all that? His world will end.'

Iris has to sit down. She now comprehends why her sister is as white as a sheet. Sol without cognitive abilities is not her father. His work is the air he breathes. It is the reason he wakes up in the morning and what keeps him young at heart. She simply cannot grasp a life for Sol without his work.

'Is there any chance of him recovering from it?' she asks hesitantly.

'Well, they'll give him physiotherapy, but the main problem may be his vision. It's the part of his brain that translates the information the eye receives that may be damaged.'

Iris looks at her sister and notices how tired she is, which obviously is not helpful for the implications of Sol's initial diagnosis. *No point asking anything more,*

'It's early days, anyway. There's nothing you can do here now. I suggest you go home and rest. Come back in the afternoon. I'll be here with him. If he wakes up, I'll WhatsApp Daisy to let you all know,' Iris assures Heather.

Heather stands up to leave and gives Iris a hug. That is indeed a surprise for Iris.

Chapter Eleven

⊂⊗ DAISY ⊗⊃

I wake up tired and for the life of me can't understand why I'm sleeping in my parents' house. I made it a rule not to stay overnight since I left this damn place. It takes me a few seconds. The memory jolts me.

Thank God Iris is here. She'll take care of everything.

Then it dawns on me. I can't build on it. Neither Iris nor Heather will stay longer than two weeks. This means I will be left to take care of Mum.

No way am I doing it.

I've worked too hard to distance myself all these years. If I needed any proof Mum and I are not destined to be together, yesterday was a prime example. I was ready to strangle her in the hospital. She was her usual overbearing, rude and demanding self. I wished the ground would open up and swallow me whole when she ordered the hospital staff around as if they were her servants. She had zero consideration for their other priorities and tasks. It became worse when it was clear she had no clue what was going on.

I have to find someone to take care of her. That's my first priority – at least until we find out about Dad's long-term prognosis. Maybe Iris could help with that? OK, now I have a plan. It's time to get up.

My plan of action decided, I feel ready to get out of bed. Stepping into the kitchen, I find Heather, Zoe and Verity finishing their tea. I glance at the clock, comprehending it is not morning anymore but well after four in the afternoon.

'Hello sleepyhead!' Heather says, welcoming me with a smile. 'Join us for some of these delicious cakes. Iris charmed the caterer into leaving us all the good stuff – he even refused to be paid! At least we can benefit from all the years Mum supplied him with customers.'

''Where's Iris? I need her urgently.'

Heather's eyes bug out at my rudeness, but she lets it go. 'She's at the hospital with Dad. She'll take the evening shift, and we'll take over tomorrow.'

'I need to talk to her now!'

I rush out of the room with my mobile to call Iris. Heather follows me into the living room.

'What's going on?' she probes while I doom-scroll on my mobile. I turn to Heather with anger, not towards her but due to the situation. I can see in her eyes my behaviour is alarming her, but I don't care. I need to find a solution for Mum before my siblings all disappear on me.

'How long before you go back to Berlin?' I enquire.

'I don't know,' Heather replies, 'I need to see if I can get another week off work.'

'So, possibly another week before you leave… How long do you think Iris will stay?'

'Knowing Iris, probably ten days to two weeks and even then, she'll be running the world.'

'And how long do you think it will take Dad to return home?'

The penny drops at last. I can see in Heather's eyes she gets the picture and the full magnitude of the situation.

'I have no idea, but certainly longer than two weeks.''

'It means I have maximum two weeks to find a solution for Mum. I'll be damned if I'm going to be stuck taking care of her!'

Heather flinches at my tone, but I'm ambivalent. I won't be the one whose job is to pacify everyone anymore. *I guess everyone has their limits.*

'Relax. I'm sure we can find a solution in two weeks!' Heather attempts to soothe me, 'Let's talk about it with Iris tomorrow, when we take over with.'

'I'm not waiting until tomorrow!' I counter. 'I have to start looking now, otherwise I'll be stuck here with her.'

'You know what? I think you're right. I'll ask Zoe to take Mum for a walk or – even better – for a bike ride! Do they still have that tandem? Then you and I can put our heads together. Does that work for you?'

I heave a huge sigh of relief. 'That would be great!'

I watch Heather return to the kitchen and overhear her dealing with Verity. *I don't have that patience,* listening to Heather overcoming Verity's objections...

'Whatever for?' I can hear her petulant voice.

'Zoe has never been to Oxford, Mum!' Heather explains. 'You're the best person to show her all the little places in Oxford no one knows. For most people, Oxford is a stuffy old University City, but you know some magical spots. Why don't you show it to her? There's no one better than you, Mum?'

Flattery always works on Mum. 'You're absolutely right.'

I can hear her call, 'There's more to Oxford than stuffy old libraries. Let's go, Zoe. I need that bike ride!'

Once I hear the front door shut, I start breathing easier. It is good to know Heather is on my side. Maybe Iris is right. Families do come together in times of crisis.

When Heather returns, I'm in a much better mood. My initial fear of having to deal with Mum alone dissipates.

'First, I need sustenance,' I declare. 'I think much better on a full stomach.' We sit in the kitchen. Heather pulls some of the delicious food out of the fridge that is left from yesterday's party.

While warming it up, Heather goes through all the ramifications of Dad's condition. I listen with as much concentration as I can muster, but my thoughts go back to who can take care of Mum. I know that no matter how bad Dad's condition is, I'll be able to take care of him, but having to deal with Mum as well is beyond my strength.

'We must find a carer to live here with Mum,' I conclude more to myself than Heather.

Heather is silent. To my surprise, she encourages me to taste some of the food. I devour everything Heather sets in front of me.

'God, I'm full! But boy, does this feel good. I feel better already,' I start laughing. 'Mike always says that before any important discussion, he makes sure I'm fully fed. Otherwise, it's a lost cause. He should have seen this!'

I'm aware Heather has no clue what I'm talking about. For her, food is only a necessity. She once told me that if it was up to her, she'd eat astronaut food: one pill with all the essential nutrients and be done with it.

Not for me.

All at once I recall something from yesterday's celebrations. 'I saw you talking with Ruth yesterday. What was she on about?'

'Oh, the usual. The only thing she had to talk to me about was how bad Mum's condition is and that we need to support Dad.'

'Did Ruth have something practical to say about how to take care of Mum? Uncle Geoff went through the same process, so she must have had some experience with it.'

'Yes, she said we need to get a live-in carer for Mum.'

'Well, that's what I want!' I screech. 'How do we get one? It needs to be someone who can handle Mum on their own without me being here.'

Heather is silent for a while, looking at me with those big dark eyes of hers when at last, she has some reactions to my frantic search.

'Let me call Ruth. She's bound to have some phone numbers.'

We both jump when at that moment my phone rings.

❧ IRIS ❧

I guess stroke patients come in all shapes and sizes, Iris thinks to herself while sitting beside Sol's bed, writing down what he dictates to her. *When listening to him, no one would believe he had a major stroke only forty - eight hours ago.*

Sol sits in his bed like an emperor, giving instructions to Iris. Yes, he speaks slowly and with great concentration, but still sounds like him. *And here I am thinking Mum is the dictator in this family. I guess I get it from both of them.*

'Go to my emails and look for one from James Price, from Andrews College, subject: "maps",' Sol orders her. 'It's essential I make some corrections on the issue. I want you to call Martin Brandies and inform him I will not be able to give the lecture this weekend.'

Iris dutifully jots them down.

'Do you wish me to explain what happened?' she checks with him.

'No need. News travels fast. They all know by now,' Sol chuckles. 'But tell him I'll give that lecture next month if he wants.'

Iris considers explaining to Sol about his stroke, which will not allow him to leave the hospital for three months at least but decides to let it go. Sol frowns with thought, or rather the right side of his face does.

'On my table, there's a foolscap folder named 'Professor Lewis' Book'. Bring it here so I can work on it.'

Heather comes in. The sisters exchange eloquent looks that say, *he has no clue about his condition.* Neither have the heart to explain the true extent of it to him. Heather sits next to Iris.

'He'll come to it,' she whispers.

A nurse enters the room with a tray. The food looks like typical hospital food, bland and unappetising, but to their surprise, Sol smiles. 'My favourite time of the day! Though they could use some cooking lessons from your mum.'

Iris is in shock. Her dad was never one to eat poor food or indulge himself. He eats half the quantities on his plate and avoids any pudding or desserts, no matter how hard Verity tries to convince him they are fine from time to time.

Hearing her father say he likes food is like hearing a stranger. She exchanges looks with Heather, but Heather pretends she didn't notice this change. Heather is focused on Sol's attempts to eat his meal with only one hand, in which he is not successful. He lacks coordination, and his food lands on his hospital gown top. Sol is embarrassed.

'I feel such a fool!' he mutters.

'Dad, give yourself a break. You're only a few days into recovery. It's going to take time,' Heather reassures him while taking his spoon.

Iris, watching her father in such a helpless state, leaves the room in tears.

Standing outside in the corridor, Iris allows herself a good cry. When she calms down, she spots Daisy in deep discussion with a woman at the end of the hall.

She approaches closer to overhear what they are talking about. The woman is handing over loads of forms to Daisy to fill out. She stands up and hands Daisy a card. 'Here's my mobile number. Call me when you've finished filling these out or if you need anything else. I know how tough it can be, just remember I'm here to help you.'

Once she leaves, Daisy starts filling out the forms with such concentration that she doesn't even notice Iris standing beside her.

ᑕᗅ DAISY ᕽᗅ

I'm busy filling the forms when, out of the blue, I hear Iris, 'What was all that about?'

It catches me by surprise that I jump. 'Where did you spring from? You scared the hell out of me!'

'Yeah, I notice,' Iris retorts. 'Who was that?'

'That is the hospital social worker,' I respond.

'Why do you need a social worker, and what are all these forms?'

I look at Iris. The look on Iris's face tells me she never in her life thought of asking for help from another person. I know she is good at delegating tasks at work, but it is a sign of leadership, not about asking for help. When it comes to private or personal matters, I remember Iris describing herself as a 'self-sustainable unit'.

For the first time in my life, I realise my big sister is proud of this but not aware of the disadvantages. Self-sustainability is hard. Seeing Iris in this new light is a revelation for me. I always looked up to her, seeing her as Superwoman. *It's not that way anymore.*

I pick up some of the forms and show them to Iris while explaining we need a carer to stay with Mum while Dad recuperates.

'Heather tells me that it will be at least three months before Dad comes back home. I need to visit him every day. I can't leave Mum on her own.'

'That's why we need someone. I also need someone to be with her when I'm working in London. Fortunately, for us, Dad, being Dad, has two private health insurance policies which cover paying for a carer, but we need to request it and provide evidence. This is where the social worker comes in. They have to sign and approve this request before the insurance covers it.'

'But do you have someone in mind?' Iris enquires. 'I mean, we're talking about Mum here… We both know how picky she can be. How will you explain a stranger coming to live with her?' I expect that question from her and smile.

'That's your job. I only made it easier for you….' I answer.

'How's that?'

'Well, I remembered Ruth was talking about Uncle Geoff's carer,' I tell her. 'She's looking for a new position since he died. Her name's Aisha. Mum visited Ruth when they were sitting Shiva and met her. According to Ruth, Mum was impressed with Aisha.'

'So…' Iris is still clueless about what I am talking about.

'I've asked Aisha to come this afternoon to meet Mum. You'll be there to make it as easy as possible for everyone. Make sure Aisha understands we need her to move in by the end of this week. I want her to get used to everything before you leave.'

I am so busy trying to find solutions I never stop to think about how it comes across to others. I only get it when Iris responds to my long speech.

'I must say, I'm impressed. It's been less than forty-eight hours since Dad had the stroke, and you've taken care of all the important things. I like this new Daisy.'

'So, you'll do it?

'Yes, ma'am!' Iris says with a smile.

I grin back and return to filling in the forms.

❧ DAISY ☙

Time stops for no one is my mantra for the next three months. Everything becomes hazy for me. I can only remember fragments, like YouTube clips. It's like one long, grey period of constant running from one place to another with never-ending tasks: an image of Dad strapped to a machine that imitates walking, allowing the body to relearn movements; me standing on the side watching him hanging helplessly.

I recall how much I struggle to cheer him up, but when he isn't looking, tears roll down my face. Times when Mum insists on coming to the hospital but is more of a burden than help with her imperious attitude.

She insists on taking Dad to a physiotherapy session only to get lost, so I have to find them both and take Dad to the session myself.

Iris comes for the odd week here and there and takes over with Dad, being with him during occupational therapy. At night she shares with me how he strains to recover the use of his left hand, how he endeavours to dress himself, or how to help him move from the bed to his wheelchair.

I will never forget the sadness I experience each time I help him put on his shirt or the effort it takes me to aid him in moving from the wheelchair back to his bed.

I know my humiliation is nothing compared to what he goes through in those moments. I can see the sadness in his eyes when he looks at me as I tie his shoelaces.

'Dad? Are you OK?' I ask, looking up at him.

He smiles and shakes his head. 'Daisy, I don't want you doing this. It's not fair,' he answers. 'You must have your life back. Promise you'll find a carer for me when I return home. I can't watch you do this anymore.'

The pain in his voice is more than I can take. I promise to find someone for him.

'So, we'll have a full house again, your mum, Aisha, me, and another carer! Only this time, we will be the children!' he jokes. When he is being funny, he doesn't slur his words so much.

110

'It's good you've not lost the Bach sense of humour,' I laugh.

The most painful moments come when I see Iris with Dad, struggling to read his manuscripts. Despite his infirmity, he isn't willing to give up on them. He can't read them, but the problem is not in his eyes, as Heather keeps reminding me; it is a cognitive problem in his brain.

What would Dad do without his beloved research? There is no point in him living without his research, I know. *What am I going to do once he's released from the hospital?*

ℭ SOL ℬ

If there is one thing Sol learned at an early age, growing up as a Jewish boy in Nazi Germany is that life is unpredictable. However, nothing prepared him for what he was going through in the past three months.

He doesn't mind the challenges with his new condition. He, in a way, cherishes it and takes it as another challenge in life. What he isn't ready for are the waves of regret that overflow him from time to time.

Looking at Daisy tying his shoelaces makes Sol sad. Not because he is helpless but because it opens an old wound in him. It reminds him of his failure to protect his girls from Verity's endless demands of them.

He knows he cannot forgive himself for the years Iris had to act as the head of the family and make difficult decisions when Verity wasn't around. He knew that in many ways, it was his fault Iris never had a proper childhood. She became an adult too soon.

He can't quite understand how it all happened, but he noticed it too late in life to change the dynamics in his dysfunctional family. Maintaining the veneer of perfection became the norm.

He ruminates upon it now: is it his own upbringing? His father has been the centre of the family, everything geared around his success. Sol's mother did everything else in the house, come rain or shine – even to the detriment of her own health.

Or was it Verity's ferocious insistence on making sure nothing disturbed him in the pursuit of his own career? He sighs.

He hasn't been there to help his girls to do what they wanted. He has a sudden urge to resolve it and try to put things right. *Maybe it's too late for Iris, but I can still do something for Daisy.*

Chapter Twelve

CR DAISY ಐ

It's been three months since Dad had his stroke. My life has turned upside down. Iris and Heather did their best to help me, but it's hard to truly help when they live so far away. I could give all the reasons why they couldn't help more than they did, but it didn't take away the sting of having my whole life collapse on me in the middle of my life. I suddenly had two elderly people to take care of. I could manage with Dad, but Mum was a different issue.

A few weeks ago, the rehabilitation centre informed me that Dad would be released. I knew it was time to move them to London. I couldn't continue commuting between London and Oxford to care for them. It's true Aisha is a blessing, but there are limits to what she can do with Mum.

I had to make a decision, but I didn't want it to be done all on my own. I wanted Heather and Iris to be on board. Thank God for Skype, where we could all meet online and discuss it even though we're all in different countries.

I first contacted Iris, who was sitting on her amazing, beautiful balcony. Within seconds Heather joined us from her Berlin apartment.

I didn't have time for chitchat, *so unlike my usual self. The new circumstances are definitely changing me...*

'Dad's time in the rehabilitation centre ends in three weeks. I decided to relocate them to London. I need one of you here to help me with the move,' I inform them. My tone is sharper than I want, but I don't want to leave any space to question my decision. I know it sounds more like an order than a request.

Iris appears impressed. *Well, she would. That's the way she would have done it.* But for me, it is new.

'I can come next week and help you,' Iris responds.

Heather takes her time in giving input, but when she does at last, it is not what I expect to hear. 'I'm not sure it's the best decision for Mum. She can hardly find herself in Oxford, let alone in a huge city like London...' *Typical Heather.*

Before Heather can continue, I explode. 'Have you any idea what's it been like for me the past three months?' I shout.

Iris and Heather are dumbstruck. Neither of them has ever seen me in such a state. *I probably sound like Mum. No doubt, the time I'm spending with her is taking its toll on me.* But I don't care who I sound like. I just need them to make that effort and help me when I need it.

I suddenly remember what Mum used to say, 'Helping someone is doing what they ask you, not what you want to do.' It sounded all wrong when she used to say it, but I can now see the truth in it.

Iris tries to calm me down. 'Neither of us underestimates what you've been doing. Heather is only trying to think through all aspects of this decision.'

'Oh, shut up, Iris! I'm sorry, Daisy.'

That's not fair on Iris, I think, as Heather explodes on her, but I have no time for the bickering between those two. They're grown-up women. They can fix it between themselves.

'Like I said, I can come next week and help,' Iris repeats. 'I'll reschedule my assignments. But I can't promise anything else – Nate is already complaining I'm never home.'

'When can you be here?' I turn to Heather.

It takes Heather a few seconds to reply. 'I'll ask my boss for a few extra days off.'

'Good!' I respond in a business-like manner. 'Anything else?'

'How will you break the news to Mum?' Iris inquires.

I laugh bitterly. 'Already done. It was a huge drama. Thank God Aisha was there! She took her out for a walk, and by the time she got back, she forgot all about it.'

Heather and Iris both look relieved.

'Well, it's good we have Aisha. Seems like it's working!' Iris remarks.

I couldn't agree more. 'I don't know what I would do without her. She keeps me sane. Every day I bless Ruth for giving us Aisha.'

Heather is curious. 'How did Mum accept Aisha?'

'It's been a spark of genius on my part,' I giggle. 'I told Mum Aisha is working with me and as I'm staying in the house, she also has to stay. I had to repeat it a few times in the first week, but after that, Mum just accepted Aisha as if she always lived with us.

'The great thing is that Aisha does everything Mum loves: she listens to her, asks her loads of questions, and keeps Mum busy, so she doesn't notice what's going on. Best of all, she has the patience of a saint! Anyway… I have to run now. Dad has another doctor coming to assess him, and I need to be there. Ciao for now.'

☙ IRIS ❧

Daisy and Heather log off, leaving Iris watching the blank screen, lost in her thoughts again. She has a heavy feeling in her chest. She is trapped between her heart's desire and her obligations.

Sitting on her balcony, she can see all the way down to the coast. Her home is her haven. It is the one place in the world where she can let go of the burden she carries.

She knew this place was her home as soon as she saw it five years ago. She and Nate had been looking for a place to retire for over ten years. When she stepped into this remote house, she knew she'd arrived.

The place is a renovated eighteenth-century Spanish hacienda with olive groves at the back of the house, orange trees and vineyards along the edges of the property. Since they moved, she and Nate became passionate about organic farming, starting their own vegetable garden and planting more fruit trees to turn the place into an edible forest. She never imagined they'd take to something as basic as farming and gardening, but somehow it gave her a sense of peace she had never experienced before.

It is off the grid, so they depend on solar energy and rainwater ponds. But for her, it is an advantage. She loved being self-sustainable; it made her feel safe, which she had always longed for.

'As long as I have my Wi-Fi, I'm as free as a bird.' She jokes with her friends. For her, this place is her own private Garden of Eden.

Her whole life, she searched for somewhere she could be playful like she was as a child, free from Verity's overbearing authority. The hacienda allows her to do just that. *I've never been as relaxed and at peace as I'm here.*

She knows that if it is up to Nate, he would also give up the Wi-Fi connection and Internet; his dream is to be like Robinson Crusoe and disappear from civilisation, but this is not for Iris.

She still has family duties. Though she loves living off the grid, her family needs her, so she keeps the communication channels open for them via the Internet.

Thinking about her family reminds her of the conversation she just had with Daisy. *Daisy looks tired,* she thinks *No wonder,* but that makes Iris feel guilty again concerning the situation.

After a while, she looks up from the empty screen to see Nate walking up the driveway. He breaks into a smile when he catches her looking at him.

She smiles back. As usual, her heart misses a beat. After twenty-five years together, she still cannot believe such a stunning man chose her as his partner. Growing up with Verity's constant criticism of her looks convinced her no man would ever desire her.

She was ready to live a life of a spinster focused on her career. She always wanted children but never dreamed of having a partner to help her. So, when Nate stepped into her life, she wasn't sure he would stay. *No one did,* she reminds herself.

In her usual condescending way, Verity said to her he was only after her money – not that she had much at the time – but still, Verity had been suspicious about his motives for years, even after they had Joy.

'Why would a striking young man like him attach himself to you?' Verity often asked.

Iris learned to stop listening to Verity long before, but somehow her criticism always had an edge. As the decades went by, even Verity realised Nate was here to stay.

Iris could finally let go of her belief she is not a beautiful woman. She began to have confidence in her appearance, not just her skills and professionalism.

Now watching her man walk up to her, she has an overwhelming surge of love. She is indeed blessed to have such a unique relationship.

He reaches her and leans to give her a soft kiss on her forehead. 'Penny for your thoughts?'

Iris grins. 'You won't like it.'

'Since when that stopped you?' he replies, laughing at her.

'Daisy wants me to come and help her move Mum and Dad to London.'

'So, you're going away again!' he contends, sounding like a spoilt child.

'Must you be like this?' Iris snaps, hurt. She immediately feels remorseful for lashing out at Nate. She paces up and down the balcony. To be fair, she doesn't feel like rushing back to London. She wants to stay with Nate in their haven. *Surely, I've earned this by now?* But she has to keep her promise to her family.

Lost in her inner battle, she hears Nate say, 'I don't get it. Your sister chose to do this. She could say no and find someone to take care of your parents. Why does she think everyone else has to pay for her choices?'

Iris goes into defence mode. No one is allowed to attack her family. 'Don't start!' she tells him, but Nate is not giving up.

'Why is it that every time someone in your family needs help, you're the one that saves the day?'

Iris stops her nervous pacing. 'You just don't get the concept of family!' she hollers at him.

Nate is shocked. He reaches out to her to calm her down. 'Of course I do! You and Joy are my family.'

Iris evades him. 'You don't understand how my family works!' she utters through gritted teeth.

Nate snorts with derision. 'No one understands your family!'

Iris stares at him. Is he joking, or is it another one of his sarcastic remarks?

'I know I'm being a pain in the arse about this,' he asserts. 'But I thought I was your pain in the arse. What's changed?'

Iris shuts her eyes in despair, realising she doesn't have the energy to explain it to him. It is something she doesn't completely understand herself. 'Nothing's changed. I can't deal with this right now,' she states.

'I know I'm not the ideal family man, but you knew that on our first date,' he murmurs, smiling at her.

It is true.

Nate's softness is the last straw for Iris. She cannot take it anymore. She collapses back into her seat, looking like a rag doll. The words just came pouring out.

'Why don't you get what I had to give up when I chose to live with you?' she mutters.

Nate is surprised. 'What? That we live abroad? I thought you wanted this just as much as I did!'

Iris has no idea how to explain it without sounding as if she is blaming him. 'No, it has nothing to do with that.'

'Then what? For God's sake, Iris!' demands Nate.

Iris summons all her courage. 'I broke my promise.'

There is silence on the balcony.

'What promise?' Nate mimes.

'I was supposed to take care of them. It's my job, not Daisy's,' Iris whispers, more to herself than to Nate.

He stares at Iris. 'Don't you think Daisy is capable of doing it?' he enquires.

Iris looks at him with weary eyes. 'Sure she is. She might be doing a better job than I can... but where does that leave me?'

Nate moves in to hug Iris as she weeps tears of release. 'Well, I guess you'll be heading there tomorrow,' Nate notes. 'I'll always be here, you know,' he adds as he turns around and walks into the house, leaving Iris sitting on the balcony with her thoughts.

Her mind is racing. On the one hand, she has lists of what she needs to do before leaving: all the appointments she has to rearrange, emails to send and packing to do. On the other hand, she already goes through all her contacts in London to see who can help them find a good place for Sol, Verity, and their carers.

She knows the criteria. Yet in another corner of her mind, a voice is nagging her. *For how long are you going to keep that promise?*

She remembers the day she made that promise to Verity. She spent the weekend with her parents. It was a beautiful spring day some decades before. Daisy and Heather were playing outside in the garden when she walked into the living room, when Verity put on one of her favourite records and asked Sol to dance with her. It was Leonard Cohen's song, 'Dance Me to the End of Love'.

She watched them, making sure not to be seen, thinking how lovely they looked in each other's arms. She recalled her thoughts at the time: *so that's what a loving couple looks like.*

There were no better words to describe it than the words of that song. Iris always remembered the first lines of it and how appropriate they were to what she was witnessing. Now, she perceives the second line as even more relevant: '*Dance me through the panic 'til I'm gathered safely in.*' Once the song ended, Verity looked up at Sol, tears in her eyes.

'I need you to take me to the hospital tomorrow,' she whispered. 'I have a lump in my breast, and they need to operate.' That was how Verity informed her family she had breast cancer.

Her mum knew about the lump for some time but refused to go and get it checked because she thought there were more important things to do, like children, work, graduating her Masters, and her endless social obligations.

When she finally found time, the tumour was so big they had to perform a total mastectomy. Iris would never forget the look of shock on Sol's face. He wasn't even angry at Verity for not telling him about it all this time. He was simply panicking. Verity saw Iris standing in the doorway.

'Iris, you're in charge of this family now. Promise me you'll take care of Daisy and Heather and help your Dad,' Verity commanded in her most imposing tone.

What else could I have said? Iris thinks when replaying that scene in her head. *Could I really have said no?* As usual, Verity

121

created the perfect circumstances, so things would be done according to her will. And ever since then, Iris had been the problem-solver of the family.

I'm the fixer, the person in charge... until now. But old habits die-hard. Iris's guilt at not being there to care for the family is not easy for her to relinquish. *So here I am, nearly sixty years old and still keeping my promise to Mum.*

Iris sighs and realises it is time to stop planning and start doing. She gets up, takes a last long look at the view she loves so much and walks into the house.

❦ HEATHER ❦

Heather keeps staring at her iPad long after her call with Daisy and Iris finishes. She has no clue why she is so rude to Iris. It's true that while growing up, Iris always tried to run Heather's life and dictate what to do, but that was a long time ago. *Why is she still pushing my buttons?* She wonders.

Then her thoughts move to Daisy. *Daisy looks knackered, no doubt taking care of Dad and Mum is playing a part in it.* She knows she disappointed Daisy by not immediately replying to her request, but she trusts Daisy to know her well enough and realises it's not because she doesn't want to come to help her but because she is not one to make quick decisions. *Maybe one of the reasons I resent Iris is because she has no problem making a choice and acting upon it immediately,* a thought crosses her mind.

Heather's way of making decisions is by evaluating every

single detail it involves and looking at the consequences for each option the situation demands. This takes time, and for that, she has her famous 'ProCon-book', as Zoe calls it.

Thinking about Zoe makes her smile. Maybe the only time she didn't need her 'ProCon-book' was when she met Zoe and decided to move and live together with her...

Zoe certainly is not her usual type. In a way, she is the total opposite of all her previous relationships. Heather's previous lovers were serious, analytical, and cautious, not like Zoe with her artistic and free-spirited friends. Come to think of it... Zoe proves that opposites attract.

When she met Zoe for the first time, she found out how much truth there was in that cliché. There is something free about Zoe, which for her means she can finally be out of the shadow of Sol, Verity and Iris, something she always longed for.

On the other hand, she knew that for Zoe being with her meant safety and something solid in the unpredictive life she had.

Zoe's life has been more of a gipsy's life. Being with Heather, who is reliable and consistent, is a novelty for her and Heather knows it. They discussed it many times.

Zoe brings out of Heather her funny and exciting side, which she buried long ago. But with it also came her explosive part, which Heather identifies she inherited from Verity. She can still remember their first fight, which came as a shock for Zoe, who had learned to avoid confrontation at all costs.

For both of them, it has been a huge learning curve. Heather grasped how profound Verity's influence was on her. At the same time, Zoe, for the first time in her life, did not run away from a relationship thinking it was the end of it, the way she used to, due to the legacy of difficult foster home experiences she carried with her from her past.

Now sitting in her apartment in Berlin, Heather knows she needs to make a tough decision. Her life in Berlin is comfortable and without stress, something she loves. She never could understand Iris's need for challenges and mountains to climb. For Heather, having a loving, quiet, easy, and comfortable life is her dream. Now that she's finally managed to create this with Zoe, she doesn't want to lose it.

However, she owes Daisy a long-life debt, which she cannot escape. Deep in her heart, she knows she needs to move back to London and help Daisy with the burden that has fallen upon her with the stroke of Sol.

This scares Heather. *What if Zoe does not want to come with me, and what would she do in London if she did? She doesn't know anyone there, and long-distance relationships never last.* A flow of thoughts and options is going through her brain. *Time for my ProCon-book.*

She gets up, takes out her notebook, sits at her favourite armchair, and opens the tattered notebook. She divides the page into two columns. On top of one of them she writes PROS, on the other CONS, and starts writing all the details that moving to London would mean. All the steps she needs to take, consequences, risks, and opportunities.

Heather is fully immersed in her process; she doesn't notice how the room turns dark and hours go by. She raises her head only when Zoe steps into their apartment.

'Let there be light', Zoe declares in a loud voice while switching on the lights in the apartment.

Heather chuckles. *Trust Zoe to bring in some lightness when serious issues are at stake,* but she is relieved to get a break from her heavy thoughts.

'What's on your mind?' Zoe inquires. 'I haven't seen this notebook for a long time. Are we making decisions?'

Heather raises her head, looking blankly at Zoe. 'What would you say if I told you I'm thinking of moving back to London?'

The look on Zoe's face proves to Heather that this is an unexpected announcement, and she fears the worst. However, the following sentence takes her breath away.

'I'd say, cool!' Zoe answers. 'If you are finally thinking of making a change, who am I to stop you?'

'No, be serious. I think I'll have to move to London for a bit. Daisy needs my help, and I can't say no.'

'No problem! I'll come with you. It'll be fun. A new adventure – just what the doctor ordered,' Zoe retorts.

'You'll come with me? But why?'

Zoe looks at Heather and smiles. 'Because I know you need to do it! Besides, I love your family. I don't understand why you hate your mum so much, but hey, it's your thing.'

'How can you like my mum? She's the most hypocritical, shallow person I know. She still hates the idea of me being gay,' Heather cries out.

Zoe nods while Heather is talking, and when Heather finally finishes her rant about Verity, Zoe gently states, 'That's not my impression of her. And why do you hate her so much? It's not as if she abandoned you.'

'I wish she had,' Heather mumbles. 'You have no clue what it was like growing up gay with her.'

'That's true. But I do know what it feels like when your own mother dumps you. All I see is a charming woman trying to outsmart a horrible disease. It'll take everything from her,' Zoe counters, determined to get Heather to see a different view.

Heather is silent for a while and then jots in her notebook, 'Zoe likes the idea of moving'. In a separate line, another point, 'Zoe likes Mum'.

She then stands up looking at Zoe, who is still in her coat.

'You're hungry?' Heather asks.

'Starving. Would kill for a hot soup.' Zoe responds.

'No worries, I thought you would. I'll heat it up'. Heather walks to the kitchen to prepare their dinner.

Chapter Thirteen

⊘ IRIS ⊘

Iris sits beside Sol's bed, reading the title of a book from a list of books she created online, waiting to hear whether he wants them to be taken to London or left in Oxford. Most of the time, he insists on them to London.

It's been a long stay this time. Every few days, she sends a message to Nate, telling him she has to stay another week, thinking she will finish everything by then. But her stay extends further and further. There never seems to be enough time to complete the move.

Iris blessed her lucky stars when she found a great new apartment for Sol and Verity in London. It's not too far from Daisy's place, so it is handy for Daisy to visit. However, the place is much smaller than the house in Oxford. The main concern Iris has is Sol's study. He will be able to work, but the room is tiny compared to the one in Oxford. There is no way they'll be able to move his entire library to the new place. Some books need to stay in Oxford.

Iris never had a hold on how many books Sol had accumulated in his lifetime. She estimates there are over three thousand books in his library, but when she takes it upon herself to make an inventory, she apprehends the enormity of the task.

In the years she's been away, the books have taken on a life of their own, overflowing from Sol's study and filling up every free space in the house. There is a moment when she thinks she is watching the famous scene from Walt Disney's 'Fantasia' of the Sorcerer's Apprentice, but instead of broomsticks carrying infinite buckets of water, she sees them carrying an infinite number of books.

After struggling for several days with the number of books, she gets Heather's help finding an app to create the book inventory. There is no way she could have done it otherwise.

'Thank God for Heather's grasp of technology!' she tells Sol. 'I'd be lost without it.'

Now she hopes Sol will agree to leave most of the books in Oxford, but Sol is too attached to most of them. As the list of books to take lengthens, Iris finds herself growing irritated. She starts doubting her father's judgment.

'Dad, explain your criteria to me,' If she knows what they are, she can make those decisions quicker and ease the move. However, when she looks at her father, she recognises he isn't really looking at her. He is staring at a spot on the empty wall behind her. She repeats her request.

'I don't have any criteria,' he answers in a sad tone.

Iris understands she has to get her father to think properly. She takes his hand. 'Dad, look at me. We can't take your whole library to London. If you need a specific book, we can always come back and pick it up for you. But for now, take only what you need for your research...'

This approach makes a difference. Sol sits straight up in his bed and looks into her eyes. 'Do you think I'll be able to continue with my research?'

Iris wants to tell him that everything will be ok. She knows Sol's heart is in his work. *If he can't work, he'll die.* How can she explain the reality of his situation to him without taking away his flicker of hope?

Iris stands up, stretching her back. She is stiff from hours of sitting and reading lists of books to him. *I'm not getting any younger,* smiling to herself.

'Why not?' she declares, sounding more confident than she is. 'You can complete the two manuscripts you were working on before the stroke.' She isn't sure if he could do new research, but working on what he already wrote is a possibility for him, with time and some help from assistants.

Sol is not reassured. He looks at a sign about visiting hours on the wall behind her. 'I can't read the sign on that wall! How on earth can I read my books?'

Iris is determined to get his hopes back up. 'First, physiotherapy will get you stronger. Then, you know, a research assistant is something you can use,' Iris states.

Sol looks grumpy. 'Yes, I know you don't like them, but now you have every right to one. You'll make one lucky student grateful for the rest of her life with such an opportunity.'

Though it appears like her point is getting across to him, Sol is still gazing glumly at her with no real sign of agreement.

'Where's Verity?' he questions.

Iris detects it is useless to press the point. He is thinking about other things. She sits down, resigned to leave the topic.

'Mum will be here shortly,' she mutters, all at once weary.

Her lethargic tone alarms Sol. 'Is she coming on her own?' he probes.

Iris hears his concern. 'Dad don't worry. Mum might be confused and forgetful, but she still knows the way to the hospital. Don't forget she volunteered here for years. It's one of the few places she knows well. Besides, Aisha is with her at all times.'

Sol sighs with relief. Iris opens the list of books on her app.

'Are you sure we can't stay in Oxford?' Sol inquires.

Iris considers how to answer, her eyes filled with compassion. It is hard for her to be the bearer of bad news, but she knows there is no way her parents can stay in their beloved home.

'Too many stairs and levels! Your wheelchair can't move around the house safely,' she explains to him, and not for the first time.

Sol gapes at the wall again. 'I've lived in that house for more than forty years. One doesn't just pack up and leave,' he mentions grumpily.

Iris cannot bear to hear the sting in his voice but can think of nothing to say to ease it for him.

'I won't be able to see our home again!' he whispers.

Iris is speechless by the agony in his declaration. Seconds of silence stretch out. 'We can organise one last farewell party,' she remarks. She doesn't expect a response from him, but when she sees the sudden light in Sol's eyes, she knows this will help him in his distress.

She is sure Daisy and Heather will kill her for the suggestion, as it is another project to be completed, but she doesn't care. Just seeing the light in her Dad's eyes is enough for her. She feels she's made a difference at last.

∾ HEATHER ∾

When Iris comes back from the hospital informing them all she promised Sol one last party in their home, Heather is surprised to notice she isn't outraged about it... well, maybe irritated and concerned how they could push it while still packing the house. However, when Iris declares she will take care of it, she can release a sigh of relief and admit that isn't such a bad idea.

The next few days go by so fast Heather experience it like watching a video on fast forward.

She is impressed at how Daisy takes control of the whole process of moving. Daisy organises a moving company to come, divides the tasks of sorting out what goes to London and what stays in Oxford between the three of them and makes sure everything goes according to schedule. *I haven't seen Daisy this assertive in all my life. Maybe because it's crucial for her that things are done how she wants.* It doesn't matter to Heather what the reason is. She is happy Iris is not trying to control Daisy and letting her do her things.

Though Iris is giving Daisy the space to run things in her own way, she also makes sure to keep Verity out of their way when sorting and packing. Taking care of Verity becomes an endless battlefield.

Most mornings, Verity wakes up confused, finding boxes all over the house. She starts taking stuff out of them and complains about the mess in the house. Heather is delighted to have Aisha's help with the constant explanations to Verity about the move from Oxford to London.

Aisha has an endless reservoir of patience, going over the details with Verity again and again. Some days, Verity is fine, behaving and acting the way she always did, which makes being with her acceptable. But occasionally, a different Verity comes out. Sometimes it is a confused, lost woman and sometimes a demon, screaming and shouting, refusing to listen to reason. It is in those moments Heather observes Iris is the only one who can handle Verity.

At times it will be Iris's soft voice relaxing Verity, and when Iris loses her patience, she screams back at Verity, which shuts up Verity for a while. In those times, Heather feels the rest of them melt away into the walls.

When Daisy tells Iris she is the only person in the world who can stand her ground against Verity when she goes into her demon mode, Heather experiences a pang of jealousy. Still, she is honest enough with herself to admit the truth in Daisy's words. They all freeze and die inside, while Iris is strong enough to push back.

When the day of the farewell party arrives, everyone is elated. The party is a success. Verity, in her element, acting as the elegant hostess, shines throughout the whole event, though Iris reminds her from time to time they need to take Sol back to the hospital for one final night. Somehow Verity is able to accept it.

To Heather's surprise, Verity even explains to Sol why they must move to London.

Daisy stands next to her, listening. 'Miracles never cease!' she whispers to Heather.

The next day, Daisy, Heather, and Iris are in the kitchen, surrounded by boxes, waiting for the movers to come. Iris has to catch her flight back home but is still giving orders.

'Relax!' comments Heather. 'You did well. Let go of the micro-management.'

'I had to be here. The farewell party was my fault.'

'It was for the best. I think it did Dad good, and even Mum was at her best, so don't feel guilty about going,' Heather responds.

It seems as if this kind of statement moves Iris. Heather has no idea why, but she notices Iris trying to control an outburst of emotions. She bends down to look inside a box full of books and blows dust off an old library book.

'Oh, look what I've found!' she mutters. 'Of all the books in the world... Anna Karenina. I always said he got it wrong... not all happy families are happy in the same way. Each happy family is different, too.'

Heather chuckles. 'Happy families indeed,' she retorts. 'Let me know if you ever find one.'

The sisters burst out laughing. It is a wonderful bonding moment as they mark the end of this life's chapter. Like many families, they can undercut discomfort with humour.

CR DAISY ☙

Mike is driving, which gives me some time to go over my emails. Lately, my multi-tasking is at its peak. Taking care of Dad, Mum and my clinics with patients have left me wishing for an extra two hours a day and one extra day a week. I know Mike feels neglected, but I have no idea how I can give him the attention he deserves.

We were returning from another fertility clinic Heather recommended. I am so absorbed with going over my emails that I hear Mike's question only when he most likely asked it for the third time.

'So, what did you think of the clinic and Doctor Williams?' he asks casually.

He's trying not to disturb me too much… how sweet of him.

'No idea why Heather recommends it,' I reply, without even raising my head from my mobile. I furiously type some quick responses to non-important emails.

'I guess Heather thinks she knows what you need rather than what you have in mind,' he remarks, careful, as ever, not to criticise Heather.

I stop my typing and look at Mike.

'Right. Never mind compassion, as long as it's scientifically accurate,' I state, smiling. I know I'm not fair to Heather, but I no longer have time to be 'nice' to people. I start understanding why people think 'the truth hurts', but I'm not in the mood or have the energy to play games or be tactful.

'Why not ask Iris?' He states, knowing Iris is a sore issue with me.

We discussed this a few times. For Mike, it makes sense to ask someone who already gave birth at a relatively late stage in life rather than asking someone knowledgeable about it but who doesn't have the experience. He doesn't understand my reluctance to check with Iris.

'I might,' I mumble after a few moments. 'It's just… you know her. She'll make a project out of it and drive me crazy.'

'She means well,' he observes. Mike understands Iris can be a bulldozer when it comes to getting her way, but he's never been on the other side of it to experience how it feels when Iris wants something different than what you want.

'But I guess that's because I'm looking at it from the outside. There are things between you three I'm not even aware of,' he adds to make clear he's not taking sides.

'You're right. But she will advocate all that New Age nonsense, natural birthing, and all that. I'm not ready for it,' I insist.

Mike laughs. 'That's probably true! Iris loves that entire Hippy Dippy lark. But all you need to do is tell her what you want and don't want. I'm sure she'll be more than happy to help.'

I stare straight ahead, playing with my hair, a habit I have when I feel conflicted about something. His remark made me recognise something I didn't like to discover.

'Actually, I'm not sure I know what I want,' I whisper.

The elevator takes me up to the upper floor of the building to Dad and Mum's new apartment, and it takes too long. I don't have much time, but Aisha insists I come urgently. It isn't like Aisha to sound desperate, which means something severe is taking place.

I must admit, each time I enter Dad and Mum's apartment, I'm grateful to Iris for finding this place. I couldn't have found a better place myself. It ticks all the boxes I need.

It takes me less than five minutes to get here from my place, and maintains all the elegance, space and comfort Dad and

Mum are used to. Besides, the view from their balcony over-looking the park is breath-taking. The park is a bonus as it allows Dad to practice his physiotherapy with Max and a relaxing place where Aisha can take Mum when she's agitated too much.

But the best part of this place is Dad's study. *'He needs to go back to his research.* I'm worried that without his work, Dad will lose interest in life. *I must find a research assistant for him. But I'm so busy! Maybe Heather could do it.*

I'm thrilled Heather and Zoe moved back to London, and, as always, it takes Heather such a long time to organize herself. *I'll give her a few more weeks, then ask her to find a research assistant for Dad.*

The elevator finally arrives at the top floor. Aisha is at the door already. Aisha is an angel sent by heaven. Even so, there are moments when even Saint Aisha is unable to handle Mum. *Maybe it's a good way for me to see how I will juggle work and motherhood.*

Her urgent calls somehow always come when I am in a middle of a session with a client or on my way to a presentation. *I'll need to find a system,* I keep telling myself. But now, all I want is to put out the fire and return to the clinic.

Aisha is in tears. This small pleasant Indian woman in her forties is the epitome of calm, but it now looks like she's going to lose it completely. Showing emotion this way is not part of her nature. It has to be something intense to bring her to this level of frustration.

'What's going on?' I question Aisha, offering her a tissue to dry her tears.

'She's locked herself in the bathroom, and I can't get her out of there!' Aisha weeps.

'Has it happened before?' I probe.

'Sometimes, but usually I manage to get her out,' Aisha mouth, sniffing. 'That's why I never bothered to tell you about it, but today it's worse than before.'

'Where's Dad?' I ask, noticing Sol is not around.

'When she locked herself in and started shouting, I asked Max to take him to the park. That's when I called you.'

'Good thinking! OK, let's see what I can do.'

I go to the bathroom door and knock on it gently. 'Mum? It's me, Daisy. Can I help with anything? Can you open the door for me, please?'

To my surprise, Mum unlocks the door at once and steps out. I'm shocked to see her wearing old trousers, a dirty torn shirt and a tatty old sweater that is missing a few buttons. I grimace. *I must talk to Aisha. She has to make sure Mum dresses smartly. Old Mum would rather die than be caught dressed like this, even at home!*

I gently guide Mum to the living room and help her to settle on one of the sofas, and I perch by her side. Mum grips my hands while I try to remember when she last held me like that. It is as if Mum is drowning and holding on to me for dear life.

'Mum, what's wrong?' I softly question.

'They think I'm not important anymore. I'm excluded from every conversation,' is Mum's reaction.

I have no idea what she is talking about, but from what I learned in the Alzheimer's family members support group, I know she needs to be reassured.

'We'll never do anything to exclude you, Mum,' I note, hoping it will soothe her agitation.

'Don't patronise me!' she snaps. 'You think I don't see what you're doing? I do. I'm not stupid. You treat me as if I'm a child...'

I breathe in deeply. This is not going to be simple. *I'd better keep my nerves in check, otherwise, all hell will break loose, and Iris isn't here to walk me through the fire.* I put an arm around my Mum. 'I'd like to understand, Mum. Maybe I can help....'

'Who's asking for your help?' she hisses.

If this is how she's going to react, I need to do something else. I conclude the best strategy is to distract her. 'Shall I read to you?'

'I don't need you to read to me! Don't treat me like a child,' Mum insists, sulking.

This is too much for me. My patience runs out. 'So why did you call me?'

'I didn't call you!' It looks like she is on the verge of saying more, but then she falls silent and stares at the wall.

That's true. She didn't call me. Aisha did, but something is bothering her, and she needs to say it. I sit there in silence, waiting for her to say something. After a few minutes, she starts talking as if nothing distressing has taken place.

'But now you're here, let me tell you something,' glancing around. 'I don't understand what I'm doing in this place. Who's this old man who lives here? I want to go home.'

I'm stunned. I was under the impression Mum understood why they moved to London. I heard her explaining it to their friends on the phone and when they came to visit. *Perhaps Mum is having hallucinations.* I know it is possible for Alzheimer's patients to have these symptoms, but I assumed it would be at a later stage of the illness.

'What old man, Mum?'

'The old man in the wheelchair. They even make him sleep next to me! What would my mother say?'

I am flabbergasted. 'But that's Dad, Mum.'

Mum's face twists with rage.

'My Dad is gone! I hate it when you lie to me!' she shouts.

I am struggling to control my own anger. 'Mum, it's Sol, your husband!' hoping that logic might penetrate Mum's dementia.

That was it. It only takes those five words to bring the house down. Mum flies at me, hitting me.

'Don't lie to me!' she screams. 'You've always been a sneaky, two-faced liar! I don't need your lies! How can you say that it's Sol? Do you even know who Sol is?'

I am momentarily paralysed by her assault, like a deer in headlights. I grab her flailing hands. I decide to give as good as I get.

'He's my Dad. Of course I know!'

'No, you don't! It's not that old man in the wheelchair. Sol is the most eligible bachelor, and I outsmarted all the other girls by marrying him...'

Suddenly, Mum looks around. It is as if she'd been transported into this reality. 'Where is he? Why isn't he here to help me?'

Once Mum starts screaming I am a liar, I am back in my old room in Oxford.

I am playing with Heather in our room, giggling but trying to keep quiet. We know Mum is sleeping. God help us if we wake her up. No matter how hard we try, the dragon will always rise and fly into our room, screaming her famous sentence: 'What part of 'no noise' is not clear?'

I will always try to pacify her by saying we aren't making any noise, but the response will always be: 'Don't lie to me!' Nothing hurts me more than her calling me a liar. It is as if she shoots arrows into my heart. I cannot stop the tears from coming. I would ask her, 'Why do you always assume we're lying to you?' But as always, Mum never listens and just shouts another of her famous lines: 'Stop crying or I'll give you something to cry about!' Thank God Heather is there with me. I can always depend on her to stand up for me: 'Stop shouting at Daisy! She didn't do anything wrong!' Mum will scream: 'I don't care who it is!' I have to give it to Heather. She has guts: 'You sound like a bad opera singer!' she says, giggling. That is the last straw for Mum, and she raises her hand to strike Heather, but as always, I will stand in her way as fast as lightning so instead of Heather being struck, I would be hit. Mum will stalk away, saying, 'You're lucky I'm your mother. Grandma would have given you the belt.'

I am jolted back from my memories by Mum's viciousness.

'You've no idea how I feel. Who do you think you are?' Mum shrieks.

That's it for me. I jump up from the sofa. 'Stop screaming at me! Can't you see I'm here to help you? If you don't calm down, I'm leaving. You can handle the old man by yourself!'

My uncharacteristic outburst does the trick. It stops Mum in her tracks.

'Fine. If that's how it is, then that's how it is,' she says, getting up and hobbling out of the room.

I collapse back onto the sofa. This is not how I wanted to handle the situation. I had every intention of doing it the 'right' way, whatever that is, according to the family support group.

I spot old photo albums lying on the coffee table. I go through the photos of family holidays to distract myself. Even so, Mum's screams from my childhood still reverberate in my mind.

Aisha comes into the living room. 'Verity fell asleep. Would you like a cup of tea?'

I barely hear her. 'I hate her so much. How can I care for someone and hate them at the same time? What if I turn out like her? No one needs that,' I mumble, flushing with embarrassment when I see Aisha's eyes full of compassion and reassurance.

'You'll be fine. Every new mother is scared. I certainly was.'

To cover my embarrassment, I gather the albums and put them back on the bookshelf. *It doesn't do to display that level of vulnerability in front of staff... I'm such a snob.* Aisha is only trying to help.

'Tea will be great, thanks. Nothing like a good cup of tea to restore normality, whatever the hell that is,' I reply.

Chapter Fourteen

CR DAISY ꙮ

I'm exhausted.

I walk back home after a full day of non-stop fires that needed to be put down. Between clients' mixed-up appointments, a group therapy session that didn't go as planned and running to Dad and Mum's place just because Mum couldn't find the remote control. Heather seems to evaporate each time I need her.

Once I get home, all I want is a shower and go to bed and sleep for days without anyone waking me up for errands that need to be done.

I'm done taking care of others!

Mike isn't at home. Oggi greets me with his usual enthusiasm. I bend down to play with him, thinking he deserves his evening walk.

'Fine!' I tell him. 'Let's go out, and I'll have a takeaway.'

An hour later, I cuddle up with Oggi on my favourite sofa, zapping between different channels on the TV, not looking for anything specific, just something to help me unwind from my day. The Skype icon pops up... Iris.

I look at Oggi. 'What do you think? Shall we take this call or ignore it?'

Oggi puts his head to one side like he is contemplating it.

143

Weary as I am, I'm familiar with my sister. She will keep calling until I answer.

I click on the icon. Before I can utter a word, Iris is on with her endless interrogation...

'How was your appointment at the clinic? How's Mum and Dad?' she demands.

I feel my energy ebbing away. I have no urge to be excellent. 'What is this, an interrogation?'

Even that doesn't stop Iris in her tracks. 'Guilty as charged. As Mum used to say, you can't teach an old dog new tricks. Hey Oggi!'

I smile at Mum's famous phrase and her reference to Oggi in the same sentence. 'Unless they have Alzheimer's,' I reply.

'Turning into a comedian, sis?'

'The other option is worse,' I retort with a sigh.

Iris allows a few seconds to pass. 'Now that the niceties are out of the way, how's it going on the pregnancy front?'

I stroke the playful Oggi, hoping to absorb some of his energy.

'Not so great. Extra hormones are not the best combination with Mum and Dad's daily emergencies. I'm already feeling pregnant but without the morning sickness.'

'Didn't know you've already started with hormone treatments. You move fast. Did you go to the clinic I recommended you?'

I realise I never thanked her for the recommendation. I'm ashamed. *I wonder why I didn't do that.* Another tiny voice at the back of my mind reacts *because you don't like to admit Iris isn't as bad as you think she is.* I didn't want to continue down that road.

'Fantastic, thanks. Mind you, I'm not sure if I'm ready for this journey.'

Iris laughs. 'None of us are!'

'That's just what Aisha told me,' I utter.

'Oh...Wow, you spoke to Aisha about it...'

'It just happened. I was upset, thinking out loud.'

Iris clears her throat. 'What would your supervisor say about that?'

'She thinks it is a good sign!' I laugh. 'Tell me something, how did you handle the fear?'

'I'm a strange bird.'

I have no idea what Iris is referring to. *Not that she isn't a weird bird, but how is that answering my question?* I want a better answer from her. God knows I need some guidance on this journey, and Iris is the only one I can ask these delicate questions. 'Explain yourself.'

Unlike Iris, it takes her a long time before she formulates her answer. 'My fears started after Joy was born. I always knew I wanted children, but what I really wanted was the experience of being pregnant.'

I'm stunned. I still don't get what she tells me, and I'm trying to process her answer. For once, Iris is quiet and allows me to do it in my own time.

'What's the difference?' I manage to say at last.

'I wanted the feeling of something growing inside of me. I wasn't thinking about being a mum for the next twenty years.'

'So, you're saying you enjoyed being pregnant and giving birth?'

'Every minute of it!' responds Iris, laughing.

'You are odd....'

'Thanks for the compliment, but this isn't about me. What do you want? Do you want the experience of being pregnant and giving birth or the experience of being a mother and caring for someone?'

I am totally taken aback. I take Oggi on my lap and hold him tightly. 'I never thought there was a difference.'

Iris smiles with genuine compassion. 'Neither did I; I discovered it later. I thought, holy shit, I need to take care of this creature for the next twenty years! This little baby is dependent on me, and I have to learn to put her needs before mine, even if she thinks I'm being cruel, so she grows up to be independent and strong.'

I wanted to resist what Iris was saying. It seemed like such a huge challenge.

'Well, whatever lies ahead, I think unconditional love is always the answer,' I mutter as if the subject is closed.

'Unconditional love is the answer, but love doesn't look the same as in the movies.'

'Goddamn it. First, they ruin romance, and now motherhood,' I attempt to be humorous.

Iris glares at me and keeps silent. I am aware Iris doesn't buy my tone. I am hideously vulnerable. I need space to process it.

'Well, you've given me lots of food for thought, Iris. I need to think about it. See you!' I end the Skype call before Iris can say anything else.

Gone are the days when I gave silent thanks for the proximity of my parents' apartment. I am running late... again. I've been so busy getting myself ready for the ceremony. I know how much Dad hates being late. *You'd think after fifty years with Mum, he'd be used to it.*

I feel like the white rabbit in 'Alice in Wonderland'. 'I'm late, I'm late, for a... not-very-important date,' I mumble to myself when I approach my parents' communal entrance but can't find the keys to the door in my oversized bag. I buzz the intercom. Max answers.

'Tell Dad and Mum they better be ready once I get up there. Otherwise, we'll be late to this damn ceremony'. I rush to the lift without hearing what Max has to say.

It has become a logistical nightmare every time we have to take Mum and Dad to one of their many social events. I hoped moving to London would mean fewer social obligations, but no such luck.

Dad is so well respected by his colleagues that they all make strenuous efforts to keep him busy, welcoming him and Mum to any event or ceremony in the city.

What they don't realise is that each time I take them out of the house entails a whole operation, including long explanations to Mum, getting Dad and his wheelchair into a lift that isn't designed for a wheelchair, and booking a parking spot for their specially adapted car that contains the entire entourage, including Aisha and Max.

I am exhausted just thinking about it. When I enter the lift, I am glad I can quickly check my image in the mirror. I had to dig deep inside my wardrobe to find this particular outfit, as I didn't own much eveningwear. I smile bitterly, realising the plain suit I have on is probably some kind of rebellion against Mum's own tendency of attending all the posh events she is invited to, glammed up to the nines. I had time to check my hair and touch up my lipstick before the lift opened on my parents' floor.

I hurry to the open door of their apartment. Dad already sits in his wheelchair in the lobby, dressed very smartly. Max is straightening his tie to make him look as dignified as possible. I watch the tenderness with which Max looks after Dad and, not for the first time, send a silent grateful prayer to Aisha, who has found him.

I remember the first time I met him. It was a few weeks after they moved to London. It was essential they have another carer. Aisha is not able to take care of both Dad and Mum - his needs are so different. We needed a strong young man who could pick Dad up, wash him and dress him. Dad is tall and heavy. Even with all good intentions, Aisha would not have been able to do it.

Aisha mentioned her neighbour's husband is looking for care work. I had no idea who Aisha's neighbour was, but I was so desperate I told her to bring him with her next time for an interview.

I am never good at having a 'poker face'. But when I first saw Max, I had to admit I was not as open-minded as I thought.

Max looked like the stereotypical Russian gangster. Terse, mostly silent, as strong as an ox and no facial expression whatsoever. It took me a few seconds to recover, but once I started asking him questions, my prejudice disappeared in seconds.

His voice is soft, his movements are gentle, but best of all, I sensed he is dedicated to his vocation. He's been a male nurse for more than ten years in Russia, but somehow, in the UK, his appearance worked against him when looking for work.

He now has a new baby and needs the money. I am also desperate; I hire him on the spot and have never regretted it. He is the best thing I could find for Dad. He is caring, gentle and treats him like a father. He clearly enjoys it and once even told me it never feels like work, even though he is being paid.

I am suddenly aware I am staring at Max and Dad; I smile to cover the embarrassing moment.

'Sorry. I know how much you hate being late Dad, Where's Mum? Is she ready?'

Dad laughs. 'I'm used to Daisy Time. As for Mum - brace yourself.'

I look from Dad to Max for more information, but both men have their poker faces on.

I walk to Mum's bedroom.

'Mum? Where are you? We need to go!'

At the sound of my voice, Mum comes out dressed in an outfit that has seen better days. Her hair is a mess, and she is definitely not ready.

I gasp. I made such an effort to prepare Mum for this occasion. I made an appointment for her at a nearby hairdresser's; I chose an outfit for her and instructed Aisha about it.

Aisha appears behind Verity, *just like a shadow,*

'What happened?' I whisper to Aisha. 'I thought I arranged everything for you.'

'She said she was too tired to go to the hairdresser's, so she stayed in bed the whole day. I tried to call you….' Aisha whispers back. There is no accusation in Aisha's voice, but it still makes me feel guilty.

I've seen those calls, but I was in the middle of sessions and ignored them. Well, the truth is I was hoping they'd find a solution to whatever crisis it was without me.

I decide I have to make Mum change her outfit. There is no way they would be allowed into the ceremony with her dressed like that. I master all my patience and resolve.

'Mum, you can't go dressed like that. I prepared a nice outfit for you. Let's go and try it on.'

Mum glares at me and puts her shoulders back in defiance. 'I can make my own decisions on what to wear, thank you.'

It is a familiar battle cry. I now understand what Dad meant by 'Brace yourself.' I am ashamed of Mum's unkempt appearance.

My spirits sink. I can't make Mum maintain the standards she used to have before the illness took hold.

'Of course, you can choose your own clothes, but you've been wearing this outfit for three days. Let's see if we can find you something fabulous.'

I take Mum by the hand, but she pulls away from me. 'What's wrong with this one? I think I look very smart.'

I stare at her in astonishment. *Is she going blind as well as losing her memory?* I point lightly at all the stains on the shirt and holes in the jacket. 'Come on, Mum! You'd never allow me to go out dressed like that. It's your best friend's celebration! Don't you want to look your best?' The second the words are out of my mouth, I regret it.

'If she's my best friend, then it doesn't matter how I dress. It's not as if we're invited to tea with the Queen.'

I have no idea what to do. I see Dad falling asleep in his wheelchair. Time is running out. If we don't leave soon, there'd be no celebration left. I make up my mind.

What the hell, it's their life. If Dad's OK to go with Mum dressed like this, who am I to interfere? I'm just the driver here. I shake Dad's shoulder gently, and he opens his eyes.

'Dad, is it OK if Mum goes dressed like this?'

Dad gazes at Mum, his eyes full of love.

'She always looks great to me,' he replies, his voice husky with emotion. My eyes fill up with tears: he is clearly seeing a much younger Mum.

I attempt to make the outfit look as good as possible by adding an expensive, brightly coloured scarf that hides some of the stains. Mum allows me to brush her hair, so it looks presentable. I step back to admire my handiwork.

'Well, that's as good as it's going to get!'

Dad, Max, and Aisha smile at me. Mum pats her neat hair. I open the door to the apartment and lead the whole entourage to the lift.

What's wrong with me? I think, lying on the examination couch, waiting for my doctor to come in. *I'm supposed to be excited and thrilled, and all I want is for it to be over.*

Mike stands next to me, holding my hand as if trying to give me the energy to treasure this moment, but I am unable to react to his gesture. All I can think about are the appointments I have to reschedule with clients. Some I transferred to colleagues, matching them up appropriately. I am stressed about it, but I have no other option. My clients lead high-pressure lives. They meet with me twice a week, squeezing me into their own busy day. Postponement is impossible.

I love my clients and, in many ways, treat them as if they are my kids, but these days there are so many unexpected events with Dad and Mum it is as if my parents are now my children. *Is this what parenthood is about? Putting out fires twenty-four hours a day?* If so, I am not sure I want this kind of life.

At last, Doctor Lewis enters the room. I relax a little. I always feel reassured when she attends me. I smile, recalling Iris, who recommended her, telling me it had been 'love at first sight'.

Doctor Lewis has a dry sense of humour that reassures me. She is sensible and sensitive. She explains medical procedures in what Mike calls 'normal people language', which is fantastic for me.

'Right then, let me bring you up to speed…' begins Doctor. Lewis.

'Can't we just get on with it?' I ask.

Doctor Lewis smiles. 'Seems like someone's in a hurry here!'

'Hurry doesn't even start to describe it.'

'I'll just give you a very quick recap, then we can start the procedure,' she responds, patting my arm and smiling at Mike.

I'm aware I'm coming off as unreasonable. 'Normally, I'd want the full explanation, but I don't think I can take it today. Please just do what you need to do and let me go home.'

Doctor Lewis and Mike look surprised. They exchange glances.

'Just tell me if there's anything special I need to do after-wards.'

'Take the day off. No tension or stress,' she answers.

My heart sinks.

'That sounds like my dream day,' I announce, feeling sad for myself. There are a few minutes of silence in the room.

'How long will it take before we know if it is successful?'

'Around two weeks. I really want you to try and relax during that time,' insists Doctor Lewis.

I laugh nervously. 'Wishful thinking.'

'Then it's time you learn how to if you want to be pregnant!' Doctor Lewis retorts in an authoritative voice. She glances at Mike. 'If you want to be a father, then you'd better make sure Daisy has proper rest for the next two weeks.'

Mike nods earnestly. 'Oh, I certainly intend to put my foot down that she will... but have you met my girlfriend?' trying to lighten the moment. 'She's very much her own woman.'

Doctor Lewis looks at me lying on the examination couch, clutching Mike's hand. She sighs. 'It's up to you how you want to play it, but if you want this to work, you'd better learn to relax and rest.'

She starts the IVF procedure, guided by the ultrasound images. Mike watches. I close my eyes. The room is silent. I try to empty my mind of everything without much success.

Once Doctor Lewis completes the procedure, she covers me with a blanket. 'Now then, I want you to stay lying down for at least half an hour. No getting up until I return, ok?' She leaves the room.

I sigh with relief. It is over. Mike gazes at me, looking awestruck.

He sits in silence and then bends down and kisses my hand. He has no words, but it feels right to be in silence.

After a while, I need to do something to preserve this moment. I sense that if I can talk to whoever is in my uterus now, it will help make it real for me. I look at the ultrasound monitor.

'I hope you like your new home. I want to make it a great place for you for the next nine months, so please stick with me. You're the best thing that's ever happened to us. I promise I'll become the best version of myself for you. So just keep snug and safe in there while I try to sort out the mess out here. You're my chance to make it. Let's work together,' I profess to the blurry white image as if it is already a growing foetus.

I forget Mike is in the room when I am speaking, but when I finish my speech, I look up at him and see he has tears in his eyes. I believe he never saw me as vulnerable as this. *We all get to have new experiences in this journey, I guess.*

❦ SOL ❧

Heather sits beside Sol after examining the apartment to check everything is in order. She asked Max to help Sol dress smartly as if going out to meet someone. Max is now cleaning up the remains of the breakfast, which Sol has dropped on his sweater.

It's as if she's expecting the Queen to come for a visit, Sol thinks, bemused. He has never known Heather to bother about how the place looks. He is curious. *What on earth's going on?* He enjoys having Heather back in London.

It is like having all his girls back at home – well, not all of them. Iris is still living off the grid on her farm in the middle of nowhere in Spain. Though he loves seeing the photos and videos she sends him, he still can't understand why she prefers living there and not in the city, or at least in England, which for him is the most civilised place in the world.

Looking at Heather, he notes that the best thing that happened since his disaster was getting his family back together. Every cloud has a silver lining. He is never one to believe in positive thinking or spiritual destiny, but somehow, he experiences being blessed, despite everything. He will never admit it, but he recognises it is the truth.

Suddenly the intercom buzzer sounds. Heather jumps up to answer it. 'Hello? Is that you, Natalie?'

Sol watches his daughter.

'We're on the top floor. I'll leave the door open for you.'

Heather stands, waiting at the open door. Sol has the impression she is anxious about it. 'Why are you so nervous? It's not a royal visit, is it?'

Heather laughs. 'Even better than the Queen! We've found a research assistant for you. Professor Gray recommends her. I just hope you like her.'

So that's what this is all about. He remembers Iris and Heather are determined to get him back to work. He wants it too, but he is dubious he'd ever be able to work as intensively as he had before the stroke. It is hard for him to ask for help on this issue.

He never had research assistants. He thought it was exploitative of young students' hard work without giving them credit for it. Secretly, he didn't think anyone could do a better job finding those important footnotes (the trail of crumbs, as he calls them) that would lead to an authentic and important discovery. Besides, he loved the thrill of the chase. He'd never give it to someone else.

But these days, he can't even read properly. When Iris mentioned finding a research assistant for him, he never thought they would actually go and look for one, but it appears they did.

He smiles at Heather. 'If she's as efficient as Gray says, then there'll be no problems.'

'Hi, I'm Natalie,' says a young woman at the door. She shakes hands with Heather.

Nothing prepared Sol for the surprise of seeing Nathalie for the first time. She is in her early thirties, bubbly, with a nose piercing and tattoos on her arms. *Definitely not your typical PhD student,*

He observes her with amazement. He makes up his mind and smiles at her.

'Max, can you take us to my study so we can show Natalie the scope of work she's facing, please?'

Max pushes Sol's wheelchair to the study.

Unlike his study in Oxford, this room is tiny. The books reach the ceiling. Many others are still in packing boxes, waiting to find their proper place in a room that has no space for them.

'Welcome to my heaven and hell. I need someone to shine some light into this space and help me keep my sanity.'

'I'd be honoured!' answers Natalie. 'Your work's been so important to me. I can hardly believe I'm here.' Natalie moves around the room, peering at the book titles. Not a lot of space to move in, but it is like finding a cave full of treasure. She softly touches some books as if meeting an old friend.

Natalie kneels and looks into some of the boxes with more books and reprints of articles that need to be filed and documented. Her face lights up each time she encounters another rare book.

Sol watches her closely. 'Are you good with computers?'

Natalie is surprised by the question. 'Sure. What specific skills do you need?'

Sol beams. This is precisely the answer he hoped to hear. He is suddenly excited at the possibilities that employing this girl can give him. 'There's a document on my desktop that I can't find. It's about my latest research. I was in the middle of editing it when I had the stroke, and now I'm unable to read at all. Would you be able to help me with it?'

'Of course!' Natalie pushes Sol up to the desk where the computer sits. She positions herself close to him so that they can work together. She enlarges the icons on the desktop. 'OK. Let's see what we have here. Can you remember the name of the file?'

After that, they are totally engaged in the work. Heather comes in. They don't even notice her. She looks at them peering at the screen, Natalie's fingers flying over the keyboard.

Heather leaves the room quietly and types a message to Iris on her phone: 'Well, you can tick one item off your to-do list....'

Chapter Fifteen

↶ IRIS ↷

Iris ponders how quickly actions turn into habits. You don't even notice you're doing them, but they become part of your day. Like brushing your teeth in the morning or having dinner at a specific time.

People say it takes time to get used to new habits, but it isn't so in Iris's opinion. For years, she did her best to avoid calling her parents. She only did it before her holidays or when she had something exciting to tell them.

Even then, Verity would say something to put her down or give unwanted advice. This became more pronounced once she had Joy. Verity did not accept Iris's earth mother style of raising her daughter. Thank God Nate was at her side on those occasions. When Verity's inevitable criticism upset Iris, Nate would take the phone and end that difficult conversation.

She is still horrified by the memory of when he'd written a long letter telling Verity that if she is bored with her life, instead of finding fault with her daughter, she should find a hobby or a lover to entertain her. *No wonder Dad doesn't like Nate either,* she muses, while still going red in the face each time she thinks about that letter.

It seemed to work, though. As the years passed, Verity stopped trying to control Iris. That didn't mean Iris made more effort to share anything with her, but it certainly made her yearly visits to Oxford more bearable and sometimes even fun.

It was important for her Joy would get to know Sol and Verity. It was essential for her that Joy would connect with her grandparents and would learn to love them.

It worked. The minute Joy was old enough to travel on her own, she wanted to spend some of her summer holidays in Oxford with 'Grannie', as she called Verity. This made Iris happy. Seeing the pleasure Sol and Verity experienced each time Joy visited them, Iris was grateful for Nate's initiative with the embarrassing letter.

Interestingly, her occasional calls with her parents swiftly graduated to weekly calls on a Friday evening, as though she was having dinner with them.

'If I were a religious person,' she'd say to Nate, 'I'd say God works in mysterious ways.'

'You might not be a religious person, but you are deeply spiritual. It's not surprising you see it that way,' Nate replies, kissing her.

Now she makes her Friday evening call with them. She gives her parents a 360-degree tour of her home. She isn't sure whether they can see much, but she hopes she gives them an experience like they are with her. She describes what the camera is showing, just to make sure.

Sol sits in his wheelchair facing the screen, Verity next to him, as close as she can in order to be in the frame too. It always makes Iris laugh when she notices her parents have no idea how to position the camera. Iris asks Max to direct their gaze to the camera; otherwise, she will be talking either to the ceiling or the top of their heads.

'Dad, how's your new research assistant working out?'

Sol's face lights up. 'She's good. I didn't expect much from her, but she managed to find several important resources. I must say she excelled in the test I gave her….'

Verity frowns and fidgets. 'You should see those two! Every time she comes, they disappear to his room, close the door, and I don't see them for hours. I came in once, and they sat next to each other - like two young lovers! I'm not a jealous woman, but he has so many young girls coming in and out of the house. He has no time at all for me.'

Sol roars with laughter. 'My darling Verity, you're such a drama queen! That's what I love about you. What young girls?'

'There's the one with that awful piercing….'

'That's Natalie, my research assistant!'

'Right… well, I must say she's nice. Got good manners. Then there's the one that came today. You disappeared with her and Max!'

'That's Lily, my physiotherapist,' Sol explains patiently, as to a little child, but Verity is having none of it.

'That's what I'm saying! All these young girls… And then there's the one that keeps telling me what to wear and where to go. She annoys the hell out of me!'

This time, Iris is roaring with laughter. 'That sounds like me, Mum.'

Verity leans towards the screen. 'I wish you were here. Where are you? None of my daughters come to visit me anymore!'

Iris sighs. She is certain Daisy and Heather are taking turns visiting their parents every day. Is it possible Verity cannot recognise her own daughters anymore? Iris doesn't even want to think about it.

'Daisy lives practically next door to you, and Heather is back in London now. Just to see you.'

Verity looks surprised. 'Daisy lives close to us, really? Then why hasn't she invited us to her place?'

Sol gently takes Verity's hand. 'We were there three days ago, my love,' he reminds her softly.

Verity stares at him, puzzled, 'Oh... my brain is like a Swiss Emmenthal; more holes than cheese.'

They all laugh, with relief as much as at the joke. Verity can sometimes apprehend the seriousness of her predicament.

Sol has tears in his eyes. It is unbearably poignant to see his wife in her condition.

Iris casts about in her mind for a way to change the subject. 'So, back to my first question, how's your research with Natalie going?

CR VERITY & SOL ℰↃ

Max shuts off Skype and wheels Sol into the living room. Verity follows them to sit beside Sol. She is troubled with something she wants to check with him but can't recall what it is. There is a warm feeling in her heart. The only person who can help her is Sol. He has been her rock all her life. She takes his hand and observes it slowly. Sol looks surprised.

'That was a nice call, wasn't it?' he attempts to uplift her mood.

Verity isn't sure what he means by that statement but knows she cannot admit it. 'Yes. But I miss people coming to visit.'

Sol understands what she is referring to. Though their London apartment is wonderful, they are still not as accessible to their old friends in Oxford. *None of us is getting any younger.*

Even though the trip from Oxford to London is not long, it is not one many of their friends can do on an impulse. Their London life has to be planned. However, he cannot say it to Verity. It will involve repeated explanations of why they had to move to London in the first place.

'The old gang from Oxford came to visit last week! It was a joy...' he reminds her.

Sol's words are like sunshine entering Verity's dark world. She beams at him. 'That's true. We laughed so much I couldn't breathe!'

'So you see, people still come and visit us, darling.'

Verity is sure Sol would never lie to her, but she also knows life is not the same. Sol has behaved in strange ways lately. 'That's not true. It's only me and you in this house, but I do love being with you,' she says, kissing his cheek.

Heather has explained Verity's Alzheimer's patterns to Sol, but he doesn't always have the patience to ignore it or change the subject. It is hard, but when Verity looks at him with such love and admiration and when she still kisses him in her special way, it is as if, for a moment, he gets the woman he fell in love with years ago back. He lives for such moments.

'There is one thing our friends told me that troubles me.'

'What?' asks Verity.

Sol's words dry up.

Their friends told Sol Verity had shared with them she had no money. Sol had been shocked by her indiscretion. He and

Verity were of the generation that never discussed financial matters. It was bad taste.

'Why did you tell them you had no money?'

'I told them I don't know anything about it. You always took care of it, didn't you?

'Yes, but now Daisy's taking care of it,' he answers.

That triggers Verity. 'Why would you give her my money?' Verity shouts.

Sol takes a deep breath. 'I didn't give her your money. She only manages it because I'm not able to, now.'

That doesn't seem to calm Verity. On the contrary, it only makes her more agitated. She snatches her purse up from the table and opens it. 'But I don't have any money. Look… Nothing in it! No money. What if I want to buy something? I can't.'

Sol is in turmoil now, thinking about it. How can he explain to her that no one stole her money? He decides to capitalise on her present good humour. 'Never mind. What I mean is, if you want to buy something, Daisy can always give you some cash.'

'Who is Daisy, and why does she have my money?' Verity snaps, her good mood vanishing.

Sol is nearly in tears by now. He rarely wears his heart on his sleeve, but lately, it has been hard to conceal his emotions. He gently puts his good hand on Verity's face to make sure she is looking straight into his eyes. 'Daisy is our daughter. We have three daughters, darling. Do you remember?'

Verity looks confused.

'Iris, who lives in Spain; Daisy, who lives next door to us and Heather, our youngest. She used to live in Berlin, but now she's back in London.' He stares deep into Verity's eyes, trying to see a spark of recognition at their daughters' names, but there is none.

'Why did you give my money to a stranger?' Verity insists.

Sol shifts in his wheelchair. It is dispiriting to see his beloved wife of so many years deteriorating into a petulant child. He decides on a more authoritative tone. 'You have enough money. I only gave Daisy permission to manage our finances because I can't,' he repeats firmly.

Verity stares at him.

'You do trust me, right?' he checks with her.

'I do. I'm just not sure about this Daisy.'

'Good. I'll make sure you're well taken care of.'

That does the trick. Verity relaxes and gazes at her husband with adoration again. 'Yes. I know you will. You're the one I can always depend on.' She stands up smiling and leaves the room.

Sol slumps in his chair. Finally alone, he allows the tears to come. He is tired and emotionally drained.

CR DAISY 80

I knew Mike has made dinner reservations for us for tonight, but, as usual, I am late. I come in rushing, dropping my heavy bag full of client's folders, at the same time trying to hang my coat, only to find myself tangled with my scarf, so I dump everything on the floor. I am sure Mike is in his workroom upstairs.

'Mike? I'm home. We can go out for dinner, but I need a few minutes with Iris on Skype before we go!'

'Get on with it then! Or I'll be starving by the time you finish.' *Sweet Mike*. He still believes some guilt-tripping would work on me.

I open my laptop. The Skype icon immediately pops up, showing several missed calls from Iris. *God! Impatient as always.*

Iris appears onscreen. 'I thought we said eight-thirty. Did I miss something?' she enquires.

I am too tired to apologise or explain. 'What's on the agenda?' I try to sound as business-like as possible.

'I spoke with Mum the other day, and she was all fired up by the fact she has no money...'

I roll my eyes. 'Don't go there. It's not the first time.'

Iris is surprised. 'What do you mean?'

I am tired and stressed out. I am torn between telling her about the money saga and Mike waiting for me upstairs and our restaurant reservation. But really, I have enough of Iris's desire to know everything. *If she really wants to know what's going on, let her come over for a few months. We'll soon see if she can manage things any better than me.* I can hear an angry voice in my head.

'You can't call in once a week and think you get to know everything that's going on here.'

I can see this hurts Iris.

'I do what I can,' she mumbles.

Now I am guilty. 'I know. I'm sorry. I'm so tired of it all. I took a day off and drove Mum to Oxford. The guy who worked in her bank still works there, handling her account. He showed her the printouts: how much money she has. He tried to reassure her all was in order, but she made a huge scene...'

166

'What do you mean a scene?'

I laugh bitterly. 'Think of the bank scene in Mary Poppins.'

'You mean Mum was dancing and singing?'

Oh, now Iris is trying to be a stand-up comedian; well, it's not working on me today.

'No. She was screaming her head off. 'Where's my money? Why are you showing me bits of paper?' She accused them of stealing her money.'

'What did you do?'

'Got her out of there as soon as I could and sent an apology to the guy by email. God, I hate her!' I utter in despair.

'You do realise she can't control it?'

'Don't you dare lecture me. This is the old Mum, screaming and shouting and embarrassing me!' I snap.

Iris has no answer to this. After a few seconds of silence, when I can calm myself a bit, I can hear her say: 'It must be hard to take care of her when you hate her so much.'

This does the trick. My anger ebbs away. I am defeated. 'It's a daily struggle.'

I guess Iris thinks the best strategy to get out of this heated situation is to change the subject, not realising we are still on dangerous ground.

'What about the pregnancy?' she probes as casually as she can.

'I'm taking a break. I lost the first two embryos. I have two more, but I can't even think of starting the hormones again. I'm stressed out, and the hormones drive me up the wall.'

'How about finding ways to relax? I know some really good techniques....'

I expected this from her. 'Spare me your airy-fairy nonsense, Iris. What I need is for Mum to disappear! I'm so scared that I'll become like her.'

Iris takes a deep breath. 'I know you think she is a terrible Mum, but maybe you're judging her a bit too harshly. Think about what she had to go through when raising you and Heather....'

'I don't care!' I scream. 'There's no excuse for what she's done to us!'

This time I am the one that pours fuel on this fire.

'Speak for yourself, Daisy. I had a great Mum. She made mistakes, and she might have fucked up big time as the years went by, but really, until you're a Mum yourself, I don't think you're in any place to judge her.'

I'm aware I'm the one that went too far, but I am still fuming. 'Oh, you and your mumbo-jumbo pseudo-psychology! You always know what's right and what's wrong, don't you? But there are some things you just can't forgive!'

I can see Iris is on the verge of abandoning the call, but she just can't hold back. 'Mum used to say, 'until you have kids you'll never know'. And I used to think - what the hell is she talking about? Except for breastfeeding, I pretty much raised you and Heather, then I had Joy and realised Mum was right. I guess what pisses us off most is not when our parents are wrong, but when we find they were right.'

I am outright dumbfounded. 'How can you justify how she treated Heather and me?... Oh yes, that's right. You took the easy way out. Once you were old enough, you disappeared, only to show your face once or twice a year. You say you raised us? Well, you might have when we were tiny, but you were never there to protect us when we really needed you!'

I know my accusations are pitiful, but I am beyond reason by now.

'Listen, I only had one child to raise. Mum had three while working full-time, studying, and taking care of Dad's PR. When you do all that, you can judge her - or me, for that matter. It's a hell of a job and an utterly thankless one. No matter what you do, it's never good enough for your kids. They'll always blame you for what's wrong in their lives. So bloody good luck with the IVF, Daisy. Get ready for the blame.'

I am silent, not for absence of words, but from the lack of ability to contain my emotions. I only glare at her and then slam my laptop shut.

I stand up. 'Mike let's go. I need some good food to calm me down!'

Chapter Sixteen

ભ DAISY ৪০

I love my work. I love everything about it, even the difficult cases of psychotherapy. One of my greatest joys is the feeling that I can actually support someone in discovering what stops them from living life to the full.

I can never get bored seeing someone's eyes suddenly shine when they manage to do something they never thought possible: when the penny drops, and a patient lets go of a belief they held for years that is limiting them or realising the misinterpretation on their part about an event that took place years ago.

My heart soars each time a patient experiences a breakthrough. I'm aware it is arrogance on my behalf to think I am responsible for effecting change in their lives. The answer always lies within the client.

There is magic and grace in this work. I never know what makes the difference between success in healing a person and mere survival. That is what makes it so exciting over all these years. There are no formulas. It keeps me on my toes all the time, finding what works and what doesn't.

Lately, however, with all the crises around me, I'm unable to give myself completely to the process, which frustrates me. I wish I could do more for my clients, but all I can hope for is that I'm not disturbed during sessions or even only keep my appointments.

I stop counting the disruptions to my routine. I start referring some of my clients to colleagues who can give them the time and energy I can't. Each time I transfer a patient, it tears a piece of my heart. It is hard to say goodbye.

I am sitting in my armchair having these thoughts while one of my patients, a woman in her forties, is kneeling on the floor, painting on a huge piece of paper. She is painting her own body outline.

It is one of my favourite processes with a client. It triggers memories that later we can discuss. It allows me to watch my patient's body language while she is working, which gives me indications that regular verbal communication doesn't.

I suddenly notice Sylvia, my receptionist, tiptoeing in as quietly as she can.

'You have a phone call from Heather', she whispers.

I trust Sylvia completely. She knows she's not allowed in the consulting room unless it is urgent.

'Tell her to take Dad to the emergency room,' I whisper back. 'I'll meet them there once I'm finished.'

'They were there this morning.'

I groan upon hearing her answer. 'You're doing great!' I tell my client. 'I just have to step out for a second. Keep painting. I'm going to put some music on. That might help you.'

I put some classical music on and step out of the room with Sylvia. I snatch Sylvia's phone. 'Heather, I'll call you back on my mobile. I have to be somewhere private.'

Glancing at the packed waiting room, I hurry to one of the empty consultation rooms, and dial Heather's number. *Why the hell can't she just take care of Mum and Dad while I'm working?* Heather answers immediately.

'Make it quick. I'm in the middle of a session.'

I know Heather doesn't do 'quick', especially when medical issues are at stake.

'This morning, Max rang to say Dad was groggy and unable to speak. I rushed to the apartment, but when I got there, he was fine. I just got another call that it happened again. I took him to A and E, but by the time we got there, he was fine again, and they refused to examine him....'

I can't take it anymore. I want to scream. 'And? What do you want from me? If you can't deal with this, why the hell did you move back?' The minute I speak, I regret it. I am not being fair to Heather.

'Dad is asking for you!'

That stops my rage instantly. I can hear Dad in the background, groaning.

'Here, Dad...I'm putting Daisy on loudspeaker.'

'Daisy!' I hear Dad wheezing. He sounds desperate.

I gasp. 'I'm on my way.'

Later that night, Heather and I sit around the dinner table while Aisha cleans away the remains of dinner. We are both exhausted. It has been a long and emotionally draining day. Neither of us has any energy to speak. Just sitting with each other in silence is a comfort. I finally stir.

'It's the third time this month,' I remark. Heather sighs.

'I think it happens more frequently than that, and each time it's worse and takes longer for him to recover.'

I put my head down on the table. 'I can't do this anymore… between Dad's attacks and Mum's demands, I'm losing clients… I might have to close the clinic,' my voice muffles.

'Can you afford to do that?' Heather knows that my clinic is my only source of income – more than that, it is my passion. What would I do without my beloved clients?

'Mike says he earns enough for both of us, but he doesn't get it. I'm not working just for the money.'

I can see Heather biting her lower lip, trying to hold back a snide comment.

'Nice if you can afford it,' she responds eventually.

I ignore the implication of what she said. 'You don't get it, either. I need something to take my mind off from caregiving or getting pregnant. I need one area in my life where I am competent.'

I don't know if it makes sense to Heather, but I am grateful for her silence. Later she holds my hand and squeezes it just to let me know she's there for me.

After a while, Heather gets up and walks to Dad's study. She brings back a pile of papers, all marked with red pen. I look at the documents without knowing what I'm looking at.

'Natalie says Dad's memory is foggy after each TIA.'

I glare at her. 'What does that mean exactly?'

Heather sorts through the papers, thinking how best to explain it to me. 'Transient Ischaemic Attack, you know, mini-strokes. Before the attacks, Dad was able to pinpoint every footnote from where it was taken, but now he's sending Natalie on repeated wild goose chases. It's as if he's losing it.'

I have no energy to even try and process what Heather is telling me. 'You're the expert. What do you think?'

'I'm out of practice, but I can ask the doctors to do some tests.'

That is good enough for me. All I want is to be back at home with Mike. I'm glad Heather knows what to do. Her next sentence makes me even more relieved. 'You know what, from now on, I'll take care of the medical issues for both Mum and Dad... that would release you at least from those obligations.'

'That's wonderful... thanks so much', I state, standing up. 'And on this happy note... I'm going home... Do you need a lift?

CƆ HEATHER ꙮ

Noticing the changes with Verity made Heather believe that caring for Alzheimer's patients is harder for their carers than the patients themselves. *They don't really know what's happening while we have to handle all the chaotic side effects.*

She never stops to think that Verity has her own demons to fight. Now she stands with her in the lobby of St. George's Hospital, giving thanks for her parents' social connections. She needed to take Verity to one of the regular check-ups but decided it was time to visit an expert that might shed some light on what else they could do for Verity. Of course, Verity had some high-flying consultants in her little black book, and she could make this appointment quite easily by just mentioning the Bach name.

They find the directions for the Cognitive Neurology and Dementia department, and she steers Verity towards the lifts.

It is a lovely spring day. Verity is enjoying the change of scene. 'Remind me, dear. Why are we here?' she asks.

Heather sighs with exasperation. 'We're going to visit Professor Ben Isaacs, your friend.'

She can see Verity is suspicious. The name doesn't ring a bell. For some reason, it makes her sad. Her Mum used to remember her friends' names, who was married to whom, how many kids and grandkids they had, who was divorced and who had taken a lover.

Verity never had an interest in historical dates, but the intimate details of her friends' lives were very much her domain. Heather can see her Mum doubts what she told her, and when she hears Verity's sniff and sees her stern look, she knows... *Here it comes...*

'I doubt if he's my friend, he's probably Dad's friend.'

'Oh Mum, he's visited you several times. You liked him. He made you laugh,' Heather mentions.

Now that is something her Mum must remember. She adores people who make her laugh.

Verity always said that not many of the stuffy professors had a sense of humour, even the important ones, so how come she can't remember Professor Isaacs? It is the first time Heather grasps what it might be for her mum.

Forgetting names isn't like mislaying her bike lock but more like walking into a room and not remembering entering it. It probably scares her, but being Mum, she has to keep appearances. Verity smiles. Hearing that this person has made her laugh probably reminds her of happier times.

'I used to laugh a lot, didn't I?'

Heather smiles back at her. 'Yes, you did, Mum. You were always the life and soul of the party with your funny stories.'

Mum beams. But her good humour vanishes when the lift doors open, and Heather takes Verity's hand to go in.

'Who are we going to see again?' she questions, her brow furrowed with anxiety.

Heather's smile evaporates as she presses the floor button. 'Professor Isaacs!'

'Well, who the hell is he?' Mum snaps. She stares at her own reflection in the mirrored walls of the lift.

The lift doors open onto a plush reception area. Heather rummages in her bag for their appointment letter as they join the queue. When she turns around, she can't see Verity. *Oh, for God's sake...*

'Mum?' she calls. A few elderly ladies look at her, confused. She hurries down a few corridors leading off the reception, but Verity is nowhere to be seen. She rushes around the maze-like department. As she keeps going down corridors that all look the same, she starts to panic.

After ten minutes of panicky search, she finds herself lost. Heather retraces her steps as best she can and end up back at reception. *She can't disappear into thin air. At least it happened in a building - imagine losing her on the street.* Looking around, she notices several doors. Heather opens a few at random, apologising when there is someone in there. By now, she's in tears.

The last door she opens is a door to a consultation room next to the lift. Verity sits there, peacefully gazing at nothing. Heather takes some deep breaths, relieved to find Verity safe. She forgets how angry she is.

Verity looks up and smiles at her. 'Where did you wander off to? I've been waiting for ages,' she declares.

'Never mind. The doctor is waiting for us. Shall we go?'

Verity stands up, looking round the room as though surprised to find herself there, but follows Heather out. Heather is holding Verity's hand so she will not lose her again. They join the queue.

'We have an appointment with Professor Isaacs,' Heather informs the receptionist when it is her turn.

'Turn left at the end of the corridor, then it's the third door on your right,' responds the receptionist, hardly looking up from her screen. Heather would usually resent the woman's indifference, but today she thanks her and gently leads Verity in that direction.

Heather remembers Professor Ben Isaacs as a cheerful, elderly man who never took life or his own position in the hospital too seriously. He used to say he'd seen too much absurdity in the world to think anything was worth breaking his heart over. He frequently stated, 'If God exists, then she certainly has a weird sense of humour!'

They sit opposite him when he repeats it, admitting how difficult it is for him to see Verity in such a condition. He keeps reminding Heather how he enjoyed her mum's cooking and her parents' hospitality all those years.

'What brings you good ladies here on this fine day?' he enquires.

'Mum was diagnosed about two years ago with Alzheimer's. I thought it would be good to have another check-up for her and see how advanced she is with the disease.'

'You're quite right. This disease has so many stages and aspects one needs to be on a regular check-up for it. Let's see what we can do.'

He turns to Verity with a smile. 'So, tell me, my dear, what's your name?'

Verity grins, flattered by this man's attention. 'Verity Bach, how do you do?'

They shake hands.

'How old are you, Verity?'

Heather can see this throws Verity off her game. She needs to save face. 'I think I'm eighty, but I'm not sure. I don't feel eighty! I certainly don't look eighty....' She tails off, looking at Heather for confirmation.

'You'll be eighty next year, Mum. Well done,' Heather reassures her.

Heather notices how Verity is watching Professor Isaacs jotting some notes on the paper before him and trying to figure out why he is doing this. Usually, this would trigger her suspicion, but his reassuring smile relaxes her. *He knows what he's doing. Mum's not his first patient.*

'Let's try something else. Just the usual questions,' he continues. 'What's the date today?'

Now Verity is confused. Heather knows she has no clue what day of the week it is, or for that matter, what year it is. Verity surveys the room for a clue as to how to answer that question. *I have to give it to her; she's using all her avoidance mechanisms.*

Verity giggles flirtatiously. 'You know, as a teacher, I would walk into the classroom and write the date on the board. Now I'm retired, every day is the same.'

Heather can see her mum is pleased with herself for coming up with this answer.

'Let's try something else. I'm going to say three words, and I want you to remember them, ok?'

Verity is puzzled, but it seems she's enjoying his company. She smiles and nods. 'Oh, I do love a game!'

'I thought you might. Are you ready? The words are - Tree, post and white. Can you repeat them for me?'

Verity laughs. 'Tree, post, white.'

'Wonderful! Not that difficult, right?'

Verity glances at Heather. She smiles back at her mum, encouraging.

'Verity, can you draw a clock for me, please? And include the hours.'

Verity is able to draw a circle but gets frustrated when she tries to mark the numbers on the clock correctly. She keeps doing it again and again, erasing what she does until it is impossible to see anything that she's drawn. Heather can see she understands she is missing something but doesn't know what it is.

After a few minutes, Professor Isaacs puts his hand on hers to stop her. She raises her head from the paper. She is tense and agitated.

Professor Isaacs smile soothes her. 'That's absolutely fine, deary,' he assures her. 'Do you remember I asked you to repeat three words? Can you tell me what those three words are?'

Verity looks at the paper where she'd attempted to draw the clock. She is defeated but quickly straightens her back and beams at Professor Isaacs. 'White, and I think, tree, but I can't remember the third one. My brain is fucked up... pardon my

French. I know it's not nice to say, but I'm not one to mince words.'

She peeks at Heather. Heather tries hard not to laugh. Her mum looks back at the drawing, still attempting to correct it.

'She's definitely in an advanced stage, though she's incredibly resourceful in how she deals with it,' Professor Isaacs admits to Heather.

Verity catches the last part of his sentence and receives it as a compliment. She smiles at him.

'I'll write my report and be aware she needs constant care, which I'm sure you've already taken care of.'

When Professor Isaacs starts writing some things in his notebook, Verity leans towards the table as if sharing a secret with him.

'They say you can help me with my memory.'

He gazes at her. Heather can see how hard it is for him to disappoint her with his answer. 'Unfortunately, there's no cure for what you have, Verity, but we can make each day count. How's that?' he explains kindly.

Verity looks terribly lost. She tries to cover her sorrow.

'I used to be a happy person,' she utters. 'But I've lost that joy. I don't know where. To tell you the truth, I have nothing to live for. I sit at home all day. No one comes to see me. I don't feel like going out. I want to die... Can you help me with that?'

Heather's heart is torn hearing her mum speak this way. She gasps, and her eyes fill up with tears.

'It's normal to feel this way in your condition, but perhaps think about simple things. Walking, swimming, dancing or even going to the gym. Get physical! Good for the body, good for the mind! It's not good for you to sit all day at home,' Professor Isaacs responds, taking her hands in his.

Heather knows it isn't the answer her mum wants to hear. Verity watches her without any recognition in her eyes and only notices her tears, which she focuses on.

'We tell her that, but she doesn't want to do anything and stays in bed most days!' Heather manages to whisper between the tears that are flowing down her cheeks.

'What did you enjoy when you were young?'

'I used to like doing things... I think. Nowadays, they want me to go to this club, but everyone there is old, and all they do is sit and watch drivel on TV. I need action. Yes, that's it,' Verity glances at Heather and adds, 'right, Heather?' showing she still recognises who she is.

'If we find something like that, do you promise to give it a chance?' Heather mutters through her tears.

'Well, of course. But it needs to be good.'

'In order to like it, you need to try it a few times, Verity. Will you do that for me?' Professor Isaacs asks.

Verity preens herself, feeling flattered. She bats her eyelashes at him. 'For you, doctor, anything.'

Chapter Seventeen

෨ IRIS ෬

Iris puts the last few things into her overnight bag when her phone rings.

'Mum, is Dad coming with you?' asks Joy. 'I've got a little surprise for him, and I want to give it to him in person.'

'Well, right now he's determined not to come, but let me check again.' She puts her hand over the phone. 'Nate?' she calls from her bedroom. 'Have you changed your mind? Joy would love to see you there!'

To her surprise, he enters the bedroom and takes the phone from her. 'What's up, beauty?'

Iris can't hear what Joy is saying to him, but a big smile appears on his face. He ends the call and turns to Iris. 'I'm coming with you.'

Iris raises her eyebrows. She has no idea what Joy said to make him change his mind.

'Not anything big. She said it might be the last time all the Bachs can be together. She has a point'.

Iris is surprised to hear Nate agreeing with anyone else on an issue he has strong opinions against, such as a family gathering.

'Your mother always said family only ever meet at funerals or weddings. I hate both, but as it's a happy event, I might as well come. We can leave with Joy the next day, which means it would be, like your Dad always says - Veni, vidi, vici...' he pauses for a second and then adds with a twinkle in his eye 'this way, I get to be the good guy.'

Iris smiles. 'In my book you're always the good guy. I'm happy you're joining us.' She can't remember the last time Nate joined her for a family occasion. He avoids them like the plague.

Small talk is not his forte - unless it is politics and climate change where his opinions rattle other people's cages. In many ways, Iris is happy Nate doesn't join her often, knowing she would end up defending him - not that he needs defending, but she cannot help herself. She never knows if she is doing it for his sake or her own. Having him join her at Sol's party would now definitely seal it as a special occasion.

Iris stands in her parents' living room, looking around, feeling as if things are falling into place and life is returning to normal, or *whatever 'normal' means anyway.*

Sol is in his wheelchair holding his latest book, Natalie standing next to him, beaming with pride, and explaining how much work had gone into making the book to whoever is willing to listen to her...

Dad has achieved his dream of publishing another book, a thought goes through Iris's head. Verity appears relaxed and happy, surrounded by family and friends. What makes Iris cheerful more than anything else is seeing Daisy pregnant.

Daisy's belly is prominent in a special outfit Joy made for

her. Joy flatly refused to make the usual pregnancy clothes for Daisy that hid the pregnancy.

'Besides,' Joy remarks to Daisy. 'You have great legs. You should show them off!' *First time I've seen a mini dress on a pregnant woman. Joy is right. Daisy does look gorgeous in it, I would never dare to wear something like that, but on Daisy it looks gorgeous,* Iris thinks.

When she surveys the room, she is surprised to see Nate being sociable. He is engrossed in a conversation with Mike, but she can't hear everything they are talking about. Heather and Zoe are entertaining everyone with funny stories. *I haven't seen Heather this funny in ages... Zoe's influence, no doubt.*

Heather sits next to Sol, going through the new book. 'It's beautiful! No expense spared by the publishers, I notice.'

Sol is pleased she observed it. 'They certainly went the extra mile.' He points out the luxurious binding, the vintage endpapers, and the hand stitching.

Iris suddenly feels Nate's arm around her waist.

'I wonder if they did that because they knew it's going to be his last book,' he whispers.

Iris's happiness vanishes at that remark. She wants to ask him why he would say such a thing but realises there is a hint of truth in what he mentioned. She must find ways to subdue her fear of Sol's death.

☙ VERITY ❧

Verity holds another copy of the book and goes through it while Natalie explains her role in the creation of the book. Anyone listening to the conversation can tell it isn't the first time Natalie tells this to Verity.

Each time she explains, Verity announces, 'Honestly, these two always look like lovers when they are working together. Fortunately, I'm not a jealous woman....'

Iris comes to sit next to Verity to give Natalie a break. She suddenly feels nostalgic. 'You always said Dad's work was his other woman, Mum.'

'Nowadays, I'm his other woman. He spends so much time in his study while I'm all by myself,' Verity states as if talking to herself.

'Mum, look...everyone is here. You're having fun now, right? That's what's important!'

Verity stares at the book she is holding. 'I'm always happy when my kids are around...' she answers in a dream-like manner. 'But why are you here?'

Heather joins Iris and Verity on the sofa. She catches Verity's last question. 'It's Dad's book publication day,' she responds to Verity.

Verity looks at her and then at Iris, sitting on both sides of her. She knows she is supposed to understand what is happening but isn't sure what it is. She looks at the two women, knowing they are familiar. She experiences a warm trickle of love for them, but it's an uncertain and tentative emotion.

Lately, she has had it with other people. It makes her feel insecure and afraid, two emotions she has hardly encountered before. She knows she is safe with these two women. They are her daughters… *of course they are!* She smiles and takes their hands.

⊂ॐ IRIS ☜⊃

Iris recognises Verity is now present in the moment with them.

'It's quite an achievement, doing all this in less than two years after a stroke, isn't it?' she says, checking with Heather if she's right in saying this and keen to capitalise on their mother's lucidity. She wants to show Verity it's a big celebration, something unique. Heather agrees and starts explaining to Verity what it all entails, which gives Iris the opportunity to go and talk with Sol.

Iris kneels opposite Sol so he can focus on her. 'What now, Dad? What's your next project?' she asks, thinking that if he has another project planned, what Nate said would not come true.

Her father's eyes are clouded. 'I don't know…' as if he is suddenly tired. His gaze drifts away from her. He looks as if he is lost in his own private world. His next words were even more alarming to her. 'I want you to burn my library when I'm dead,' he declares.

'Dad, I'll do no such thing! It goes against everything you taught us. If you want, I'll find a good home for it,' Iris suggests, shocked to her core.

Sol looks at her, bleakness in his eyes.

'I don't need them anymore,' he expresses softly.

The fear of what Nate had noted floods back. She isn't willing to give in to it. 'Oh, is this your swansong then, Dad?' she manages to verbalise.

Sol laughs at her sarcasm. Iris's hopes rise.

'You do know swans don't really sing before they die... but I might,' he asserted.

This is too much for Iris.

'Your glass is empty, and I need a drink.' She gets up to cover the awkward moment and heads towards the kitchen, her mind working overtime. She needs reassurance from someone that Sol isn't serious. Without his work, Sol will become a ghost. She isn't willing for that to happen. *I need to find him a new project.*

She finds Aisha, Zoe, and Heather in the kitchen, organising food and drinks to be brought into the living room. She is shaken from her conversation with Sol. She leans on a counter.

'Do you know what Dad just told me?' They all look at her. 'He just asked me to burn his precious library when he's dead!'

She expects to hear some cries of shock, but Aisha and Zoe exchanged looks while Heather shrugs. 'He keeps changing his mind about it. He's not himself lately.'

That takes Iris by surprise. Except for this exchange, Sol sounded perfectly well to her. The fact he and Natalie were able to complete the book is proof of this to her. 'What do you mean?'

'Most days he sits in his wheelchair, listens to music, and doesn't talk. It's as if he isn't here anymore,' Heather explains.

That doesn't fit the picture for Iris. 'But tonight, he looks good....'

'That's the problem. You never know when it's going to happen.'

Iris, not knowing as much about the medical side as Heather, tries to think of something to ask. 'And has he been examined recently?'

That is a trigger for Heather. 'What do you think? That we were going to hang around waiting for you to tell us to do it?'

Iris, determined not to ruin the festivities, decides to ignore her sister's resentment. 'Well?'

'Of course he has! But it's difficult to work out what's going on,' Heather snaps.

Iris shuts her eyes and counts to ten. Opening them again, she sees Aisha and Zoe have left the kitchen. 'There must be something we can do.'

'And what would the resident genius suggest?' voices Heather sarcastically.

That is too much for Iris.

'Back off, Heather. I didn't say you were doing anything wrong. I meant that there must be another solution,' Iris professes.

'When you come up with one, let me know and I'll do it,' Heather snarls back at Iris.

Zoe hurries back into the kitchen with an empty tray. She takes in the situation at a glance. 'Dahlinks!' she vocalises in a fake Transylvanian accent. 'Let us eat, drink and be merry! There vill be time for ze drinking of ze blood later on.'

That breaks the tension. Iris and Heather laugh. They all return to the living room, where everyone is cheerfully accepting champagne from Aisha.

'Oh, I do like a nice cold glass of champagne!' Verity affirms, beaming. 'I do love a party. Any excuse to celebrate!'

Sol hears her and raises his glass. 'To my daughters! The best thing we ever created!'

CR DAISY ꙮ

End of a chapter, I thought to myself on the day after Dad's book publication. I was on my way to return the keys to my clinic. With a heavy heart, I had decided to let it go. I knew I wasn't serving my clients as well as I wanted to. Giving up my business would mean closing a chapter in my life, but it would allow me to start a new one as a mother, which I'm looking forward to.

I never thought I would, but lately, as my pregnancy advanced and the baby started to move and kick inside me, unexpected new emotions appeared.

Just before reaching the clinic, I remember I have to take Dad to the hospital for an examination later that day. I phone Max to tell him to get Dad ready. Max assures me he will have Sol ready to go the minute I get there.

I enter my old clinic. The new owner has already reorganised the space to fit her needs. I feel like an intruder. It is the last sign that conveys that this episode of my life is over.

When I step out of the building, I turn around and look at the space sending my thanks for giving me years of satisfaction and fulfilment. I pray it will do the same for the new owner. I am just about to finish when my phone starts ringing. I look at the screen; it says MAX.

❧ SOL ❧

The day after his book launch, Sol is still in bed. Max tiptoes into the bedroom, gently waking Sol and helping him to get into his wheelchair. Max pushes him into the shower.

Soon, Sol is showered, shaved, and dressed. Max checks him over carefully, which Sol appreciates.

'Dignity at all times,' Sol remarks.

Max smiles and nods. He has really come to care for this gentle, scholarly man in the time he's worked with him. Not having a father figure growing up, Sol became a paterfamilias for Max. He pushes Sol to the dining room table and goes to the kitchen. Sol is staring into space, watching how the morning light plays on the walls, casting shadows of the tall trees outside into the room.

After a few minutes, Max returns with Sol's breakfast and sets it for him on a small tray on his wheelchair.

'Is there anything else I can get you?' Sol shakes his head.

'Then I'll go and clean the shower. Call me if you need anything,' Max says, leaving the dining room.

Sol is happy to have this time on his own. He relishes the moments when no one is fussing around him as if he is a fragile object that might break. Sol slowly eats his breakfast of scrambled eggs. He savours each bite. When he finishes, he looks around.

The golden morning light shines in. He takes it all in. The light reflects off pictures of Verity and himself on their wedding day, photos of Iris, Daisy and Heather, and various photos of them all on holiday all over the world. His gaze falls on the coffee table where his latest book is lying. He sighs with contentment, knowing it is time.

'Today's a good day, no need for more,' he whispers. His head nods slowly down to his chest. The golden morning light embraces him.

ᑳ DAISY ᑴ

'Daisy, you must come NOW. Something is terribly wrong with Sol. I called the ambulance. They should be here in five to ten minutes, but you need to be here now.'

'I'm on my way,' is all I can say to Max. *It must be serious if Max, who is able to keep calm in all situations, is as worried as he sounds.* I note to myself as I hurry towards my parents' apartment. On my way, I text Heather, telling her to come immediately to their place. No matter the situation, I know I need Heather by my side.

When I enter their place, a few paramedics are busy connecting Dad to the defibrillator. Even for me, it is obvious Dad is gone, but they are still doing everything they can to bring him back.

While they are working on him, Mum strolls into the dining room—Max nor I know what to do. I am certain that trying to explain to Mum what is going on would be a mistake. Lucky for me, Aisha follows her in. Realising what is going on, she ushers Mum into the kitchen.

'What's going on here? Who are those people?' I hear Mum say in a plaintive voice.

'Sol isn't feeling well, and those people are helping him. I'll make something for you to eat, shall I?'

'Do I know them? Are we having another party?' Mum insists.

'No, they're medical people helping Sol,' explains Aisha.

Not for the first time, I admire Aisha's ability to stay calm with Mum. Max's strength lay in his physical care for Sol's disabilities. *Had lain…* it hits me.

The door bursts open, and Heather rushes into the apartment. She's out of breath. I look at her and we both know… Dad is gone. There is no time for us to process our emotions. Heather stares at the labouring paramedics.

'He's dead! Why are you doing this?' she demands.

One of them turns to her. 'By law, we have to.'

Heather can't watch. She goes into the kitchen. Soon the paramedics stop trying to revive Sol.

Max, despite his usual stoic manners, is numb with grief. He walks to the linen cupboard and takes out a sheet to cover Sol.

'You have to wait for the police before calling the undertaker,' the paramedic informs us. 'I'll ring the doctor for the death certificate.'

Max sees the paramedics out. Heather and I look at each other and Dad's body.

I feel as if the world has turned upside down, and I'm spinning without a point of reference in the world. It's as if I lost my North Pole and am lost in the universe.

❦ HEATHER ❦

When Max covers Sol's face with the sheet, the knowledge that Sol is gone hits Heather like a Tsunami wave. She looks at Daisy and sees that she's in an even worse condition holding her belly and swaying back and forth.

'Sit down before you fall,' she says and brings Daisy a chair.

'I can't deal with this or Mum,' Daisy retorts.

'Where's Iris when we need her? She'd love all this. Can't you just see her organising the 'funeral project'?' Heather grunts.

But Iris is already halfway home. There is no way of reaching her for the next few hours until she lands. *At least she'll have Nate,* Heather thinks.

'I wouldn't want to find out through a WhatsApp message. Maybe it's best to wait until they get back home. What do you think, Heather?' Daisy manages to say.

'She'll kill us if we don't let her know as soon as possible. I think we should send a message to Nate. He'll know what to do,' Heather responds.

'Good thinking. I'll tell the family,' Daisy states. 'You take care of the rest,' scrolling through her phone.

'Leave Mum to me... the wheel has turned.' Heather articulates reading Daisy's main concern of having to take care of Verity.

At that moment, Verity strolls into the living room. She observes Sol's body, covered with a sheet.

'Why is this sheet on the floor? Someone might trip. It's dangerous!' she utters, clearly annoyed.

Daisy cannot find the words and just shakes her head. It's obvious that if she could, she would strangle Verity.

Heather takes control of the situation seeing Daisy in such a state. She takes Verity's hand and leads her to the sofa.

'Mum, I have something to tell you. That's Sol under the sheet. He's dead,' she clarifies as gently as she can.

Verity blinks in disbelief and puzzlement. 'Where is he?'

Heather needs to explain it in a different way. She takes Verity to sit on the floor next to Sol's body. She lifts the sheet gently so that Verity can see Sol's face.

Heather watches her Dad's face too. He looks peaceful. Verity stares at him. She has the bewildered innocence of a child, yet she seems to understand. She kisses his forehead, covers his face tenderly, gets up and walks back to the sofa. 'What am I going to do now?' she sounds like a lost little girl. 'Dad always took care of me.'

Heather experiences a sudden flood of tender love towards her mum for the first time in years as she takes her mum's hand. 'You've got us. We'll take care of you,' she replies.

○꒰ IRIS ꒱○

Iris and Nate are on their way to catch the last train from the airport to their village. They must be quick, as there are only two trains a day that stop at their station. If they miss the train, the next one is only the following day.

Iris has so much work piled up she cannot even think of missing it. As they rush through the airport to the train station, her mind is working overtime, prioritising all her assignments so that once she arrives home, she can start first thing… She hears

Nate gasp. She doesn't give it much thought and hurries on, only to find Nate is not with her.

She stops and turns to see him standing still, reading a message on his mobile, looking pale. *Oh God, I hope nothing's happened to Joy!*

'Darling, what is it? Is it Joy? What's happened?' Nate's expression is unreadable.

'Joy's fine. It's your dad.'

Iris can breathe easily now. She is light-headed. But she can't understand what Nate is saying about Sol.

'He was in excellent form! You saw him yourself last night,' thinking about Sol wanting to burn his library.

Nate walks towards her and takes her hands in his. 'He's dead.'

Iris's legs turn to jelly. She staggers. Nate supports her, guiding her to a nearby bench. Iris looks at him, stunned.

'Could you say that again? I'm not sure I heard you correctly,' she whispers.

'Your Dad is dead, Iris. I'm so sorry,' Nate repeats gently.

Time stops for Iris. She isn't sure what she is supposed to do. The humdrum activity around the airport completely recedes from her. She feels like she is sitting in a sealed room, with no air in or out.

Nate squeezes her hand. 'You sit here. I'll bring you something to eat, and then we'll decide what to do.'

She stares at him. It is as if he is a hundred miles away. Then the noise of the airport breaks in again. This shakes her. 'I need to talk to them.'

Nate shakes his head. 'Look. It's been a long day. Let your sisters deal with it for the moment.'

But Iris is not listening.

'No, I need to talk to them, I need to talk to them!' her thoughts whirling in her head.

Nate hugs her. 'Listen to me. Daisy says your Mum's doing well, considering the circumstances.'

Nate knows exactly how Iris feels. She always had to go to where the crisis was. *It would be good for her to just let things be,* he thinks to himself but doesn't dare to say it.

It looks as if Iris read his thoughts. 'I need to do something. I'd rather throw myself into coping mode. You're all trying to make me redundant!' she wails, putting her head in her hands.

Nate rubs her back. 'There will be plenty for you to do once you get there. Aren't you always saying we're human beings, not human doings?'

Iris glares at him. 'I don't want to just 'be' now. I want to 'do' anything that would make me feel something. I hate being useless!' she weeps.

Nate knows only too well what she means. 'Look, I'll contact Joy and get us flight tickets back to London. Let's find something decent to eat. The army marches on its stomach. Am I right?' he playfully nudges her.

Iris appreciates the sense of this and smiles. Nate can always bring her around.

People huddle around Sol's coffin. On a bleak afternoon, it is an oasis of calm against the stormy Oxford skyline. The whole family is here, plus carers, friends, and university colleagues. It is a splendid turnout.

Iris stands next to her father's grave, getting ready to say a few words about him. She looks composed and dignified in a simple black dress. She holds a piece of paper with a few notes scribbled on it, but she knows what she wants to say by heart. It is just an excuse to hold on to something. It will keep her strong. She glances down at it, then scans the crowd before her and clears her throat.

'A poet once wrote, 'After my death, say this when you mourn for me. There was a man and look, he's no more. He died before his time. The music of his life suddenly stopped. What a pity! There was another song in him, and now it's lost forever.' That man was my Father....'

Verity stands between Iris and Heather. She fidgets and turns around to look at everyone around her. Each time she recognises a familiar face, she waves to them as if they are at a party. Heather keeps a firm grip on her arm to prevent Verity from wandering off. Verity tries to wriggle free of Heather's grasp. Iris hopes Verity won't make a scene.

'... Some might say eighty-four is a good age, but his best work was not done. He still had one more song in him,' she utters and suddenly falters.

She detects the emotions she had the night of Sol's book launch. He'd known it was his swansong, and so had she, but she couldn't bear to acknowledge it. The memory of it chokes her, and she is unable to continue. Daisy notices and immediately moves to Iris's side to carry on.

'Dad died the way he lived - simple, humble, and quiet. He achieved such a lot, but his journey ended too soon. His work remains unfinished. I'll miss you, Dad,' she adds.

When all the eulogies are given, the mourners approach Verity to offer their condolences. Verity basks in their kindness, greeting them with hugs and kisses. Heather accompanies her, hoping to keep her mood buoyant.

'Isn't the party going well?' Verity remarks. 'Look, there's James! I'm going to say hi to him....'

'He'll come to you, Mum,' Heather responds. 'That's how it works. People come up to offer their condolences.'

Verity frowns. 'What condolences?'

Heather sighs. She cannot find a delicate way to say it. 'It's Dad's funeral.'

To her astonishment, Verity laughs. 'Oh! Yes, he suddenly jumped on his horse and disappeared into the sunset. I don't know what got into him. He left me just like that without any explanation...'

Her mood is as mercurial as a little child's, crying one minute and laughing the next.

'Oh look, there's Ruth. These days people only ever meet up at funerals or weddings,' she mentions gaily as if nothing had happened.

Heather is grateful to see Ruth. If there is anyone in the family who knows how to deal with Verity's mood swings, it is Ruth. She'd seen it all with her own father, Verity's brother. Ruth and Verity hug.

'Verity, you look so well,' said Ruth.

'It's because of this party! Parties keep me young!' Linking arms, the three women walk away from the grave to the waiting limousines.

Chapter Eighteen

∝ DAISY ∞

My nights are now filled with terrifying dreams. I am afraid to fall asleep only to wake up in the morning, either tired or restless, knowing my sleep will not be peaceful but stressful.

Sometimes, I cannot remember my dreams, but I know they were important. I've always believed dreams carry with them a message. I'm not a fan of Freud or Jung or their interpretations of dreams, but I am certain dreams carry information from my unconscious mind. I am desperate and determined to get to the root of that knowledge.

One night I dreamt Dad came to talk to me. He said the strangest thing I've ever heard, 'your children are all around you… look around, and you'll see them in each of your patient's faces,' he said and vanished. At first, I doubted whether it was him, but in my gut, I knew it was.

The next night I had the recurring nightmare of walking through a dark valley. I am pregnant, and with every step I take, a dead baby falls between my legs. It is like I am walking in a forest, and the dead babies are the falling leaves. The woman that is me doesn't even cry or scream in horror. It is as if it is natural for her, as if that's how life is.

Every time I have this dream, I wake up with sweat and tears in my eyes and terror in my heart. *What does all this mean?* I cannot share my fears and dreams with Mike. I sense he's going through his own doubts about the whole pregnancy, kids, and parenthood, and it doesn't feel right to discuss it with him until I know what I truly want.

One night I woke up in cold sweat and watched Mike tossing and turning on his side of the bed, mumbling incoherent words. The only thing I could hear was, 'I can't do it... I can't....'

I have no clue what haunts his dreams, but I am sure we are both tormented with doubts and fears for the future. It feels so lonely not to be able to share it with him, but I am determined not to do it until I am certain about my own decision.

A few days later, I wake up in bed soaking in my own blood. By now, the familiar experience of a miscarriage is known to me. I am not horrified by it as I was the first time it happened. In a way, it is kind of a relief. It is consistent with all my nightmares and dreams.

I am calm when I call Mike to let him know I'm taking a taxi to Doctor Lewis's clinic. Mike says he'll meet me there and acts as calmly as I am. True to his promise, he is waiting for me in the clinic. Unfortunately, we're both experienced by now with the procedure that follows.

After a few hours Doctor Lewis, in her efficient yet kind way, enters my room.

'How we're doing?' she asks.

I never know how to answer such a question in situations like this. *What am I supposed to say, give a detailed description of how I feel? or am I supposed to give a neutral polite response that means nothing?* I opt for the latter.

'I'm fine, not my first rodeo...' trying to be stronger than I am with my favourite avoidance mechanism of turning things into light humour.

But Doctor Lewis is not fooled by it. 'You are allowed to mourn and be sad, Daisy', she articulates my own unspoken thoughts.

'I'm not sure whether I'm sad ...I've been having doubts lately about this whole thing, and I'm not surprised this happened,' I quietly admit to her. There is something in Doctor Lewis that makes me feel safe with her to tell her my innermost thoughts. *Maybe that's why Iris recommended her so much.* Whatever the reason was, I'm grateful now for it.

'It's natural to have doubts in this process. Why don't you and Mike take some time off and check if it's still what you want? You still have one embryo in case you decide to give it another chance... and if not... there are other options... The most important thing is that you'll be certain of your choice.'

I am beyond grateful to hear those words from her. Mike enters the room just in time to hear her last sentence.

'That's good advice, doctor,' he says as he approaches my bed and sits down beside me, holding my hand.

'I'll leave you two to discuss things.'

Doctor Lewis walks towards the door. Just before she leaves the room, she turns around and adds, 'Just remember Daisy, it isn't written anywhere that as women we all must give birth or be mothers... For some of us, it's not our destiny or path.' And with that, she leaves Mike and me on our own.

Mike holds my hands, and for a while, neither of us says any-thing. I know Mike is waiting for me to express my thoughts or feelings, and I appreciate his patience with me. *Where do I start?*

'I've been having nightmares...' we both say at the same time when the silence is too long.

'I know...' we both complete each other. No doubt we're in tune.

'You first,' Mike states to me.

'I'm not sure where to start, but to cut a long story short... I don't know anymore whether I want to get pregnant, have children or even be a mother,' I tell him. 'I also suspect you're having doubts too... I heard you the other night mumbling in your sleep...'

'I can't tell you how relieved I am to hear you say this... I didn't know how to tell you that I'm having doubts about this whole thing... It was supposed to be simple and easy, and now I feel like we're struggling to push a huge bolder up the moun-tain only to have it roll back on us each time... it's not natural... It isn't supposed to be this hard....'

Mike has tears in his eyes when he speaks, and I can feel his love and care for me.

'It's so hard for me to see you like this,' he tells me. 'Each time you have your hopes up only to have them trampled upon by your own body... I really think that if it were meant to be, it would have happened by now... it troubles me to have you go through all these procedures only to be disillusioned again... I can't take it anymore, and I didn't know how to tell you that.'

I didn't need this speech to know how much Mike loves me but hearing him express it in this way makes it clear that not only he loves me, but he also really understands who I am and what I am going through even when I try to play it strong.

'So, I guess, for now, we both agree we don't want to pursue this anymore... I mean... In the end, when we started it all, it was because I wanted to make sure I wouldn't have regrets later in life... now, I can say we tried, and it didn't work... no regrets for trying and maybe no regrets for not giving birth... I do feel complete on this issue.'

Mike bends down and gives me a kiss. 'Agreed,' he says. 'And now... rest... I'll let Doctor Lewis know about our decision.' He stands up and walks out of the room, closing the door behind him and leaving me with my thoughts.

Heather will rejoice, and I wonder how Iris will take it, but it's none of her business...' However, there is still a voice in my head that reminds me of Iris's question: *Do you want to be pregnant, or do you want to be a mother?* I know I no longer wish to be pregnant, but whether I want to be a mother is something else for which I have no answer at this moment.

Mike and I agreed to keep our decision between us. Obviously, everyone knew I had another miscarriage, but no one dared to ask me if I was going to continue trying.

A few weeks later, I find myself packing some of Dad's clothes to give to charity when Heather comes into the room. 'Heard you're Kondoing Dad's stuff, and I came to see if you need any help.'

I look surprised at Heather. Organising and tidying stuff is not her strong point. If it were up to her, she would live a minimalist life and still manage to have a mess around her. Thank God Zoe brought some colour and beauty into her life and, with it, a sense of order.

Though I'm surprised to hear her say this, I accept her help gracefully. After a few hours of emptying Dad's wardrobe, separating items into different piles and folding those that would go to charity, Heather and I are tired. It looks like the task took more than just physical effort; it also drained me emotionally.

Aisha enters the room where we are working just in time as we seal the last box.

'Tea?' she checks in her soft voice.

'I'd kill for one,' Heather answers.

'No need to kill anyone, I made a fresh pot, and it's in the living room,' Aisha informs us.

Heather and I move to the living room. Mum is asleep on one of the sofas. Lately, she has been sleeping a lot, which makes my life much more peaceful. However, I'm aware that within a short time, I would need to decide what to do with her. This apartment is way too big for her and Aisha, and the costs are extreme.

I can't think about it now, I tell myself. *If not now, then when, and if not you, who?* a voice chimes in my head. I am so busy with the voices in my head that I don't hear Heather asking me something.

'I'm sorry I'm arguing with myself and didn't listen to your question… what was it?' I admit to her.

'Now worries… I know it's none of my business, but I'm curious … are you thinking of trying to get pregnant again?'

Here it is… someone dared to ask the question, and now I'm

unable to escape it... *well, you still can... she did say it's not her business.*

I stare at Heather and realise she is curious, not because she wants to gossip, but because she's honestly concerned. Heather and I have been each other confidants for so many years, and somehow the last few years, we never managed to have a proper heart-to-heart conversation. I also feel I want to share my decision with someone. *She'll understand more than anyone else.*

'No... Mike and I decided not to try again. We do have another embryo, but we both feel it's not right.'

'I agree... I always thought it went against what you really wanted... remember, we promised each other, long time ago, we both would not have kids,' Heather says triumphantly.

'You're wrong, Heather. My decision not to try again has nothing to do with that old promise. Who I am today is not the young woman I was when we made that promise... I didn't say I abanded my wish of being a mother. I just said I'm not going to try getting pregnant.'

Heather looks as if she has been struck by lightning. It is definitely not what she expected to hear from me. I could see she was trying to regain control over her emotions, and I decided to let her do it in her own way.

'No matter what your reasons are, I'm happy to hear this,' she is finally able to say.

I am about to get up and leave it at this when a suspicious thought comes into my mind, which scares me.

'Heather, did you feel betrayed by me when I decided to get pregnant?' I blurt. *God, I hope I'm wrong,* I say inwardly once the words are out there.

If I thought Heather appeared shocked before, now it is obvious. Cool and calculated Heather has streaks of tears running down her cheeks, and when she is ultimately able to say anything, it comes in fragments of speech.

'Yes... I thought you were my ally... It was as if it was 'me and you' against the world... not willing to accept what Mum, Dad, Iris, or society expect us to be... and then you suddenly announce you're accepting their view on what happy life is... I felt betrayed, and you didn't even notice.'

Hearing Heather share her agony so honestly makes me feel ashamed of myself for not realising this earlier. I understand our promise to each other on this issue came from totally different reasons. Mine was my fear of being a mum like Verity, but Heather's was from who she was.

It didn't feel right to point this out now. It didn't matter anyway. What I need to do now is to find a way to comfort her and apologize for not seeing her or being there for her.

.'I'm sorry you had to go through this pain. I didn't mean to hurt you...' I start to say, but Heather stops me.

.'It doesn't matter. You're right. We're not the same women as when we made that pact between us. What is done is done, and we're back at the same spot as we were before... let's just keep it between us... I don't think Iris would agree with you, and as we both know, there's no point in trying to argue with Iris when it comes to the issue of what family is.'

I don't agree with Heather about how she views Iris, but it is not the time or place to start that debate, *and, in a way, she's right... it would be harder to get Iris to accept my decision,* a voice in my head whispers.

Chapter Nineteen

⚬ DAISY ⚭

I'm not happy to discover that once someone dies, taking care of all the bureaucracy can take weeks, months or, in some cases, even years. I'm hoping it won't be years in Dad's case, but it keeps me busy, which is a blessing. It distracts me from the nagging feeling in the pit of my stomach concerning our decision.

I keep telling myself I will only deal with a few urgent things on my To-Do list, and then I can reopen my clinic. The thought of being able to help others is the best remedy for my agitation, I believe. *I know, I know,* I remind myself. *Some might call it… denial.*

'Am I doing the right thing by throwing myself into all these activities?' I ask Doctor Lewis when I come to say goodbye.

'Well, it's not a bad thing to do,' Doctor Lewis says kindly. 'I think this is a good coping mechanism for you.'

I sense a warm rush of gratitude towards the woman. 'Thanks! I guess I needed to hear that. I know I'm not your patient any-more, but – this is going to sound stupid – I see you now as part of my family!'

'That's very sweet of you. By the way, my first name is Rose, so you can stop with the 'Doctor Lewis,' she smiles. 'Funny enough, Iris said the same thing… that I felt like family to her when we first met years ago at university.'

Only then I realise how close Rose and Iris are. It dawns on me that maybe Iris knows me better than I think. She knew which doctor would be a good fit for me, even if in the end the result had not been what she anticipated it to be...

'Were you Iris's doctor when she was pregnant with Joy?' I probe to change the subject.

'No, Iris had already gone to live abroad,' Rose states, a little wistfully. 'I wish I had. I might have been able to help her after, well, you know...'

I nod as if I understand this allusion. It is something between Iris and Rose that is best to leave for the moment. *If Iris had wanted to share it with me, she would have done it a long time ago*, I tell myself. Besides, I have enough on my plate without dredging up the past, although I am a bit curious if I'm honest with myself.

'I'll tell you what I told Iris then... though I'm a gynaecologist, or maybe because I am one, I know very well that giving birth and being a mother are two totally different issues. Your decision has nothing to do with your wish of being a mother.'

I can't believe she's telling me this. *She's probably the one that got Iris to think that way.*

'Now I know you and Iris are close friends,' I reply with a chuckle. 'This is exactly what Iris told me when I started this path.'

'She's right... but it's not about her we're talking about. It's you... and no matter what you decide, remember you have one more embryo just in case you wish to become a mother and create your own family in some other way.'

Interesting... I never thought of other possibilities for creating my own family. I guess these days, we have so many options we should not be stuck with the old formation of what we know, but I didn't have a lot of time to contemplate this. One thing is for sure; Rose opened a whole new world of opportunities for me.

A few hours later, I find myself squatting on the floor in Dad's study going through boxes of papers. The table is covered with invoices, bank statements, insurance papers and salary slips going back thirty years.

The whole place is a mess. I have to go through everything to understand the status of his accounts. I might not be as efficient as Iris, but through the years I found my own way of working, which is quick and efficient. I organise everything in small files hoping it will all make sense to me later.

'Is this a treasure hunt?' I suddenly hear Heather's voice and jump out of surprise. I feel mildly guilty. Heather is always trying to get me to rest.

'You could say - I'm looking for Dad's will. Feels like I'm searching for the Holy Grail.'

That takes Heather by surprise. 'Did he even have one?'

I am baffled by her throwaway remark. 'This is Dad we're talking about! I'm sure he did, but I can't find it. The only thing I can find is what he wanted to do with the house in Oxford.

'I thought it would be more important when Mum... you know.'

I look at Heather in exasperation. She is such a competent doctor, but financial know-how eludes her. *Thank God for Zoe, again...*

'It's important now! We must take care of Mum, and I don't

know if we have the means to support her,' I reply, opening another dusty box of papers.

Heather smiles and nods as if she understands what I'm saying. Looking at her, it dawns on me. The truth is money is not important to Heather. She is like Dad in this regard. She lives a simple life and loves going to flea markets and charity shops. I suppose it is her way of revenge on Mum and her fervent 'keeping up with the Joneses', which Heather always loathed. If Mum had to live frugally now, she'd be horrified.

'Didn't Dad have a financial advisor? I mean, he and Mum knew all sorts of people,' Heather remarks.

I sigh heavily. 'That's what I'm trying to figure out. He certainly had bonds, security accounts and things I don't even know the names of. It looks as if he had some kind of a portfolio.'

Heather's facial expression tells me she didn't understand half of what I mentioned.

'That sounds good!' she utters.

'Yes, but I don't know what it all means!' I respond in despair.

'Let's track down the financial advisor, for starters,' Heather suggests.

'I agree,' I express, grateful the unworldly Heather is trying to help me for once. 'But there's no point asking Mum...'

'What about Iris?' suggests Heather.

BAMM! I slap my forehead.

'Of course! Why didn't I think about that in the first place? I'll call her tonight...' scribbling a note to myself, knowing that without it, I might forget it by the end of the day.

'At least we can do something constructive with her all-encompassing knowledge of this family,' Heather comments bitterly.

I send her a look. I don't care for Heather's tone. 'Go easy on Iris, Heather. Try seeing things from her perspective, for once.'

'What perspective? As a mother-substitute? No thanks.'

I knew Iris has always been a thorn in Heather's side, especially since the responsibility for organising Mum's care now solely came down to Heather after Dad passed away.

My energy for the discussion ebbs away. Life is too short.

'Try listening more, Heather,' I announce firmly. 'You might learn something.'

Heather opens her mouth to speak but stops herself for some reason.

'Fine!' Heather finally states. 'When she stops being a total control freak, I'll cut her some slack. But I think it's time she did something in the name of the family she holds so dear!'

I'm surprised by the viciousness in Heather's voice but decide to let it go and continue examining the different boxes in Dad's old study.

CR HEATHER ED

Heather watches Daisy go through the different boxes in Sol's old study. Just being in that room feels strange for her without having Sol in it. She keeps turning her head to the door, hoping to hear Max rolling Sol in his wheelchair into the room, only to remember that this is not going to happen. Again, she feels the sharp ache of loss in her belly.

She didn't expect it to be so hard. She isn't prepared to feel that emptiness that follows her everywhere after his death. To her surprise, she finds herself constantly talking to Sol in her head, and when faced with a decision to make, instead of going back to her ProCon notebook, she now has a new way which is, what she calls, the WWDD system – What Would Dad Do. It helps her focus and make decisions faster than before, which she knows makes everyone happier.

Looking at Daisy frantically going through the boxes to find the will, she doesn't know how she can help anymore. *Daisy is right, my financial IQ is not high, but I'm too old to change this. I can find other ways to help her.*

'I know you're concerned about financial issues and how we can care for Mum in the best way,' she comments, 'but have you thought of other possibilities?'

Daisy raises her head from one of the boxes. She looks as if she is astonished to still see Heather in the room.

'What do you mean?'

'What if we sell the house in Oxford? That will bring in a lot of money. We then use the money to put Mum in a nursing home. With the money the sale of the house would bring we can pay for the best nursing home there is.'

Daisy appears flabbergasted by Heather's suggestion. She drops down to the floor in disbelief at hearing it.

Heather is not sure what in her suggestion is so outrageous. 'I mean, both of us don't have much love for Mum. Why should we be burdened by her now? Her condition will only worsen, and she will need professional people to care for her. Within a few months, it would not make a difference for her who takes care of her… even today, she finds it hard to recognise who we are.'

Daisy stares up at Heather with an expression like a fish out of water trying to gasp for air.

Heather decides to sit next to her down on the floor. As she does, she takes Daisy's hands and stares straight into her eyes. 'This will also give you the chance to return to work and open your clinic again… It would be your chance to do what you truly love and are good at: taking care of your patients… can't you see it's the best way to go?

Daisy can at last find her voice. However, the first words that come out of her mouth are not what she planned them to be. 'Iris would kill us both… not just her….'

'I don't care about what Iris thinks. If she thinks differently, why isn't she here to carry this load called 'family' … I look at you and think it's time you took care of yourself and not for someone who will never appreciate what you have done for them… Mum will never be grateful for what you did for her, even if she would recognise you,' Heather cries out in frustration.

'It's not about Iris... it's about me… I'm a Bach... we don't throw someone out of the family just because they are in need… it's not how we do things… as Bachs, we stick together through good and bad times… I might not agree with Iris on many things, but I do agree with her that as a family, we should take care of each other.'

'Who says we're not taking care of Mum… I'm only suggesting that a nursing home would give her more than what you, Aisha and I can give her… it's the logical thing to do.'

Daisy has nothing to say to Heather in response. However, Heather senses Daisy is not sure about this solution and certainly not happy with it.

'I have to think about it,' Daisy replies as she gets up from the floor.

'What is there to think about? You know it's the best solution. Why can't you accept that, for once, I came up with a better solution than Iris would ever have?' Heather calls in anger.

Daisy glances at Heather with disdain but decides not to take the bait Heather and leaves the room, letting Heather and her anger cool down between the dusty papers and boxes.

❧ DAISY ☙

Later that evening, at home, I'm organising papers from Dad's study, reading through them, checking online to get additional information, while all the time Heather's suggestion is pecking at the back of my mind when the Skype icon pops up. Iris. I log on.

'Iris, you're a mind reader,' I cry out as Iris's tanned face comes on screen.

Iris laughs. 'No, just emotionally connected.'

I cringe inwardly from the implied criticism. 'I need some financial guidance. I'm starting to panic….'

'Why?' Iris' voice sounds baffled.

'I can't find Dad's will. I don't know where we stand financially concerning Mum.'

'Can't Heather help you find it?' Iris remarks.

I frown. 'Give me a break. She's terrified of anything to do with money. She's good with Mum, but anything else - she's useless.'

Iris has this Ahh look on her face.

'Did you speak with Jeffrey White?' she asks.

'Who?' I'm lost. I never heard this name before.

'He used to be Dad's lawyer. I'll call him tomorrow and see if he has it,' Iris replies in a matter-of-fact voice.

Trust Iris! I'm so relieved.

'You should see the mess!' I profess while I sense how the relief transforms my face.

'Don't worry. I'll call you tomorrow once I speak with Jeff. Do yourself a favour and go to bed. You mustn't get too stressed.'

Mike enters the room and overhears the last sentence.

'Hooray! I agree. Thank you, Iris. The best place for Daisy is in bed, next to me,' he waves to her.

Iris looks happy to see Mike.

'Hi Mike!' she says, waving back. 'Make sure she rests. I'm still hoping to be an aunty, you know….'

'You what?' Mike replies.

Immediately my finger hovers over the 'end call' button. 'Gotta go, Iris! Speak soon,' I announce, hanging up on Iris's startled face. Mike glares. I make myself busy with paperwork, avoiding his look.

'Is there something you're not telling me?'

I grin at him. 'Oh, you know Iris, the soul of sensitivity!'

The next day, still in my PJs, I drag myself downstairs to the kitchen to prepare breakfast when I hear Mike speaking on the phone with someone.

'She's still asleep. I'll let her know. Thanks.'

I step into the room and kiss him. 'I'm not asleep, and what do I need to know?' I ask him.

'Iris spoke with Jeffrey. He has the will. Iris will be here this evening.'

That's not like Iris. Dropping everything and rushing to London for something we could do here.

'Is it that serious?' I wonder aloud.

Mike shrugs. 'I don't think so, but Jeffrey says all beneficiaries should be present. Your sisters and Verity, basically, plus whoever else.'

I'm still puzzled, but having Iris here to help take care of business is a relief. I switch on the coffee machine. 'Nothing like good news to start the day.'

A few days later, I find myself back in Dad's study, this time with Iris. It is still a mess though we managed to clear the table so we could work on it.

'I did some calculations based on the information you gave me,' Iris declares. 'Everything stays as it is until Mum dies. Then it will be divided between us. The only question is what we do with the house in Oxford.'

I am about to speak when Mum breezes in. She appears a bit surprised to see us there.

'So this is where the party is!' Mum announces as she surveys the room. She picks up a file and blows the dust off it.

'Why did you make such a mess? Dad will be furious! Did he say when he is coming home?' she questions us.

I smile at her. 'He didn't say, Mum. Why don't you go for a walk with Aisha until he comes back? Meanwhile, Iris and I will clear up the mess.'

Mum flashes her a stern look. 'You want to get rid of me! He's gone. I'm all alone, and there's no one to take care of me,' crying suddenly like a little child.

I can see Iris's eyes starting to tear too, listening to Mum. I, on the other hand, can only roll my eyes. I've heard this drama before.

'We're here, Mum,' Iris divulges. 'We'll take care of you!'

Mum stares at her, weighing her up.

'Well, that's very good of you, dear. My own daughters don't even bother to visit me, you know. Disgraceful!' she responds, dabbing at her eyes with the hem of her tattered cardigan.

I'm all too familiar with Mum's changeable state of mind. I watch Iris, keen to see how she would handle the situation.

'Mum, we are your daughters. I'm Iris, and this is Daisy, remember? We're only here to help you.'

There is a moment of silence. Mum glares at both of us. She opens the file she holds and flicks through it. 'If you say so. We did well with our daughters. That's what Sol always tells me. This needs a wipe with a damp cloth... Aisha!' she calls. And with that, she hurries out of the room.

'Did Mum just pay us a compliment?' says Iris, amazed.

'This is what I have to deal with every day,' I explain. 'It's getting harder and harder.'

Iris decides to change the subject. She's right. Better to stick to practicalities.

'Like I said, I did my calculations. I have a suggestion,' Iris articulates, wiping her tears away.

'Go on. I'm all ears.'

Iris takes a deep breath. It seems as if what she has to say might not be to my liking, but I don't care. It's not like Iris to hesitate in expressing her opinions. It has to be something big if she takes so much time to prepare her speech.

'I looked at all Mum's expenses: this apartment, Aisha's salary, the different activities she takes her to. I also thought about you having to close your clinic, which I know you love, so I'm thinking of a financial solution that might work for everyone,' she finally says, stopping for another second.

So far, so good. I smile at her to encourage her to continue...

'Mike always says the more problems you get, the better your solutions,' I affirm.

Iris smiles nervously. She paces around the room. *Come on Iris, whatever it is, I can take it. There is no way out of it. Rip the plaster off and let it bleed!*

'You and Mike should rent out your place in London and move back to Oxford... with Mum,' Iris finally explodes with what she has to say.

This is definitely not what I expected. I can feel the blood draining out of my face...

'Are you nuts?' I yell. 'You think I should live with her? Have you heard a word I've said, Iris?'

I flop down into Dad's old swivel chair. I stare at Iris.

'I know it sounds... terrible, but hear me out for a moment,'

Iris replies quickly. 'This way, we save money on the rent of this place. You'll have the money from the rent of your place. You can set up your clinic in the Oxford house, so you won't have to commute. There's enough space for you, Mike, even a new baby!'

My eyes narrowed. *Why is Iris playing the baby card? Is she really that desperate?*

'You could even have a separate wing for Mum and Aisha,' continues Iris, warming to her theme. 'Mum's old Oxford friends will visit her. Even if she can't remember anyone, she'd still have company, which is what she needs.'

I'm too furious to even shout at Iris, so I say in the coldest tone I can master: 'Let me spell it out for you, Iris. I hate Mum. I can't wait for her to die so I can be free of her! I can't believe you think this would work!'

I storm out of the room, slamming the door shut.

❧ IRIS ☙

BAMM... The door of Sol's study slams, and Daisy runs out of the room. Iris stands in the dusty room, looking at the closed door.

That went well, she thinks to herself bitterly. She'd known it would not be easy to convince Daisy to accept her plan but did not expect such a fiery response from her sister.

Iris doesn't know how to pass the time until she has to return to Daisy's, where she is staying. Finally, when she considers it is late enough, she tiptoes in, doing her best not to disturb anyone, but worse luck, Mike and Daisy are having a late supper.

'Iris, you dirty stop-out! Would you like some pasta? We've saved some for you,' calls Mike from the dining room. He sounds cheerful. Daisy obviously didn't tell him about her proposal.

Iris has no way of escaping Mike's invitation and goes in. Daisy acknowledges Iris with a curt nod. Mike smiles and ladles some pasta on a plate, oblivious to the tension between the two sisters. They are drinking a nice Spanish red Iris brought over. Iris perches on the edge of her chair like she might need to run for it. Daisy looks daggers at her.

'How did it go with Jeffrey?' asks Mike, pouring her a glass of wine.

'Ok, thanks. Got a few things cleared up.'

Mike passes her some salad. 'So, are you rolling in it now?'

Iris has to smile. Good old Mike. 'Not until Mum dies,' risking a glance at Daisy.

Daisy drains her wine glass in a single gulp. Even Mike is taken aback by it.

'Whoa! Easy, tiger!' he utters to Daisy.

Daisy holds her glass out for a refill. Mike obliges.

Iris has no option but to change the subject. She also knocks her wine back. 'So, anything to report on the parenthood front?' she probes.

There is silence. Mike refills Iris's wine glass and stands up.

'I think I've got another bottle of this. Won't be a minute,' he says, kissing Daisy's forehead.

Daisy shifts uneasily in her chair. She waits until Mike is out of earshot. 'I don't know yet. I need more time to adjust.'

The wine has gone straight to Iris's head.

'Do you have the luxury of time at your age?' Iris asks thoughtlessly.

Daisy can't believe it. 'Bloody hell, Iris!' she hisses. 'For Christ's sake, leave it!' She throws her napkin on her unfinished pasta, carries her wine to the living room and slumps down on the sofa.

Iris follows her, determined to get a decision from Daisy on Verity's care. 'Look, I'm sorry if I upset you earlier, but I was being honest with you.'

Daisy knows Iris is being truthful but is surprised at how insensitive she is. She knows Daisy hates Verity.

'You really don't know me,' Daisy whispers, closing her eyes.

'I'm trying to be practical,' Iris comments.

Daisy shrugs. She is so tired of it all. 'I couldn't get away from that house fast enough. And in any case, Mike and I made a few decisions about our future. Thank you for asking.'

Iris pricks up her ears. Something is about to be revealed. 'What do you mean?'

'Mike and I decided not to try for another baby,' Daisy announces flatly.

Iris feels guilty. 'Look, sorry about mentioning your age. I didn't mean…'

Daisy shakes her head. 'It's got nothing to do with my age. I took the last miscarriage as a sign. I would have been a terrible mother. I would have turned out just like Mum.'

Iris finally understands, cursing herself that she didn't recognise it before. She moves to sit next to Daisy, wanting desperately to hug her, but Daisy would have pushed her away.

'I can't return to that house,' says Daisy sadly. 'Too many bad memories.'

Iris takes Daisy's hand. 'You're nothing like Mum... you never were. Maybe if you put yourself in Mum's shoes, you might see a different picture. She's a shadow of her former self. Just let it all go. Surely, your miscarriages can teach you that life's too short.'

Iris stops herself, as she isn't sure she has the courage to say her last sentence. She looks Daisy straight in the eye. 'Isn't it time you forgave Mum?'

Daisy stares at her.

'That's illogical!' Daisy cries out.

'I agree. Logic isn't the solution. Forgiveness is,' Iris replies.

Daisy bangs her wine glass down on the coffee table. Wine goes flying. Daisy stands up and looms over Iris. 'Fuck you and your whole New Age airy-fairy bullshit! There are some things you should never forgive! And bad mothering is top of the list!'

Iris gives up. It will have to wait. She gets up and heads for the door but old habits die-hard. Just before she leaves the room, she turns and looks back at poor, broken Daisy. 'Let's say you became a mother. Do you think you might make some mistakes with your kids?'

'What's your point, Iris?' Daisy says coolly.

'Is it possible, do you think?'

'Sure.'

'Would you want your kids to hold that mistake against you for the rest of your life?'

'No.'

'Right. So, why won't you forgive Mum?'

'Because of her, I don't have kids and never will,' says Daisy.

'Exactly my point,' asserts Iris. 'So, here's the logic: maybe you need to forgive Mum first, then if you have a child, you won't turn out like her. Think about it.'

Daisy stares at Iris. 'Good night, Iris,' she pronounces coldly.

Iris gestures she understands Daisy's request and leaves the room. *Oh well, it was worth a try...*

Only when Iris is gone Daisy collapses back onto the sofa. She scoops up a cushion and screams into it. Mike comes in, holding another bottle of red.

'Did you tell her?' he checks.

Chapter Twenty

ᏪᏋ IRIS ᏪᏊ

Iris does not sleep well that night. She knows she has outstayed her welcome at Daisy's, so early morning, she leaves and goes to stay with Verity. There isn't much to do, but she feels her time is better spent there than bearing the weight of Daisy's unhappiness.

After Sol died, Iris became aware of how precious time was. She wants to spend more time with her mother, even if Verity has no idea who she is most of the time. She sits with Verity, reading from old journals Verity used to write. Iris uses her finger to point to the line her mum is reading so Verity doesn't get lost. It certainly gives Iris a glimpse into Verity's early life.

'My father loved oranges,' reads Verity hesitantly. 'For him, oranges were a symbol of joy. He would come home with a basketful of oranges and save them as a treat for after supper. Then he would peel them.

'It was a magical moment. First, he cut the top in a circular movement, as if cutting out the shape of a little hat. Then he would score lines along the skin of the orange, which made the orange look like a globe with longitudinal lines.

'Next, he peeled those parts away. When all the outer orange skin was off, he took off the white pith. It was done slowly, delicately, as if he was undressing a lover. When the orange was stripped naked, he would sometimes offer half to Mum as a gesture of his love. I always knew that when he did that, it meant he probably had done something to upset her. This ritual with the orange was his way of asking for forgiveness.'

Iris is enthralled by this description. She can practically see the whole scene-taking place as Verity reads. Verity always had a way with words, but Iris never knew she wrote so vividly. She is touched by it, as it brings back happy memories of her grandparents and summers spent on their farm.

'Mum, this is so beautifully written. There's so much poetry in it!' she says.

Verity looks at her, astounded. 'Did I write this?'

Iris nods sadly.

'Well, if you say so, dear,' Verity replies.

'Yes! Now, you know you wrote this. Now, you enjoy this moment with me. Now…is all we have,' Iris states, hoping this reassures them both.

Verity slowly agrees. It is an uncertain gesture.

'I'm afraid I'll forget it,' she whispers, stroking the yellowing pages.

Funny how it works, or maybe not. Mum's always been the one who wanted something beyond the now. She always chased the pot of gold at the end of the rainbow, thinking that once she got there, all would be well: Dad's career, our education, our ambitions… None of it was ever enough. Maybe it's time the now becomes enough for her.

'Mum, shall we go on? I'm really enjoying this,' Iris suggests.

Verity looks distracted. She lets the journal drop to the floor, stands up, and leaves the room without a backward glance as if Iris isn't there.

Iris finds these sudden departures difficult but continues reading the journal, which makes her even more emotional. At last, she can cry in private now. *Must be my age.*

Suddenly the door flies open, and Heather storms in.

'There you are! Where the hell have you been? Try answering your phone, for God's sake!' she shouts.

'Well, excuse me. I wanted some quiet time with Mum, so I turned the damn thing off. No need to get all worked up!' Iris attempts to explain.

'Listen, holy fucking Mother Theresa!' Heather yells. 'You don't get to float in here and control everything, you know?'

Iris is hurt but maintains her calm. She glances down at her mother's journal. She is clutching it so hard that the whites of her knuckles are visible.

'What's brought this on?' she inquires, her face impassive.

Heather is clearly on a roll, or she would have registered Iris's stony expression - always a danger sign.

'You fly over here like you're Mary Poppins, but instead of fixing things you just add to the burden! Just go back to your perfect life and leave us be, why don't you?'

In any argument, it only takes one word to escalate it into a full-on war. This time it is the word 'perfect'. It is Iris's turn to lose the plot.

'Perfect? What the hell are you talking about? What do you know about my life? When was the last time you ever visited me? What did I ever do to you that you keep attacking me each time we meet?' Iris's cold rage is like torrential rain on a forest fire.

Heather blinks in surprise.

'Daisy says you told her and Mike to move back to Oxford. Since when are you Lord God Almighty?' Heather replies, still seething.

Now things are clear to Iris, but she isn't willing to back down. She just had about enough of Heather's hostility.

'I didn't say that's what she must do. I suggested it might be the best step financially, bearing Mum's care in mind, plus renting the apartment and Daisy's need for new premises. But what would you know about finances, Heather? Having a Ph.D. in neuroscience didn't help you much in that department, now did it?' Iris retorts coldly.

'Oh yes, throw that in my face! Where were you when Dad died? Where were you when Mum was found walking down the street in her nightie? Have you changed anything in your life since all this happened? No, you carry on living in paradise while Daisy and I have to make massive changes in our lives to take care of family - the one thing you're very good at lecturing us on - while you keep your distance, living your bloody 'Y Viva España'.'

Iris reels. That hurt. Heather just voiced something Iris had been afraid to admit to herself.

'If you want me to move back here, Heather, all you have to do is say so,' she contends casually. 'Daisy asked me to come and take care of the financial situation because you weren't doing anything except babysitting Mum, so please don't go lecturing me about commitment and duty.'

Iris turns away from the glowering Heather. Verity stands there looking at them, confused. Verity is wearing a pair of Sol's striped pyjamas; the trousers held up with a clothes peg.

'What's going on? Why are you arguing? I always say to my girls that if they must fight with one another, they should do so in a civilised way,' Verity mentions, her lucid manner totally at odds with how she is dressed.

That is all it takes for Iris and Heather to sweep back to reality. Iris focuses on her mother.

'Sorry we disturbed you, Mum. How about we go out and have a walk together?' She shoots a look at Heather. 'It's too stuffy in here, anyway,' she adds.

Heather rolls her eyes but says nothing. Verity is delighted.

'That would be lovely. I'll get my handbag....'

Iris hurries towards her. 'Let's get something warmer for you to wear.'

Verity stops and looks down at the pyjamas. She blushes.

'Yes, stripes are rather last season, aren't they?' she expresses brightly.

'Well, quite!' Iris laughs. She is grateful her Mum's illness occasionally has its lighter moments.

Verity and Iris head towards the bedroom. The next thing Iris can hear is the door being slammed to inform everyone Heather has left the building.

CR HEATHER ВО

Heather can still hear the slammed door vibrating through the hall even when she enters the lift going down. It is as if her whole body is shaking in sync with it. When she leaves the building, she walks as fast as she can to get as much distance as possible between her Verity and Iris.

It is as if demons are chasing her. When she finally gets far enough, she finds a deserted bench and drops down on it. *Why does Iris trigger me so much?* A voice whispers in her head.

Heather grits her teeth. She knows there is some truth in what Iris said to her, particularly about the finances. Heather is ashamed. She's been fighting Iris all these years and lashing out at her when she didn't deserve it.

What did Iris do that I have to fight her all the time? It can't just be that she's so dominating. Heather can't put her finger on it. She sits there in the moment and takes a few more deep breaths before she realises what it is.

Iris did not stand by her when she came out.

She wasn't there to stop Verity's snide remarks about her choice of girlfriends and hadn't been there when Verity went out of her way to make Heather feel like a freak.

Heather winces, remembering when Verity hissed at her, 'Remember you're a lady – and a Bach! Don't turn up at my parties looking all butch!'

Heather realises she internalised Verity's homophobia and had gone out of her way to look very feminine. That would have to change. In the future, she'd wear what she damn well pleased. Even Heather's successful career had been down-played.

Verity insisted it was thanks to her vaunted family name, not her own merit. Heather seethes, oblivious to people passing by. Then the feeling recedes. All the years she blamed Iris for not protecting her from Verity, Iris had her own griefs to deal with. Heather wraps her arms around herself.

I was only sixteen when I came out. Iris should have known how Mum would react to it. She should have come and put a stop to it! Heather's childish inner voice was saying - the same voice that lashes out at Iris every time they meet. Heather recognises that voice. It is the one that surfaces whenever she comes back to visit her family.

But you're an adult now. You don't need her to protect you anymore, so how about a ceasefire? Says a calmer, unbidden voice. *Not only that. Think how brave you were when you did come out. You knew the risks, you knew what would happen, and you still did it against all the odds and got to live according to your truth. Why do you still think Iris should protect you? You are braver and stronger than her!*

Time to let it go.

Heather suddenly feels lighter. She relaxes. The sun is lower in the sky, and the shadows are lengthening. She'd been sitting here a while in her internal struggle. A sense of pride dawns on her. She smiles, breathing in the cool evening air. She stands, feeling giddy, and turns for Zoe and home. She steps lightly. The weight of years is falling away.

ଔ IRIS ଓ

When Iris and Verity get back from their walk, Verity is tired. It surprises Iris that her mother, who was on the go constantly - Alzheimer's notwithstanding - gets tired these days from the gentlest activity. *Shows you how attached you are to your mental image of her, not who she's become,* says the irritating voice in her head. Her practical side concluded that it is better to deal with Verity's reality.

Aisha has lunch ready. Iris insists Aisha eats with them. She enjoys her company, and it gives her the opportunity to express how grateful they all are for Aisha's dedication to Verity. If Aisha is embarrassed by Iris's constant expressions of gratitude, she doesn't show it.

'I just don't want you to think we take you for granted, Aisha,' Iris repeats herself, more to reassure herself than the capable carer.

'I'm really very fond of your mother, you know.'

Verity goes for an afternoon nap. Aisha refuses Iris's offer to help with the washing up, so she wanders the London streets for a long time. She has the urge to fly home as surely as a bird needs to migrate south for the winter, though her flight back is only a week ahead. There are things she still wants to say to her sisters, but she knows her words would fall upon stony ground, so why bother? She'd tried her best, and it hadn't worked.

Time to let go and say goodbye.

Iris has a peculiar sense of lightness, like a weight has been lifted. She is letting go of her childhood fantasy of happy families. *Let the family be what it is. It's time I focus on Nate and Joy and stop taking care of everyone else.*

Nate and Joy don't need you! Verity says in her head.

Shut up! Her sensible voice shouts back.

You know I'm right... says the irritating voice smugly.

'True, but if I don't take care of them, who's left?' Iris cries out loud. She glances about, self-conscious. She is alone. She waits. There is silence, inside and out.

She sits on a nearby bench, dizzy with the realisation she is right. She gets up and walks back to Daisy's with a spring in her step. Ever the multitasker, she rings the airline and, as she walks, changes her flight for later that same evening.

She is worn out and rather emotional when she gets back to Daisy's.

'Iris?' calls Mike from the kitchen.

Tears run down her face as she hurries upstairs to pack. She doesn't want to see Mike right now. He will be kind to her, and she'll break down completely. She is so busy stuffing her clothes in her bag, she is unaware Daisy is standing at the bedroom door, watching her.

'I thought you were staying a few more days.'

Daisy's voice startles Iris. She wipes the tears away with the t-shirt she is holding. 'I've had enough of accusations from you and Heather. I'm done being your punch bag,' she responds, surprising herself with her own resolve.

'Not like you to be bitter, Iris.'

'Heather came to Mum's and informed me what a controlling bitch I am. So, I'm done...You can take care of yourselves. You don't need me,' she says, turning away to avoid Daisy's penetrating gaze. Once she finishes packing, she tries to hurry out of the room, but Daisy is still at the door, blocking her way.

'But I do need you,' Daisy reminds her quietly.

Iris stares at her. 'No, you don't, Daisy. I should have recognised it a long time ago. It would have made my life easier and certainly yours. You're the head of the family now, and I finally have my life back... so there we are. Everyone gets what they wanted all along!' she insists, her tone business-like.

Daisy steps aside. Iris brushes past and heads downstairs. Daisy trails in her wake.

They get down to the entrance hall and look at each other. It is profoundly awkward. Impulsively, Daisy hugs her sister. After a second's hesitation, Iris hugs Daisy back.

'Before I go, let me give you my final piece of advice. Don't give up on being a mother. Maybe you're meant to be a mother, even if it doesn't mean giving birth. Promise me you'll think about it.'

Daisy bows her head. Iris picks up her bags. Daisy opens the front door while Iris hurries out, hails a taxi, and gets into it. At the last moment, she turns around and waves goodbye to Daisy. *When shall we three meet again?* rings in her head.

CR DAISY ∂

I remain standing at the door, watching Iris's taxi disappear around the corner. My head is in turmoil. *Why is it ending like this?* Iris is gone. It feels odd to think I might not see my sister for a long time. I know it is final; I am the head of this family now.

I close the front door and lean against it. The entrance hall seems to reverberate with Iris's presence. I walk into the living room only to find Mike standing there. He watches me silently. I drop down onto the sofa, staring into space.

Mike sits next to me. As ever, silence honours the moment of high drama.

'Tea?' he suggests.

I look into his eyes. 'Good thinking. How long were you standing there?'

'Since Iris came in crying,' Mike replies.

'That's so not like her,' I mumble, more to myself than to Mike.

Mike squeezes my shoulder. I know Mike, the great peacemaker, has something contentious to say to me. I look at him. 'Well? Out with it.'

'It's actually very much like her, I think. You need to watch out for her. She's not as tough as you think.'

I frown. 'Meaning?'

Mike doesn't answer. I nudge him.

'Probably doesn't matter....'

That's too much for me. 'Oh please, 'probably doesn't matter' is code for 'this is vitally important'. Just say it!'

Mike takes a deep breath. 'I think Iris has a point in what she is suggesting to you. It makes sense if we move back to Oxford and live with Verity.'

I can't believe I'm hearing what he's saying. I'm not sure even if I see him through the haze in front of me. It's as if he's a million miles away.

'Darling, do you hear what I said?' he checks with me.

I finally come out of my reverie. 'Yes, I heard what you said. I'm just not sure how I'll be able to live with Mum, even if I do forgive her,' I mutter.

'Verity isn't the same person. When I look at her, I see a nice old woman who's unravelling. All her sharpness is gone. I don't hear her complain like she used to. In some ways, she's become a better person since the Alzheimer's, don't you think?'

I literally start giggling at this.

'Let's not exaggerate,' I remark. 'But I do agree she isn't as controlling as she used to be.'

'We don't have to decide now. Give yourself some time.'

I smile sadly. 'I will. Maybe it's a case of tolerating her but not loving her.'

Mike nods. 'That's the spirit!'

We cuddle. Mike then plays his trump card with any Bach woman. 'Restaurant or takeaway?'

I burst out laughing. 'You know me so well!'

Chapter Twenty-One

❧ NATE ☙

Nate is waiting for Iris at the train station. He is inquisitive. Iris is back earlier than he expected. *Something's gone terribly wrong.* She usually wouldn't bother dragging him all the way to the train station to pick her up. She would take a taxi home – or ask him to leave the car parked somewhere so that she can drive herself.

But this time, she sounded different on the phone. There was something in her voice, but he knew better than to interrogate her. It could wait until they were together again.

Twenty-eight years together taught Nate that behind his partner's tough façade was a soft, fragile woman. Yes, she is practical, down-to-earth, and business-like, but that is how she masks her vulnerability. Nate feels a rush of protectiveness towards Iris; no one is closer to her than he is. It is Iris and Nate against the world, they joke between them.

He glances at his watch impatiently, pacing up and down the platform. It is as if she built a glass vitrine around herself, whereby the world can see her, and she can see the world, but no one can truly touch her – except him. No wonder Sylvia Plath's 'The Bell Jar' is her favourite book.

However, getting her to talk about this latest mysterious development requires his compassion and innate gentleness.

He knows that waiting on the platform instead of in the car will delight her.

When the train arrives, it is easy enough to spot Iris. Not many people get off at this remote station in low season. Iris's face lights up when she sees Nate. She walks steadily towards him – not in her usual hurry. He knows this walk. She is thinking about how to tell him her story with enough details to satisfy his curiosity but to leave her fragile self-undamaged. He is ready for it.

When she finally reaches him, he hugs her so tightly he can hear her breathing stop. She pulls away, cupping his face in her hands.

'Looks like you missed me,' she pronounces matter-of-factly.

'I'm just glad you're back so quickly!' he replies, taking her luggage. They walk out of the station and head to the car.

'I made a reservation at your favourite restaurant.'

Iris smiles at him. 'Darling, would you mind if we go straight home? I just want to be alone with you!'

Nate didn't expect this. 'Things must be serious if you don't feel like a good meal!' he mentions with a chuckle.

Iris avoids his gaze. Nate is bursting with questions but knows to hold back.

They drive in silence, though he can hear the wheels in her brain going round and round. Iris has a tendency to make a story sound close to the truth but without the most painful parts—however, this time, he wants to know what truly took place.

When they get home, Iris drops her bags in the hall.

'Let's talk,' she announces.

Under normal circumstances, she would first unpack her bags, put the washing on and take a shower as soon as she got through the door. *She wants to get it off her chest as fast as possible,* Nate recognises.

They sit in her favourite place on the balcony, sipping the local wine and looking at the magnificent view as she articulates everything that happened in London with Daisy and Heather.

'I'm done. I finally understand now. I've been making the most terrible mistakes these past thirty years. I've been trying to parent Daisy and Heather, but I'm not their mother. It's funny. With Joy, I knew the difference between having a baby and being a parent. Once she was eighteen, I finished being a parent. True, she'll always be my baby, and I'll always be here when she needs me, but I'm not trying to parent and control her. With my sisters, I didn't stop being a parent. I had to compensate for Mum's control-freakery and ended up being a control freak myself. Does that make sense?' she looks at Nate for confirmation.

Nate had been trying to say that to her for years, but she'd never listened.

'The best lessons are self-taught, don't you think?' he responds.

Iris nods, tears in her eyes.

'Well, I'm free now. No more dashing off to London to pull everyone's irons out of the fire at a moment's notice. I'm thinking, how about that trip to South America you've always wanted? We can stay at your friend's place in the Peruvian jungle… really and truly off the grid,' she suggests, her face lighting up with future plans, something she loves.

Nate is gobsmacked. It has been his dream for a long time. Iris found it impossible to contemplate between her family and work commitments. Nate hugs her.

'The great outdoors, no phones, no internet, you always at my side – my idea of heaven!' he asserts.

CR DAISY ED

I'm not looking forward to moving. It is bad enough clearing my own house out, never mind Mum's apartment. The memory of clearing the house in Oxford and moving them to London four years ago, is still fresh in my mind; the stress, the long hours, and the sheer quantities of stuff we had to go through before the moving company came in to help.

It is Iris's idea, I remember, to find a company that will pack up our parents' possessions carefully. This saved some time and stress, but still, having to sort out a lifetime's worth of their things was enough to give me a headache.

Thinking of doing it all over again now made me dizzy. There is no way I can ask Iris to come and help after the way we parted. In the occasional moment of weakness, I call her only to get to voicemail. I never know what to say, and Iris never rings back. Iris is certainly off the family grid. The gulf between us is now simply too wide.

I can't count much on Heather either, as Heather finally found a research position that uses her experience and knowledge but doesn't force her to work hospital hours or even meet patients, which has never been her forte. The job demands much of her time and energy, but she doesn't complain as the salary is also good, which is important as Zoe is still a struggling artist. Between her new job and taking care of Mum, Heather barely has time for herself.

There is no way I can get on with packing when Mum is around. Mum would stroll into a room, open the packing boxes, take things out and hide them. I find them days later, thinking I've already packed them. I feel like I'm going mad.

Once, Aisha and I found Mum's old mobile phone in the freezer, boxes of tissues under her mattress and the TV remote control in the microwave. At least Mum didn't try to cook it. These days, before I arrive at the apartment, I make sure Aisha takes her out when the weather is good.

On the plus side, I discover that support can occasionally come from unexpected quarters. Zoe is the first angel of mercy. She always liked Mum, from the first time they met at Dad's eightieth birthday party. Having a lot of free time on her hands and not many friends in London, she often pops round on rainy days and enjoys entertaining Mum. She has the patience to listen to her stories. Being an artist, she finds ways to occupy Mum in a way that absorbs her yet taps into her latent creativity.

I sometimes take a break from the packing and watch the two of them in fascination. Why Zoe is so interested in Mum is beyond my comprehension. Maybe it is because Zoe didn't know the old, sharp Mum, forever criticising and undermining. The only thing that makes sense is something Heather once told me.

'Think about it, Mrs Psychotherapist!' Heather remarked. 'Zoe's Mum left her with an Aunt when she was only six and never came back for her. When her Aunt died a year later, Zoe went from one foster home to another until she was old enough to live on her own. Verity's her idealised mother-figure.'

'More like a toddler figure, I'd say,' I replied, but I got Heather's point. On her lucid days, Mum is still an impressive woman with amazing stories to tell and a sweetness of nature that we didn't witness growing up. On her bad days, Mum would start a sentence, then forget what she wanted to say and either move to another subject or, more often than not, let her words fade to silence.

'I don't know how you do it, Zoe,' I note as we watch a euphoric Verity putting her hands through the sunlight as though she is trying to catch the rays.

'Well, no two days are the same,' Zoe replies. 'I think your mum's lovely.'

I smile, covering up my surprise. I am grateful to have Zoe around when I am packing.

The other angel of mercy is Joy. In my bitter moments, I suspect Iris told her to come just to keep an eye on what was going on and report back.

'Oh, Aunty Daisy!' Joy says, laughing. 'Mum and Dad are on a one-way trip in the jungles of Peru! I barely hear from them. That's how I know they're ok.'

'Whatever are they doing there?' I inquire.

Joy shrugs. 'God knows! Though it's always been Dad's dream. I bet he loves having Mum totally to himself.'

This answer is profoundly unsatisfactory to me, but I embrace my niece warmly all the same.

'So, what are you up to in London?'

'I got offered a job as assistant to the head designer of a famous fashion house – can't tell you which one yet as I haven't signed the contract - They're creating the costumes for a new West End production – can't tell you about that either, I signed a non-disclosure agreement! Anyway, I'll be in charge of the project,' she announces.

Joy takes it upon herself to go through Dad's clothes. 'Oh, these are great!' she cries out loud when going through them. 'All these Harris tweed suits… it's a shame to send them to charity shops. Can I have them? I can create new costumes for a fraction of the budget and impress my boss!'

She also helps with keeping Verity busy. She enjoys it just as much as Zoe. Hearing the three of them laughing together makes me feel cross and excluded. What Iris said about for-giveness flashes through my mind. *Maybe I'm not seeing things properly,* as I seal yet another packing box.

It reminds me of the famous story I used to tell my clients: 'If one person tells you you're a horse, then they're drunk. If someone else tells you you're a horse, they're crazy, but when a third person tells you you're a horse, go to the barn and check if you like hay and have a tail!'

Now other family members find Mum so personable and charming; maybe I am the odd one out. It is certainly starting to feel this way. I brush these feelings aside. There are too many things to take care of. *I'm going to be living cheek-by-jowl with her in a few weeks. I can deal with it then.*

❧ DAISY ❧

Finally, the day of moving arrives. It is, I reflect, like organising battle lines for a war. The removal lorry arrives at the Oxford house on time but has to reverse up the drive to start the unloading, which takes ages or feels like it. Mike and Heather arrive in their cars but can't find anywhere to park, so that takes time.

I stalk the driveway like a sergeant-major, barking orders at the movers about where to put everything. Mike and Heather are not exempt from my peremptory rudeness about being careful with things, especially Dad's writing desk. I smile for the first time when I see it coming out of the lorry. It has returned to its rightful home.

Once the movers leave (an apologetic Mike tips them handsomely), Mike, Heather and I stand staring at all the boxes and furniture.

'Right, time to make this into a home,' I say, rolling up my sleeves.

Heather looks at me with a twinkle in her eye. 'If anyone can do it, it's you,' surprising me with this observation. 'I'm off to London to fetch Mum and Aisha.'

'Cool. I'll arrange their rooms first. You take your time,' I tell Heather, walking out with her.

Mike and I stand together in silence after Heather has left. It is a daunting feeling with all the boxes. The house of my childhood feels simultaneously old and full of ghosts, yet it holds the promise of a future where things can change for the better. I take a deep breath. Mike puts an arm around me.

'You ok?' he checks.

I nod. 'Let us begin.'

To my surprise, it didn't take me too long to change the dusty, neglected house into a warm living home. My resistance to living here is a thing of the past. My unhappy memories do not haunt me anymore. Within weeks of moving back, it's as if London has been but an interlude.

With my passion for beautifying things, I managed to transform it into a place that is safe and cosy for everyone. I painted walls and re-carpeted, stripped floors and re-varnished. The only thing I didn't touch is the big back garden. It has always been perfect in my childhood; my happy place, and I want to keep it that way. It is my inspiration and a place of meditation.

I turned Dad's old study into my own office and clinic. I enjoy the same view overlooking the garden that he did for more than fifty years. I now understand why he loved that room. It is beyond just being a sanctuary where one can work; it is the view and the heavenly scent of the garden that comes through the wide French doors, which I keep open as often as I can. I feel as though I embrace time and the seasons passing by and becoming part of them.

I'm working on a paper I've been asked to write for a psychotherapy magazine. I find myself stuck and need a specific book for a quote but can't find it on the shelves. I know I've done all the unpacking, but as usual, there are always some boxes that are left for 'later'. Of course, later never comes. I think the book I need is in one of those boxes.

I go upstairs to the little box room to look for it. When I open the door and flick the light switch on, I nearly fall over a box. It has no label but is still sealed. *What the hell is this? Mum's moving things again…* I kneel to open the box, only to discover it contains Mum's old journals. Out of curiosity, I open one of them at a random page and start reading it.

'Silence, finally. It's midnight. All the kids are asleep. I'm exhausted. I've just finished ironing the last pile of clothes. I had to do it; Daisy was complaining she had nothing to wear. My back is killing me, but I have to finish marking papers, and then I can finally go to bed. Sol went to bed hours ago. It's so much easier for men. They only have to focus on their career. Mother always said that every woman needs a wife.

'That's what I need! I feel like I'm wearing four different hats, and I don't look good in any of them, as the girls so frequently tell me. I wish Iris would come back and help me, but I suppose she has her own life. I'm happy for her, but I feel I'm failing with Daisy and Heather. I really try to understand them, but somehow, each time I want to get closer to them, I say the wrong thing, and it ends with an explosion. I don't remember it being this tough with Iris.

'I wish I knew what to do. I wish I could really have a talk with Daisy. Other people tell me she's such a wonderful, loving girl, but I don't see it. I only bring out the worst in her. She's the one with the biggest heart. And still, somehow I'm unable to tell her that. I feel she hates me, and all I try to do is show my love. I know she doesn't feel it. This is the cross I have to bear.'

I swallow painfully. My throat is as dry as sandpaper, and my eyes are burning. Tears are starting to roll down my cheeks— blood pounds in my ears. For the first time in my life, I get to see things from Mum's perspective. If I forgive Mum now, what difference would it make? It would mean nothing to the fading Verity, but to myself?

Was this the way forward I've been looking for? I clasp the journal to my breast as though it is a baby and walk back to Dad's study.

I return to my writing but can't concentrate. I am restless and emotional. I keep writing and deleting. It's not a good sign. I glance at Mum's journal, propped up on my desk. *What other stories of her past are buried in those pages?*

I finally stand up, grab the journal, and step out into the glo- rious garden. I find my favourite place: the bench under an ancient oak tree rumoured to be three hundred years old.

I sit and read the whole journal. When I finish, it's twilight. I can hardly make out my mother's elegant copperplate writing in the gloom. There is only one other person who can help me make sense of all this.

I pick up my mobile and dial. 'Heather! You'll never believe what I've been reading....'

Chapter Twenty-Two

❧ VERITY ☙

Verity wakes up. It takes some time to understand where she is. Lately, she isn't sure if she is awake or in a terribly realistic dream. On the one hand, things seem familiar, yet also strange.

Perhaps it is the colour of the walls...

She gets out of bed and hobbles towards the door, only to find herself opposite an old woman she doesn't recognise.

'May I help you,' she asks her, but it appears the other woman is asking her something too. Her mouth is moving, but the poor thing isn't making a sound.

Or maybe I need to go to the doctor to have my hearing checked.

'Wait here,' she informs the other woman. 'I'll go and get Sol. He'll help you.' She opens the door and steps out into a bright corridor. It smells of furniture polish. For a moment, she isn't sure where to turn. *I think I know this place,* but things look different. *That bureau moved for a start. Hmm, the cleaner was here. I need to talk to Sol about this,* she thought.

'Good morning, Verity!' someone says brightly behind her. She turns around to see a small Indian woman who looks kind, smiling at her as if she knows her.

'Shall we go and have breakfast?' she asks.

Verity has no idea who she is but decides to be charming.

'Your English is very good!' she tells the woman, who laughs.

'I should think so. I was born in Bradford,' says Aisha, holding her arm out. Verity slips her hand into the crook of it and feels more stable on her feet. Aisha leads the way. She seems to know the house.

'Are you the cleaner?'

'Sometimes! Would you like breakfast outside? It's a lovely day and you do love to sit in the garden.'

Verity nods. She likes the garden very much. 'I need to get it ready for a party, you know,' she remarks. 'We haven't had a party for a long time.'

'Good idea,' responds Aisha. They pass through a beautiful room that leads to a patio overlooking a wonderful garden. Aisha shows Verity to a seat and helps her sit down. The table is laid with white napery and gleaming cutlery.

'I shan't be a minute.'

The day is bright and sunny, and Verity enjoys the warmth of the sun on her face. It makes her sleepy, and she dozes off for a moment. When she wakes again, she isn't sure where she is. She can smell bacon cooking and hear a woman's voice singing.

'We can delay lunch!' Verity calls. 'Sol's not back yet!' No reply. 'I'll go and meet him at the library....' She stands up and crosses the garden to a door she can see from where she is sitting.

When she reaches it, she tries to open it, but it doesn't budge. She looks closely and notices something brown sticking out under the door handle. It has a name, but she can't recall what it is. She is fascinated by the red-brown colour of it and the ornate shape. It looks so beautiful sitting there in the door. She touches it, feels the odd texture, and turns it. She hears a click.

She tries the door handle again, and to her surprise, the door opens. *Magic!*

'Open Sesame!' she says, chuckling. Once on the other side, she finds herself on a street. She remembers she wants to go and fetch Sol from the library. She looks around for her bicycle. It is nowhere in sight. *Oh well, I'll just have to walk to the bus station.* She starts walking, but nothing looks familiar.

Verity stops a young woman with headphones. 'Excuse me, I'm looking for the bus station...' but the young woman just scans her up and down. Verity is wearing a puce-coloured candlewick dressing gown and maroon slippers. The young woman averts her gaze and hurries off.

Luckily a young man approaches her. 'Excuse me, are you lost?'

Verity beams at him. 'Not at all. I just need to tell Sol lunch is ready. He's at the library, you know.'

'Where do you live?' the young man asks.

Verity frowns. Where do I live? London? No, that's not right...

'Why do you want to know?' she asks, backing away from him.

Traffic roars past. Verity nearly stumbles off the pavement into its path. An older woman catches Verity's arm, steadying her. Verity stares at her rescuer. The young man shrugs and hurries away. The older woman smiles kindly at Verity.

'It's Verity Bach, isn't it?' inquires the woman.

Verity doesn't hear her; she is captivated by the woman's deep blue eyes. 'We met at a faculty dinner,' the woman indicates.

'Your eyes...' observes Verity. 'They remind me of the fjords Sol and I saw once.'

The woman laughs. With her blue eyes and white hair, the woman looks like a fairy. Verity is mesmerised by her beauty.

'Oh my, do you know how beautiful you are? No, really you are,' she utters.

'Come on,' responds the woman. 'I think your family might be wondering where you are.' The woman gets her mobile out. Verity wanders off down the street, the woman following her. Verity turns to find herself face to face with a young woman with tattoos on her arms, nose rings and many earrings.

'Hi lady, are you lost?' the young woman cries to her.

'Aren't we all?' replies Verity, distracted by the woman on the phone behind her.

'Are you lost, dear?' The young woman looks her up and down. *How rude!* She stares closely at the lost young woman.

'What's all that on your face? Look in the mirror and see how beautiful you are! You don't need all that... that....' Verity lost the word she is after. '... rubbish!' she says, pleased with herself. To her surprise, the young woman sulks.

'Silly old cow!' she answers, stalking off.

Verity glances behind her. The white-haired woman is still behind her, muttering into a phone. Verity spots the bus stop. She goes over the timetables, but the words and numbers swim together in her vision. She is tired and isn't sure anymore whether to wait for the bus or go back home. Sol is waiting for her – *or is he in the library?*

'I need to think,' she tells the white-haired woman, who smiles and nods. Verity sits down on the bus stop bench. The woman sits next to her.

Graham Miles is watching them from his window. The Bachs

have been their neighbours and friends for over thirty-five years, and he was sad to see them leave but even sadder to see Verity return a shadow of the formidable woman she used to be and without Sol. Their excellent parties were the stuff of legends.

Verity's child-like state has been difficult for him and his wife to witness. They tried visiting Verity a few times, but their presence distressed her so much, Daisy told them it was ok not to visit. Even so, Graham feels he cannot ignore the situation any longer.

Verity starts to feel hungry when an elderly man approaches her, smiling as if he knows her. She is relieved and feels safe with him. He is good-looking, too.

'Hello Verity.'

'Did you see those people?' she remarks. 'They don't know how beautiful they are. Isn't that sad?'

Graham agrees.

'Hello Graham,' the white-haired woman interrupts. Verity is annoyed by her familiarity with the man.

'Hello Monica, I'll take over from here if you like.'

'Of course! I rang the police, but God knows when they'll get here,' Monica notes.

'Why, what's happened?' says Verity.

'Nothing at all! It's a lovely day, isn't it? Why don't we go back home? I'm sure Daisy is looking for you.'

Verity smiles flirtatiously at him. 'I know we've met... remind me of your name?' Verity adds.

'It's Graham, and I live next door to you. Shall I walk you home?' taking her by the hand.

'Yes, Sol should be home by now, and I need to get dinner on the go.'

In no time at all, Graham and Verity are walking up the drive to the Bach house. Monica watches them from the street.

'I'll ring the police and cancel the call!' she calls. Graham turns and waves. Verity takes his arm possessively.

'Who is that lady? Wasn't she beautiful? And so kind,' Verity mentions while Graham rings the bell.

൦ർ DAISY ൠ

I am working on a new article in the study when I hear the doorbell ring. I want to finish it, and I'm on a deadline. Mum's journal inspired me. I decided to write a piece on early childhood perceptions and their influence on adult life.

'Aisha!' I call. 'Can you get the door?'

The doorbell rings again. I'm mildly irritated at being interrupted, and I run down the corridor leading to the front door and open it.

Graham and Mum stand there, arms linked like an elderly bride and groom on a wedding cake. Mum smiles and looks up at Graham with adoring eyes. I'm at a loss. *What is happening right now?*

'I found her walking down the street. She was telling people how beautiful they were - like a life coach!'

Mum doesn't even know what a life coach is. 'I didn't want a coach! I wanted the bus so I could go and look for Sol in the library. He wasn't there, but this wonderful man helped me to get back. He's an angel. But you must remind me of your name…,' she asks him.

'It's Graham, Mum,' I tell her patiently. 'Do come in!''

I invite Graham, grateful he rescued Mum.

We all walk inside the house. Mum looks around as if it is the first time she's ever seen the place.

'What a lovely house you have. It's so beautiful' I know there is no point in correcting this impression. I simply accept the compliment. *I'm learning… Not before time.* Verity takes my face in her hands and gazes into my eyes.

'You shine!' she states. 'You're so beautiful - like an angel!' I switch between embarrassment and disbelief. Since when did my mother become so adoring? I glance at Graham, who also looks stunned.

The old Verity has been witty and sharp. Unconditional worship has never been part of her character, *except perhaps towards Dad.* I gently disengage myself from Mum.

'Seeing we have a guest, why don't we all sit down, and I'll make us some tea?' I suggest. 'Graham, would you like one?'

'No, thanks. I just wanted to make sure she got home safely….' He hesitates, clearing his throat. I brace myself. Mum strolls towards the living room, her adventure forgotten.

'You shouldn't let her go out on her own, you know. It's dangerous.'

'Actually, I think she escaped, but I take your point,' I say briskly, keen to end this particular conversation. I am mortified.

'Well, I'll leave you to it.'

'Thanks for your vigilance, Graham,' I manage to articulate, stiffly seeing him out. He'd made me feel like a misbehaving child. I deadlock the front door, just in case.

I return to where Mum is sitting, staring at the garden. I follow Mum's eye line, and I can see the garden door is still ajar when I realise what happened. For a moment, I thought Aisha had left the front door unlocked.

'Mum, next time you want to go out, let me know. I'll come with you,' I mention.

Mum gives me a bright smile. It lights up her face. 'You're so kind. I bet your mother is really proud of you,' her face radiant.

I'm speechless. If I need any other proof that the old Verity had gone, these words are a confirmation. I had never heard my mum so positive. *Oh well, got to make the best of every moment.*

I go out into the garden and shut the old door. I lock it and take out the rusty key, making a mental note to beef up the security in the house, starting with cameras in every room so I can watch from my computer in the study if needs be.

Aisha comes into the garden from the basement kitchen with plates of food. 'Oh! Where's Verity?'

I'm thinking about taking her to task, then change my mind. Aisha is only human. The old me would have sacked her on the spot. *Maybe I'm changing too,*

We both look into the living room, where Mum has fallen fast asleep. She is snoring gently. Aisha sighs.

'Here,' I say. 'I'm starving.'

I take a plate of food and go back up to the study while texting with my free hand to Heather. 'You'll never believe what Mum just said to me.'

As time passes, I find living with Mum becoming progressively easier. Not only that, I'm starting to enjoy my life in Oxford, away from the hustle and bustle of London.

'I guess, as you grow older, you prefer the quieter life,' I share with Mike one evening when we sit in the garden, listening to the birds. Mike nods. He also adapted to life in Oxford, working online and travelling (if he has to) to meet clients. If anyone asks, he answers he's a Digital Nomad.

'How is Verity today?' he asks.

'She is talking about a safari she and Dad went on in the eighties. She describes the elephants but can't think of the right word, so she says, 'you know, big grey things with long noses,' then she goes like this...,' I stand up, wave my arm around and make trumpeting noises.

Mike falls back, laughing.

I grin. 'I said 'elephants?' and she goes, 'no, that's not it'. Honestly, I just can't win. It's like arguing with a small child.'

'You've got to admit, it has its moments, though.'

'Yes, it makes up for a lot. Funny how these days I don't lose my patience with her. The only thing I feel towards her now is compassion.'

I gulp at the rawness of this admission. 'Maybe it's as close as I can get to loving her.'

Mike is listening attentively. He takes my hand. 'I think your roles have reversed. She's the child, and you're the mother,' he mentions gently.

My first instinct is to deny it, but I sit with it for a few seconds and realise there is truth in Mike's observation. I also remember what Iris told me about not giving up on being a mum. There are other ways of doing it. Suddenly it all falls into place for me. I turn to Mike, my face shining.

'Do you still want to be a father?'

Mike stares at me.

'I think we should adopt.'

Mike's face breaks into a wide smile. 'It's like you're reading my mind. It'll be hard because of our age, but it can't be any worse than what we went through with the pregnancies.'

'You've been thinking of this for a while, haven't you?' I remark. 'Why didn't you say anything?'

Mike shrugs his shoulders. 'Well, how could I? There's been so much turbulence; your dad, Verity's illness, moving... I think we need some stability in our lives, don't you?'

I berate myself, realising he had that speech ready for a long time. I've been too busy to consider his feelings. I've taken total advantage of his laid-back character.

After the initial rush of adrenaline, the doubt sets in. Am I ready to go through another journey of hope and possible disappointment if we are turned down? It would be another loss.

'You know what? Let's take it one step at a time. Let's start the process and see where it leads us. No big plans, no to-do lists, nothing set in stone. ok?' Mike suggests, kissing me as twilight deepens in the garden. The flowers seem to glow around us. I'm unable to speak, overjoyed by his kindness and understanding of my fears.

As time goes on, there are fewer and fewer social occasions I need to take Mum to. Mum's sleep pattern changes. She is often up all night with the ever-patient Aisha and asleep all day.

Many of her friends died or moved into care homes or closer to their own families in other parts of the country. Mum is starting to outlive her old circle. In a way, it is a relief for me not to scrabble around for things to occupy her with.

In any case, she shows less inclination to go anywhere these days. Just like me, the garden is Mum's sanctuary. But when Heather is promoted to senior researcher, I find it a good excuse to celebrate it properly, like we used to do when Mum and Dad were in their prime.

We agree it will be dinner together at Heather's: just the family and a few of Heather's friends, who know Mum and will accept any of her strange behaviour.

I start the preparations early to avoid rushing. Nothing sets Mum off like tension.

I decide to enjoy it. Like I often tell my clients: 'happiness is a choice.'

I spread out a few outfits on Mum's bed so she can make her selection. Aisha helps Mum in taking a shower and washes her hair.

'What would you like to wear for this evening, Mum?' I ask.

Mum looks at me blankly. 'Where are we going?'

'Heather's been promoted, and she invites us to a dinner party!' I repeat for the twentieth time in an hour. I am so chilled; the endless repetition doesn't rankle me anymore.

'That's nice. I like parties,' Mum responds.

'Yes, you do. So, what would you like to wear?' Mum looks at the different outfits on the bed, but I can see she isn't sure what she is supposed to do.

I chose her lovely gowns made of chiffon and sequins in ice cream colours. Her shoulders sag. I bit my lip. *Come on, Mum…*

'If it's Heather, I don't need a fancy outfit, do I?' she remarks.

I am prepared for this. 'Let's pretend we're going to tea with the Queen. What would you wear for that?'

Mum has a broad smile on her face. 'The Queen? I've never met the Queen. That'll be nice.'

She chooses a turquoise chiffon dress with long sleeves and a diagonal spray of sequins across the front in the shape of a peacock. I help her into it, noticing she had lost some weight.

'I'll blow dry your hair and make it look good,' I suggest.

'Yes, please dear, give it some volume if you would,' Verity replies, as though at the hairdresser's. She sits down on a low chair facing the dressing table and its antique mirror.

I stand behind Mum, gently brushing her white hair, as fine as gossamer. The movement of brush through hair is almost hypnotic. Mum, who always enjoyed having her hair brushed, closes her eyes.

I feel myself going back in time…

I am back in my old bedroom, dressed for school. Heather is still in bed. Mum is vigorously brushing my hair. I flinch; I've long since stopped complaining that mother is too rough.

'Iris, have you made sandwiches for your sisters yet?' Mum shouts.

'I'm doing it as we speak!' Iris yells back.

Heather pulls a pillow over her head. Mum frowns and kicks Heather's bed.

'Heather, get up! You've got ten minutes!' she barks.

Heather groans. I shut my eyes and count to ten under my breath. By ten, Mum would finish plaiting my hair.

'Does anyone know where my glasses are?' Dad's plaintive voice comes from downstairs. 'I can't find them anywhere!'

'In the kitchen, darling!' Mum calls. 'You left them on the draining board last night!'

Finally, Heather gets up. I open my eyes to look at her. *Five, six, seven…* Heather is still wearing yesterday's clothes, all crumpled and dirty. Her fingernails are filthy, and her hair is greasy. Mum looks on the verge of tears, taking this in. I shut my eyes again to avoid the scene.

'Iris!' Mum screeches. 'I thought I told you to organise Heather's bath last night. She slept in her school uniform!'

'I can't hear you…' Iris shouts back.

I smirk. *Nine, ten.* Mum sighs heavily and finishes plaiting my hair. I escape to my bed and grab my school bag.

'Nine minutes!' Mum mumbles. 'Let's see how much I can squeeze into that and still be on time!'

Heather rolls her eyes and slouches out of the bedroom.

'God, you're such a martyr, Mum,' Heather says over her shoulder.

I never saw Mum look so angry. She snatches up a vase. I run out of the room, pulling the door closed as I go out. The vase smashes against the door.

'I am your Mother!' Mum shrieks.

I come out of my reverie and give Mum's sparse white hair one last gentle brush.

'You look lovely, Mum. Shall we go?'

It is a wonderful evening at Heather's. Though I am a bit nervous about taking Mum to a relatively new place, it is actually all right. Mum's coping strategy is to withdraw into herself. She is there, yet strangely absent. It looks strange watching Mum become an introvert; in the old days, she'd been the life and soul of any party, making it all go with a swing. Now she is still centre, smiling benignly while people eat, drink, laugh and toast to Heather's success around her.

There is no denying Mum's new approach makes it easy for me to enjoy the evening, too. Midnight strikes. The party breaks up. We head back home.

'Good to be out of the house. Such nice people! Where were we?' Mum says as Aisha brings her a mug of cocoa.

'At Heather's. She got promoted.'

Mum takes a sip of her cocoa and smacks her lips. Then she drops the mug and clutches her stomach. Cocoa soaks into the relatively new carpet. I'm unconcerned. The old me would probably be cross. The old Mum would blow her top.

'I don't feel so good,' she mutters. Aisha runs to get a cloth.

'Maybe it's something you ate,' Mike suggests. Mum sinks

back on the sofa and shuts her eyes. Aisha comes in with the cloth and soaks up the worst of the spill.

'Come on, Mum,' I say. 'I'll get you some Alka-Seltzer and put you to bed.'

৫০ HEATHER ৫০

Heather is at work trying to catch up on all the new assignments she is given now that she's been promoted. It's been a long time since she had a job that involved so many responsibilities, but she's enjoying it. It is exactly the type of work she loves: research, analysing other people's research and being at the front of all the developments in her field. Her focus is disturbed by a phone call. She looks at the ID and sees it's Daisy. It's one of the few IDs she will always respond to.

'Heather, I need you here urgently,' she hears her sister on the other side of the phone.

Heather can never refuse Daisy's requests, and they both know it.

'What is it?' she asks, only to hear Daisy's unstoppable rant going.

'Mum is still complaining about pains in her stomach since the dinner at your place. The GP recommended to take her to the ER, but I have a deadline for my article, which is today. I don't have the time to sit there only to find out that it's nothing. Could you get here this afternoon and take her?'

It's a rhetorical question; they both know it.

'I'll just finish something here, and I'll be there. Don't worry…
Heather to the rescue…'

Once Heather puts down the phone, she completes a few last
things on her desk and starts going out of her office when she
remembers that Joy, who finished working on the musical, is
also in London. *Let's bring Joy and Zoe with me, and we can have
some celebration time in Oxford*, a thought goes through her head.
Oh my God, I'm starting to sound like Iris!

Heather didn't hear anything from Iris or about her, neither
from Daisy nor Joy since she last saw her at Verity's apartment.
*I wonder what she's up to… maybe family does come first. Oh well, at
least we'll have Joy here. The kid's well-named.*

When Heather, Joy and Zoe arrive, it is indeed a joyful celebration, maybe not to Iris or Verity's standards, but there is a
lot of wine and good food with many jokes and stories going
around the table. Verity stays with them for a short while, smiling but silent and pale.

Heather wonders if the referral to the hospital is necessary
but supposes it is better to err on the side of caution. Verity
nods off at the table, having eaten very little. Aisha helps her
up to bed.

The next day Heather takes a sleepy Verity to the hospital.
She still doubts whether there is a need for it, but once she
describes the problem to the doctor, she knows something is
seriously wrong with Verity.

The ER physician informs her that they suspect Verity
had her appendicitis torn and she needs immediate surgery.
Heather recognises the severity of the situation and decides to
call Daisy.

'You'd better come to the hospital,' she urges Daisy.

'Oh God, what is it?'

'Easier to explain in person,' She hangs up, knowing Daisy will not like it but is confident she would be grateful for her later.

Meanwhile, both the surgeon and a social worker approach her with some papers.

'Due to Verity's age and her condition, we need to know whether you have a DNR for her or whether you wish to have one.'

Heather has no clue about it. She really needs Daisy by her side now, and if she's honest with herself, Iris would have taken care of this situation better than any of them. *Where is she... what have I done to make her disappear for such a long time.*

Heather is surprised to hear the last thought. She didn't think she had anything to do with Iris's disappearance, but apparently, deep inside, she knew she did. *I don't have time for this now,* she tells herself.

At last, she sees Daisy rushing down the corridor towards her.

൦൪ DAISY ൽ൦

'What's going on?' I shout across the corridor to Heather. I'm a bit torn between being angry at Heather for not helping me when I need her and the nagging feeling that something is seriously wrong with Mum.

'Mum needs an emergency operation. We need to decide whether we want to sign a DNR for her and these other forms.'

I'm in shock. I thought Mum was only constipated. How could I be so blind to her situation?

'Her appendix has burst, and the infection has spread,' Heather's face impassive. She is good in crisis. I feel my heart go cold.

'When is she going into surgery?' I inquire, my heart pounding.

'Until we sign this DNR, they will not take her in, and we have a problem. We need Iris's signature too on this form,' explains Heather and now I get the full picture. I understand why she looks so devastated.

'But Iris is in Peru!' I cry in a panicky tone.

Heather tries to hug me, but I dodge her.

'They're trying to help us. Trust me; they don't want Mum to die here!'

A woman approached us. 'Good afternoon. I'm Brigitte, a social worker with the hospital. Are you the daughters of Verity Bach?'

We both nod.

'I understand there's another sister?'

'She's somewhere in Peru,' I respond.

'We're doing our best to expedite matters, but without your third sister's consent, we can't move forward.'

'What do you need from her?' Heather asks.

'Just her signature on these papers.'

Heather nods.

'How the hell do we get that from her in the short time that we have?' Heather whispers to me.

I have an idea. 'Let me scan the document. Will you accept a photo of her signature on it?' I check with Brigitte.

'Usually not,' replies Brigitte, 'but in this case, we can even make it easier for you. Let her sign through Hellosign.com, and it will be fine.'

We hurry to Brigitte's office. I scan the document onto my phone.

I send it to Joy with a message: 'Hi Joy, Grandma is in the hospital. We need your Mum to sign the attached document through Hellosign.com for the hospital to operate. You're the only one your Mum will respond to! Please get her to do it ASAP.'

I shiver in a cold sweat. *What if this will not work?* I hide my fears with a meek smile at Heather and Brigitte.

'If anyone can track Iris down, it's Joy,' I announce, sounding more confident than I feel.

Brigitte nods. 'Here's my mobile number. Ring me the second you have that signed.' Brigitte hurries off down the corridor.

Heather stares at me. 'Now what the hell do we do?'

'We wait. Personally, I could murder a coffee,' I respond.

We go down to the hospital cafeteria and get some coffee. I glance at the other diners. Maybe it is the awful lighting, but everyone looks haggard.

'Is it my imagination, or does everyone else look as desperate as we are?' I whisper to Heather.

We find a corner table in the crowded cafeteria. I flick through a discarded newspaper and check my phone every twenty seconds. Nothing. I can scream.

'Stop checking!' Heather commands me. 'You'll run out of battery.'

'Well, what are you doing on yours?' I ask, infuriated.

Heather's thumbs are twitching on her phone. 'Playing a game. It calms me down.'

I put my phone face-up on the table and sit on my hands. The minutes drag. My coffee goes cold.

Twenty-five minutes later, a text comes through from Joy: 'Where r u?'

I text her back. Within minutes, Joy meets us with a signed document from Iris, not just on her phone but also printed out. I punch the air and hug my clever niece. We did it.

'What did I tell you?' I say to Heather. 'Let's take this to Brigitte.'

Chapter Twenty-Three

❦ DAISY ❦

Heather and I stand watching as Mum is being wheeled out of her room. Mum looks small and frail, already sedated and hooked up to a drip. I hurry to keep up with the bed. I press Mum's hand.

'We're here for you, Mum!'

The waiting room is full of people in the same boat as we are. Heather looks for a place to sit—Joy waves to us from a corner where she saved two chairs. Heather and I sit down while Joy sits cross-legged on the floor at our feet.

I look at my niece fondly. There is no drama with Joy. She just gets on with it.

'Nothing to do but wait,' I whisper, as though I'm in church. The atmosphere in the room is very subdued.

'I hate waiting!' says Joy. 'Wish I'd brought some work with me, now.'

'You are so your Mother's daughter,' Heather notes.

Joy looks at Heather suspiciously. 'I'll take that as a compliment,' she replies.

'You can go, you know,' Heather mumbles. 'It might take hours.'

Joy bridles. 'She's my Grandmother!' People look around at us. 'You might not love her, but I do.'

I frown at Heather. *Not now!* Heather clears her throat and tries to think of something less controversial. 'What's your mum doing in Peru?'

I roll my eyes.

'Staying away from you,' Joy shoots back.

Heather's face shows her anger.

'This isn't the time or the place, you two,' I hiss.

'Sorry,' Joy mutters. 'I'm not sure. Finding herself, I guess. Basically trying to figure out what her role is.'

Heather seems puzzled. 'Why would she want to get away from me?'

'Seriously?' utters Joy.

I decide to take control.

'Keep your voices down! Heather, come on, you were pretty rough on her the last time she came to help,' I remind her.

'I guess I was, but I was only trying to protect you. You just had your third miscarriage… how dare she suggest you look after someone you hate!'

I watch Heather with compassion. 'But in the end, she is right. I may not have a child of my own, but I'm calling on that side of me to look after Mum. She's my child now. My life has come full circle. How can I hate her?'

Heather shakes her head, clearly upset. Joy stares at us with amazement.

'Ever since I can remember, Mum and Dad explained to me that their role in my life as parents would end when I turn eighteen or in my twenties,' says Joy briskly. 'They taught me to think of parenting as a job description. A parent's job is to make sure their child grows up healthy, strong, and independent.

After that, their job as parents is over, and it's up to the young person to live his or her life the way they choose.'

Both Heather and I are speechless.

'Haven't you two lived your lives as you chose?' Joy asks.

We nod, chastened.

'Well, maybe Grandma didn't do such a bad job, then,' Joy continues, checking her phone. She switches it off. 'When Mum lost her baby…' Joy mentions casually.

'What?' Heather and I say in unison, drawing angry looks from other people.

'What do you mean she lost a child? I hiss.

Joy is shocked. 'She never told you?' searching our faces. 'That figures! Maybe she was too busy being strong for everyone. God forbid she was ever vulnerable. That's what she's doing in Peru, learning to live with her own vulnerability. Good for her, I say.'

Joy, red-faced, switches her phone back on. Heather and I look at each other.

'Joy, what happened?' Heather probes, horrified.

Joy looks up. *Old head on young shoulders,* I realise.

Joy hesitates, conflicted. This is her mother's story. She looks down at her phone again.

'Mum had four miscarriages after she had me,' Joy states in a matter-of-fact voice. 'Then she had a stillbirth when she was seven months pregnant. I was really looking forward to having a brother or a sister, so I insisted she takes me to the hospital with her for the check-up. I wanted to hear the baby's heart-beat. I was only five. The doctor told her something was wrong. There was no heartbeat. They admitted her right away, and

Dad came to pick me up. But apparently, during the night, they had to operate. It was dead. I mean, he was dead. She never even had a chance to say goodbye. I think that's why she was so determined you keep trying on, Aunty Daisy.'

Joy looks at us, her young face open. There is a long silence between the three of us. I start crying. Heather goes white as a sheet.

'I'm sorry, Joy,' Heather mumbles. She puts her head in her hands. 'God, what have I done?' she moans.

Joy shrugs. 'I don't know… Just talk to her. It's never too late to mend fences, you know. Something else I learned from Mum.'

She stands up. I look up at my niece and experience a mixture of emotions: gratitude, humiliation, grief for all of us really, but especially for Iris.

❧ IRIS ❧

The rain rattles on the tin roof. Iris smiles as she hears the frogs singing out in the jungle. After months in the rainforest, she got used to the perpetual noise. She'd even started to like it, finding any sudden silence disorienting.

It has been one of the best decisions in her life to come here and take stock. For years she thought she knew her place in the world. She was centred, her feet planted on the ground. But Sol is dead now, and Verity is unravelling, Daisy and Heather refuse to let her in, and even Joy is all grown up and doing fantastically on her own, so no need for Iris either to parent her sisters or even mother her own child.

It has been a mistake to take on patronising Daisy and Heather. It has prevented her from being their big sister and friend. The Spanish farm is ticking over nicely with tenants in place. Sol's death meant she wasn't really a daughter anymore. Verity is more a child than a mother. *So, if I'm not a mother, or a daughter or a career woman, what am I?* She wonders, tussling for her own identity.

She feels as if she is drifting out into deep space, a redundant satellite with no homing beacon. Technically, she isn't even a wife, as she and Nate rejected conventional marriage as impossibly bourgeois.

When Nate proposed coming to this healing centre in the middle of the jungle, she jumped at it, thinking it the ideal opportunity to tune in to her own needs. What she didn't expect were interesting experiences with 'teaching plants', principally Ayahuasca. Nate was enthusiastic.

'I can't wait to try it, can you darling?' Nate declares one evening.

'You're on your own!' Iris replies, laughing, not taking him seriously at first. 'Don't the shamans make you sign a legal disclaimer in case you die?'

'I'm serious. I think you should do it too. It might give you some answers.'

Iris frowns at him. 'It's a trip into the unknown. Aren't you worried about getting addicted?'

Nate sneers. 'Don't believe everything you hear. It's about letting go of ego.'

Iris turns away from him so he wouldn't see how disturbed she feels. *Without my ego, who am I? There's nothing left...* She is nauseated from the thought.

'I'd rather you didn't, but I can't stop you,' she responds in a small voice.

Nate hugs her from behind. 'Don't wait up,' he comments, rushing out of their shack.

Iris hears Nate shout greetings in Spanish to someone, and then they are gone.

Iris's eyes fall upon a book on the table by Carlos Castaneda, 'The Fire From Within'. She opens it. Nate's untidy handwriting annotated sections and underlined paragraphs. She knows Castaneda has written extensively about Ayahuasca, the substance Nate was going to ingest. Squaring her shoulders, Iris decides to do some research and settles on their bed, reading.

She finishes the book in a day. It is enthralling. One sentence struck home with her: 'The basic difference between an ordinary man and a warrior is that a warrior takes everything as a challenge, while an ordinary man takes everything as a blessing or a curse.' She'd been taking everything as a curse, it seems.

Three days later, Nate is back, wired, dirty, yet euphoric from his experience. He holds Iris in his arms, staring at her as though seeing her for the very first time.

'Well?' says Iris, relieved he is in one piece.

'It was amazing! Worth ten years in therapy, I'll tell you that right now,' his eyes intense. 'I dreamed I was naked in the jungle, and I was shrinking, like in Alice in Wonderland – I shrank to the size of an atom. The jungle was immense around me. The tiniest bugs were the size of dinosaurs! It was a metaphor. I'm so tiny, and the universe is so vast, but I saw myself in relation to it...' he falters.

'Sounds terrifying!'

'No. It's actually fine,' adds Nate, his voice full of wonderment. 'I embraced it!' A few minutes later, he is asleep.

Iris gazes at him for a long time. Even in the abandonment of sleep, Nate looks different. There is a serenity to him now. This is what he'd been looking for in his quest to live truly off the grid.

Iris decides to try it herself. In a way, she has nothing left to lose – except her life, perhaps. Even so, she signs the disclaimer along with the other Ayahuasca tourists. For once, in her well-organised, over-planned life in which everything is predictable, she will let go of control.

The shaman grins at her in his Manchester United T-shirt. Nate is thrilled and goes with her. The party heads into the rainforest. As the night settles, the shaman reappears, unrecognisable in his tribal paint. Ayahuasca is offered around the circle of eager travellers.

It is bitter and hard to swallow. Iris feels her head swim with the fumes—her stomach cramps. Hours or maybe minutes later, she throws up. She lies down in Nate's arms, staring up into the darkness of the canopy.

She can hear the frogs singing, not just nearby but all over the rainforest, their song becoming so loud it is a cacophony. She tries to raise her hands to her ears to block out the noise, but she cannot move. She wills herself to move, terrified. The urge to flee becomes unbearable. The song of the mating frogs rises to a shriek and stops.

Now, she can hear the gurgling of a baby. *It's him…* she thinks. She sits up and there he is, nestled next to his sleeping father. She picks him up and cradles him. He waves his chubby fists at her and smiles. She gets up and walks into the forest with him.

The canopy sways gently overhead. Water drip on them in the humid air. Iris finds herself on the banks of a fast-flowing river. She knows what she has to do. She plucks a large leaf from a nearby bromeliad. It is curved and smooth, ideal for holding water. It is like a Moses basket. The baby fits in it perfectly. She kisses his forehead, and he closes his eyes. She puts the leaf and her baby boy into the river and watches as the current snatches it out of her hands and away. She waves goodbye. The river turns a bend, and the baby is gone.

When Iris returns, it is noon of the next day. She has a banging headache. She sits up, feeling shivery. Nate and the shaman are cooking food on the central fire. Iris realises how ravenous she is. Judging by the look of the other tourists, they feel the same. Nate sees she's awake and brings a bottle of water over to her.

'Well?' he says, grinning.

'I've got so much to tell you.'

Back at the shack, Iris tells Nate what she experienced. Like Nate's experience, it is, in a sense a metaphor: she had to say goodbye to her son in the dream, as she wasn't able to do in real life. Her overbearing attitude to Daisy and Heather in adulthood was a symptom of her need for control in the face of death; her baby's, Sol's and of course, inevitably, Verity's. Maybe that is why she finds it so hard to connect with Heather.

Her younger sister has become a doctor, holding the power

of life and death in her hands in a way Iris never could. Iris understands that if she had shared with Daisy about her still-born son, it would have been a bond between them.

Nate is right. She had to let go of her ego in order to see her path. She now understands it. As if a window is opened and the sun streams through, she can picture herself growing organic herbs on the farm in Spain. She could become a herbalist, hold workshops, and heal bereaved people… Just thinking about it made her heart expand with joy.

Something is released inside of her. Iris grasps she needs to find someone to teach her, but who? *I will find a way. All I need is a direction, and now I have it.*

Her mobile vibrates on the little tin table, startling them both. The signal could be intermittent here.

'Ignore it!'

Ordinarily, Iris would have. They were supposed to be off the grid after all, but the Internet seemed intent on encroaching on the rainforest too. Iris knows with complete certainty she must see the message.

She opens the text from Joy. Nate's Ayahuasca afterglow fades as he braced himself for the inevitable summons from the Bach family. They weren't even safe from them in Peru.

'Do they have a printer here somewhere do you think?' she asks Nate. The local shop did. They print the document, Iris signs it, photographs it and sends it back to Joy while the signal is still there.

'I think it was meant to happen,' she remarks.

'Aren't you worried?' Nate checks with her. 'I mean, she might die. We can go back if you want.'

'I am ready to go back, but not because of Mum, but because I know why we came here. I let go and saw my path.'

The look on Nate's face is worth it...

'What?' says Iris, laughing at his loving intensity.

'Well, I was going to say I am glad you're back, but actually I suspect you're not the old Iris anymore,' he remarks.

'Oh darling, this is the new me.'

He grins. A huge weight is lifted off her shoulders.

'Let's go home,' she declares.

ℭ℞ DAISY ℰℭ

Heather, Joy, Zoe, Mike, and I sit in the deserted waiting room. There are empty takeaway containers spread on the table.

'It's been more than eight hours!' complains Zoe. 'How much longer can it take?'

We all look at Heather.

'Gastrointestinal surgery isn't my field. Sorry.'

Mike picks up the takeaway cartons and chucks them in the bin. 'Tell you what, I'll go home and get some blankets. Looks like you're in for the night. Anything else you want me to bring?'

I look at him, eyes red-rimmed with exhaustion, yet not so tired that I didn't bless my good fortune in Mike for the hundredth time.

'No thanks, darling. Just update Aisha, would you? We'll need her for a few weeks after the surgery. Joy and Zoe, why don't you go home with Mike? We can take it in shifts.'

Joy nods and stands up, swaying a little with tiredness. She, Mike, and Zoe leave. Heather makes a cup of tea for us.

A tired-looking surgeon in green scrubs comes in. 'Are you the Bach sisters?'

We both nod.

'How is she?' I ask, bracing myself.

'Right now, she's stable, but she's not out of the woods yet. The next twenty-four hours are crucial.'

Heather nods. I feel like my brain is on fire.

'What do you think her chances are?' Heather inquires.

The surgeon looks down, weighing her words. 'I won't lie to you. They're not good. Her age, the extent of the infection and the fact she has Alzheimer's...'

I'm not willing to accept this. The last months living with Mum, and especially reading her journals, have made me appreciate Mum's flawed humanity.

'You don't know my mother,' I tell the surgeon. 'She's a fighter.'

The surgeon smiles wearily at me.

'You're right. I don't know your mother. But you've asked me for my opinion, now you got it. I hope I'm wrong, I really do,' she says.

I frown and bite my lip. Tiredness is making me combative.

'Can we see her?' Heather checks.

'Of course, but only for a couple of minutes.'

She shows us into the ICU where Mum is lying, connected to a life support machine, heart monitor, and an IV drip with hideous plastic tubes up her nose and down her throat. She looks so fragile and small in that big bed.

I stare at my mum. I lean forward and kiss her on the fore-head, overwhelmed with emotion. I tuck her hair to one side. My eyes are filled with tears. Heather moves in to hold my hand. The machines beep and whirrs rhythmically like music, keeping Mum alive.

'I forgive you, Mum,' Heather whispers.

CR IRIS &O

Iris and Nate are at the airport when the news of Verity's death reaches them. It feels like *deja vu* when Nate receives the news. However, this time Nate does not have to worry about Iris. It seems as if she has said goodbye to Verity back in the jungle.

'I was there when she was alive. That's what really counts,' Iris answers Nate when he checks with her on how she is. 'I'm glad Daisy and Heather were with her.'

CR DAISY &O

Mum's funeral is on a clear, cold spring day. Heather, Iris, and I stand around Mum's coffin, which is covered with bouquets of irises, daisies and heather and lying next to Dad in an open grave.

It is a much smaller group of people around the grave than for Dad's funeral. We preferred it this way: a small, private cer-emony. I insisted on leading the tributes to Mum.

'The woman we say goodbye to is not my mother. I lost my mother to an unseen enemy called Alzheimer's. My mother was a fighter. When she wanted something, nothing stood in her way. Not cancer, not other people's opinions, not social etiquette. She didn't want to miss anything. She was always on the go: one more project, one more party, one more adventure, one more place to see. If there's one phrase that captures her spirit, it would be 'Carpe Diem' – seize the day. It wasn't always easy living with her....'

Heather and Iris smile and nod. A couple of the older mourners smile too, remembering Verity's sharp wit – only fun to witness, never to be the target of.

'I won't lie, for the old Verity, nothing was good enough,' I continue. 'But it had its positive side. My Mother taught me to become the best I could be, even when I didn't want to learn. She kept pushing me out of my comfort zone when I grew complacent. She never gave up on me, even when I left Oxford, trying to put as much distance as I could between us.'

Iris breaks down and cries quite openly at this. Heather looks stunned. *The old Iris would have kept a tight lid on her emotions,* I think to myself as I pause to allow her to regain control over her emotions... Heather hugs her and gives her a tissue. Iris hugs her back. I wait a few more seconds.

'The woman we bury here, the new Verity if you like, taught me all about love. When Alzheimer's stripped away the layers of the old Verity, a new version of her appeared. She'd given up the fight. She would say right at the beginning of Alzheimer's: 'I wish I had cancer all over again. At least then I could fight it. But with this, I don't even remember what I need to fight.'. I like to think of this as her real essence. She might not have been the mother I grew up with, but she's the one who taught me what motherhood is all about.'

Iris looks up, staring at me. Nate and Joy are standing directly behind her. Iris glances questioningly at them. Joy nods in affirmation, smiling.

'Life works in mysterious ways. Sometimes it gives us what we need through harsh lessons. The journey I've been on with my Mother was a painful one, but it helped me to love the woman who gave birth to me. I wouldn't have missed it for the world. Bye, Mum. May you find peace, and if not peace, then a few really good parties in the afterlife.'

With that, I take some soil with a spade and drop it into the grave.

Walking back to our cars, after all the condolences and farewells, the three of us find ourselves walking together.

'God, it's just like Mum used to say: people only meet at funerals and weddings. Next time let's have a wedding. I could do with something to celebrate,' Heather remarks.

We all laugh. I glance around. 'Hmm, let's see who we can marry off?'

I observe catching Joy's eye, walking behind us with Zoe.

'Don't look at me!' says Joy. 'Perhaps Aunty Heather should make an honest woman of Zoe.'

'Zoe, will you marry me?' Heather declares teasingly.

'Let me change out of my funeral clothes first,' replies Zoe.

'Spoken like a true Bach!' I note.

Funny how life turns out to be, I think to myself, as I walk towards Dad and Mum's grave with flowers in my hand. It's been three years since Dad died, and here I am, visiting my parents nearly once a month and talking to them. Who would have thought I would be able to be closer to them when they were dead than when they were alive.

I don't feel regret, but I find it interesting. Today more than any other day. I made it a habit of coming here once a month and sharing with them what was going on with us, Mike and I, Iris and Nate, Heather, and Zoe and even Joy. It feels as if I'm keeping their legacy alive by letting them know the family is all together again, and that all is well in the world.

Today I have special news for them. *You have a wonderful new grandson;* I whisper as I lay down the flowers on their graves. I'm not sure how they would react to this new arrival in our special family, but I see it as another miracle of life, and I want to share it with them. In the end, there are more reasons to get together than just weddings and funerals, and today is such a day.

I arrive back home in time to see Heather all giddy and excited. 'Good, you're here. We can start.'

It is her day, just as it is our day. When I look around the garden, all decorated and ready for the party, I can't help remembering the last big party we had here, Dad's eightieth birthday... what a world of difference.

This time Heather runs the whole show, and both Iris and I

can be spectators of the entire show: no stress, no planning, just the pure joy of being together.

Zoe steps out from the living room dressed all in white, an outfit that Joy made for her, which looks magnificent on her. Joy never fails to make the most unique and special outfits. She has created amazing outfits for today for all of us. She called it her 'Bach spring collection.' *It should have been in a magazine*, I think to myself, and direct my attention to Zoe, who brings our son and hands him to Mike and me.

In the end, Heather never married Zoe, but Zoe found the best way to create a celebration event. She became my surrogate, and we had an amazing son who we named Matan.

The Rabbi approaches, and the traditional ceremony of brit begins. When Matan bursts into a cry at the end of the ceremony, three mums and a dad are trying to relax him while the rest of the people smile and accept it as normal.

Nate approaches Mike and me, leans over Matan and says: 'Welcome into the Bach tribe. It's about time we had reinforcement to the male side.'

Mike bursts into laughter and agrees with him.

At the same time, I can hear Iris saying to Joy, 'You see, I was right all these years. Happy families are each happy in their own way', and I say,

'True, you just have to define what happiness is for you and create it for yourself...'

THE END

LEAVE A REVIEW

Did you like this book? Don't forget to let others know.

Every review matters, and it matters a lot!

Head over to Amazon or Goodreads
to leave an honest review.

Thank you!

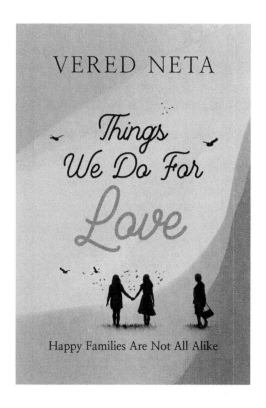

FULL CIRCLE

Historical Novel by Vered Neta
Publication Date - December 2023

When Russians invade Prague, a young medical student kills a soldier in self-defense. As authorities hunt for her, she is smuggled beyond The Iron Curtain and sneaks across borders to reach the USA.

****

When the Berlin Wall falls in 1989 and The Velvet Revolution swiftly follows in Prague, Ana's own daughter Yael wants to know her mother's secretive story, which Ana shares with her.

All Ana ever wanted was to become a doctor and use her skills to help people. However, when she reconnects with her childhood friend Jan, her entire life is turned upside down. She finds herself in opposition to her parents, the university, and even the local authorities, and eventually, the Russian government.

As a Jew, Ana's mother Helen experienced unimaginable suffering and cruelty in the concentration camps during World War II. These experiences left her with lifelong psychological difficulties. Ana's father Pavel and Helen worked hard to shield Ana from the horrors they had faced during the war.

However, as Ana becomes more involved in activism in Prague with Jan, Helen becomes increasingly fearful for her only child. She worries that Ana will reject her experience and warnings.

During the Soviet invasion of Prague, Jan and Ana find themselves on the front lines of the protest. In the chaos, Ana accidentally kills a soldier and lives in constant fear of being discovered. She turns to Jan for comfort, only to discover that he is becoming increasingly withdrawn and erratic. Ana hopes her love can pull him back from his extreme ideas, but tragically, Jan self-immolates as a political statement.

Ana is crushed by Jan's death, as helping people was her life mission, and all her hopes and dreams are now in tatters. She doubts herself and everything she once believed in. Knowing that the Soviets will soon be hunting her down, Ana formulates a daring plan to be smuggled beyond the Iron Curtain to the United States. Helen is heartbroken to let go of her only child but knows it's the only way to ensure Ana's safety. She makes Ana promise to never look back and focus on her new life in the United States.

Twenty years later, Ana is still keeping her promise. With the election of a new president in Czechoslovakia, Ana knows it's time to return to Prague and close the circle with the ghosts she left behind.

Full Circle questions what is more important in life: sticking to one's ideals and principles, or doing whatever it takes to stay alive? It challenges us to have a second look at what freedom, bravery, and strength really mean.

Printed in Great Britain
by Amazon

25584545R00169